She rubbed her hands together. They made a chafing sandpaper sound, emphasizing the chill silence of the room.

"May I offer you refreshment?" she asked belatedly.

"No, thank you. Indeed, I will get straight to the point."

"Please do." She exhaled with relief. "I much prefer blunt speech."

He straightened his shoulders and shifted to face her more squarely as though putting his mind to an unpleasant task.

"Miss Martin, I need— May I have the honor of your hand in marriage?"

Author Note

I fell in love with the drama of the French Revolution when my mother and I attended a showing of the movie *A Tale of Two Cities*.

To say the film was old is an understatement. Even in the '70s, it bordered on antiquity—a black-and-white 1935 release with Ronald Coleman as Sydney Carton. But that film captured my imagination in a way that few films have done, before or since. I remember blinking dazedly at its conclusion, literally feeling as though I had been transported to another place and time and was myself waiting on that tumbrel.

Those timeless words "It is a far, far better thing that I do, than I have ever done; it is a far, far better rest that I go to than I have ever known" continue to thrill—thank you, Charles Dickens.

Later I became fascinated with the history of the revolution, its ideals, which so soon dissolved into bloodthirsty chaos, and its impact not only on France but on the world.

One day I will set a novel based at its epicenter. But for today I am thrilled that *Married for His Convenience* at least touches this fascinating period.

Eleanor Webster

Married for His Convenience

HARLEQUIN HISTORICAL

Recycling programs
for this product may
not exist in your area.

ISBN-13: 978-0-373-30751-7

Married for His Convenience

Copyright © 2016 by Eleanor Webster

This edition published by arrangement with Harlequin Books S.A.

For questions and comments about the quality of this book, please contact us at CustomerService@Harlequin.com.

® and TM are trademarks of Harlequin Enterprises Limited or its corporate affiliates. Trademarks indicated with ® are registered in the United States Patent and Trademark Office, the Canadian Intellectual Property Office and in other countries.

Printed in U.S.A.

Eleanor Webster loves high heels and sun, which is ironic as she lives in northern Canada, the land of snow hills and unflattering footwear. Various crafting experiences, including a nasty glue-gun episode, have proven that her creative soul is best expressed through the written word. Eleanor is currently pursuing a doctoral degree in psychology and holds an undergraduate degree in history. She loves to use her writing to explore her fascination with the past.

Books by Eleanor Webster

Harlequin Historical

No Conventional Miss
Married for His Convenience

Visit the Author Profile page at Harlequin.com.

In memory of my mother, who loved history
and books and inspired me with that love.
To my father, who loves history, the English
countryside and all creatures great and small.
To my childhood pets, who greatly added to
my joy, and to Oreo, a special rabbit
who shared our home for all too short a time.

Prologue

November 8th, 1793

The severed blonde curl lay in stark relief against the polished wood of the desk.

'Hardly conclusive evidence of my wife's demise.' Sebastian Hastings, Earl of Langford, kept his glance dispassionate as he lifted his gaze from the silken strands.

'This might be more convincing,' Beaumont said, removing a single sheet of paper from the inside pocket of his coat and smoothing it out with meticulous care.

A death certificate.

'I did not realise the *citoyens* of the Committee of Public Safety had sufficient time to document Madame La Guillotine's every victim,' Sebastian drawled.

An ugly colour suffused the other man's features. He was tall and had quick eyes set within a narrow face; everything about him was angular except for the pouches under his eyes and a lax softening of his chin.

Sebastian had always disliked Beaumont, but that was a pale sentiment compared to his hatred now.

Sebastian wanted to kill him.

He wanted to squeeze the man's throat with his bare

hands until his eyes bulged and his face purpled into life-lessness.

But he would not do so. He could not do so or any hope of recovering his children would be lost.

'Given my wife's apparent demise, might I enquire after the welfare of my children?' he asked instead, keeping his face expressionless and his tone bland.

'They are in my care.'

'How reassuring. And what will it take to get them out of your care and into my own?'

Beaumont smiled, the thin lips curving upward to reveal neat white teeth. He leaned over the desk and Sebastian smelled the cloying sweetness of the man's cologne. 'Your children will be returned for a price.'

'And if I am unable to meet that price?'

Beaumont reached for the blonde curl, twisting it through his well-manicured fingers. He moved it slowly—around, between, under and over. 'Efficient lady—Madame La Guillotine.'

Sebastian stood, the movement violent and impossible to contain. His chair crashed against the wall. It fell sideways and banged to the floor.

Beaumont jumped back, but Sebastian rounded the desk and was on him. He had the man by the throat, pulling him so close he could see the pores of the man's once-handsome face.

'I promise you one thing,' Sebastian ground out between his clenched teeth. 'If my children are hurt, you will not live.'

Chapter One

April 7th, 1794

Sarah Martin lifted her skirts. Her feet sank into the mud and water dripped rhythmically from the bushes bordering the woodland path.

Neither fact lowered her spirits.

Smiling, Sarah sniffed the earthiness of the English countryside and held her skirts higher than was respectable.

Mrs Crawford would have frowned, but then Mrs Crawford spent considerable time in that occupation.

Sarah's sun had risen, metaphorically, shortly after luncheon with a last-minute dinner invitation from Lady Eavensham to even the numbers at her dining table.

Such events did not often happen to Sarah, although they occurred with delightful frequency in her writing. Her current heroine, Miss Petunia Hardcastle, had just recently made a stunning entrance in a diaphanous blue dress created from her grandmother's ball gown.

Unfortunately, Sarah's dress was neither diaphanous nor blue, but a serviceable grey. Moreover, unlike Miss Hardcastle, Sarah's longing for fashionable company had nothing to do with romance and everything to do with London. The mere mention of that city gave her a wonderful thrill of hope, a prickly sensation like the goosebumps she used to get at Christmas.

One day she would go there. One day she would keep her promise. One day—

A crackle of twigs and leaves startled her out of her reverie. She stopped. A second scuffle caught her attention and she peered into the ditch. *'Pauvre lapin,'* she spoke quickly in her mother's language.

A rabbit lay, sprawled among the weeds and grasses. Its back paw was entangled in a poacher's trap, its brown sides moving in frantic undulation.

Sarah bit her lip. Kneeling, she placed her valise to one side. She eyed the trap, but did not touch the mechanism for fear of hurting herself or causing the animal harm. She was familiar with the device, but it was vastly different to manipulate its jaws whilst they were empty than to contemplate doing so while this petrified creature lay within its grip.

Carefully, holding her breath, she pushed her fingers against the metal. It felt cold and hard and did not budge. Then, with a snap, it released.

The animal lay briefly frozen before bursting into frenetic life, its hind legs sending a tinkling cascade of pebbles into the ditch.

'No, you don't.' She caught the creature and, pulling her shawl from her shoulders, immobilised its hindquarters within the folds of cloth.

Bending closer, she inhaled its dusty animal scent as her arms tightened against its soft, warm weight.

Now what? The animal was injured and would be fox fodder if she let him go. But she had no time to go home. Already, daylight was dimming and the air shone with the pewter polish of early evening.

Besides, in many ways, Eavensham was more her home than the stark austerity of the Crawford residence. Shrugging, Sarah made her decision and, tightening her hold on the bundle, picked up her valise and stepped forward.

Some five minutes later she exited from the overhanging trees and on to Eavensham's well-manicured park, the change between woodland and immaculate lawn joltingly sudden. Without pause, Sarah skirted the impressive front entrance, veering away from the lamps and torches bidding welcome.

She would hide the rabbit in the kitchen or scullery. Hopefully, the butler would be elsewhere. Mr Hudson was not overly fond of rabbits.

Except in stews.

The path wound towards the kitchen garden, a narrow track sandwiched between the house and dairy. As she expected, the kitchen was bright and the smell of cooking wafted into the garden.

Carefully, she stepped towards the window, then froze at the snap of a twig. She caught her breath and turned, scanning the darkened outlines of the hedge and vegetable frame.

Nothing. She stepped back to the kitchen. Likely she'd only heard a fox or stable cat. She was too practical for foolish fancy.

But even as the thought passed through her mind, a hand clamped across her mouth and she was pulled against a hard, muscular figure.

She tasted cloth. Her heart beat a wild tattoo. Her body stiffened, paralysed not only by fear but an almost ludicrous disbelief as she allowed her valise to slip from her hand.

Dramatic events never happened to her. Ever.

'If I remove my hand, do you promise not to scream?' The voice was male. Warm breath touched her ear.

Sarah nodded. The man loosened his hold. She turned. Her eyes widened as she took in his size, the breadth of his shoulders and the midnight-black of his clothes.

'Good God, you're a woman,' he said.

'You're…you're a gentleman.' For the cloth he wore was fine and not the roughened garb of a common thief.

She grabbed on to these details as though, through their analysis, she would make sense of the situation.

'What was your purpose for spying on me?' His gaze narrowed, his voice calm and without emotion.

'Spying? I don't even know you.' The rabbit squirmed and she clutched it more tightly.

'Then why are you hiding?'

'I'm not. Even if I were, you have no reason to accost me.' Her cheeks flushed with indignation as her fear lessened.

He dropped his hand, stepping back. 'I apologise. I thought you were a burglar.'

'We tend not to get many burglars in these parts. Who are you anyway?'

'Sebastian Hastings, Earl of Langford, at your service.' He made his bow. 'And a guest at Eavensham.'

'A guest? Then why are you in the kitchen garden?'

'Taking the air,' he said.

'That usually doesn't involve accosting one's fellow man. You are lucky I am not of a hysterical disposition.'

'Indeed.'

Briefly, she wondered if wry humour laced his voice, but his lips were straight and no twinkle softened his expression. In the fading light, the strong chin and cheekbones looked more akin to a statue than anything having the softness of flesh.

At this moment, the rabbit thrust its head free of the shawl.

'Dinner is running late, I presume.' Lord Langford's eyes widened, but he spoke with an unnerving lack of any natural surprise.

'The creature is hurt and I need to bandage him, except

Mr Hudson, the butler, is not fond of animals and I wanted to ensure his absence.'

'The butler has my sympathies.'

Sarah opened her mouth to respond but the rabbit, suddenly spooked, kicked at her stomach as it clawed against the shawl. Sarah gasped, doubling over, instinctively whispering the reassurances offered by her mother after childhood nightmares.

'You speak French?'

'What?'

'French? You are fluent?'

'What? Yes, my mother spoke it—could we discuss my linguistic skills later?' she gasped, so intent on holding the rabbit that she lost her footing and stumbled against the man. His hand shot out. She felt his touch and the strangely tingling pressure of his strong fingers splayed against her back.

'Are you all right?'

'Yes—um—I was momentarily thrown off balance.' She straightened. They stood so close she heard the intake of his breath and felt its whisper.

'Perhaps,' she added, 'you could see if the butler is in the kitchen? I do not know how long I can keep hold of this fellow.'

'Of course.' Lord Langford stepped towards the window as though spying on the servants were an everyday occurrence. 'I can see the cook and several girls, scullery maids, I assume. I believe the butler is absent.'

'Thank you. I am obliged.'

Tightening her hold on the rabbit, Sarah paused, briefly reluctant to curtail the surreal interlude. Then, with a nod of thanks, she stooped to pick up the valise.

'Allow me,' Lord Langford said, opening the door. 'You seem to have your hands full.'

'Er—thank you.' She glanced up. The hallway's flickering oil lamp cast interesting shadows across his face, emphasising the harsh line of his cheek and chin and the blackness of his hair.

She stepped inside and exhaled as the door swung shut, conscious of relief, regret and an unpleasant wobbliness in both her stomach and knees.

That wouldn't do. Petunia Hardcastle might swoon, but Sarah Martin was made of sterner stuff.

Besides, Petunia was always caught by the handsome hero and no hero would catch a poverty-stricken spinster of illegitimate birth lurking within the servants' quarters.

With this thought, Sarah straightened her spine and hurried into the Eavensham kitchen.

Sebastian rolled his shoulders, trying to loosen the tension knotting his back. Goodness, the strain must be affecting him if he was reduced to accosting servant girls.

A branch cracked. Instantly alert, Sebastian slid noiselessly into the shadows. He heard a second louder crack and smiled. This was no French spy, or at least one very poorly trained.

'You can come out, Kit,' he drawled.

The foliage opposite trembled and swore. Sebastian clicked open his gold snuffbox. He took a pinch and inhaled. The 'English Lion' chose unlikely messengers and Sebastian would have lost patience with his eccentricities long ago, except his methods worked. The Lion had saved many lives from the guillotine.

Besides, Sebastian didn't have the luxury of choice. Right now, the Lion was his son's best hope.

His only hope.

Kit Eavensham emerged from the bushes. The young man wore a dark cloak clutched about his person and had pulled the hood low to cover his face and fair hair.

'You got my note?' He spoke in a hoarse whisper.

'I could hardly miss it as it was in my chamber pot.'

'I thought that a good place,' the lad said.

'A trifle obvious to the servants, but no matter—what is your news?' Sebastian swallowed. His throat hurt and every particle in his being waited for Kit's answer.

'I met the Lion at Dover.'

'Yes—and—my son?' Sebastian pushed the words through dry lips.

'The Lion contacted every source in Paris, but found no record of Edwin's execution or evidence of his death.'

Sebastian breathed again. It seemed his heart had missed a beat and was now thundering like a wild thing. 'And Beaumont?'

Kit shrugged, the thick cloth of his cloak rustling. 'The rumours are true. He escaped the Bastille.'

A mix of hatred and relief twisted through Sebastian. Beaumont had seduced his wife and kidnapped his children. Sebastian wanted him dead and yet, conversely, his survival gave him hope.

'We must find him,' he said.

'He has not turned up here? In England?'

Sebastian shook his head. 'I have heard nothing. Your mother tried to help by befriending the French *émigrés* in London. Until she broke her ankle. I'll have to find some other female now, I suppose.'

Sebastian sighed, for once regretting his lack of female relatives—other than a great-aunt who lacked tact, or basic civility, for that matter.

Kit nodded, raising his hand towards Sebastian's shoulder as though to offer comfort but, perhaps seeing Sebastian's expression, allowed his palm to drop with a soft thwack against his leg.

Then, nodding a quick farewell, he left.

Alone again, Sebastian scanned the darkening landscape; the garden was tranquil except for the muted clatter of pans from the kitchen and, overhead, the rhythmic, feathered movement of a bird's wings.

'No record of his execution or evidence of his death.' He repeated Kit's words, giving them rhythmic cadence. 'No record of his execution or evidence of his death.'

There was hope.

And while it hurt to hope, the alternative was unthinkable.

When Sebastian entered the drawing room, he saw that Lady Eavensham sat alone beside the fire with her ankle propped on a stool.

'Lovely to have your company, dear.' She smiled her welcome. 'Lord Eavensham is showing the others a painting of his new horse, but I chose to remain seated. Getting around is still not easy. Anyway, we're not missing much as it is not a good likeness. Animals are so difficult to paint, don't you know, and can look dreadfully stiff. Make yourself comfy and pour yourself a brandy.'

She spoke in a trumpet of a voice, her husband being many years her senior and going deaf. Sebastian complied, sitting close to the fire's crackling warmth. His parents had been friends with Lord and Lady Eavensham until his mother had slept with Lord Eavensham, cooling the friendship. Of course, his father's friendships had been largely cooled with everyone—except the bottle.

She was dead now—his mother, that was.

Sebastian had remained friends with Lady Eavensham, but had seen her most frequently in London. He hadn't been to the country estate for years, but felt an instant familiarity with the place. It typified all that was good in a country house: the huge fireplaces, shabby comfortable chairs, worn rugs, thick curtains and the mingled smells of food and smoke and dog hair.

A mirror hung over a massive stone mantelpiece and

ubiquitous cupids decorated the ceiling, all pink-skinned legs and plump bellies.

'The leg is improving?' he asked, belatedly remembering his manners. 'And you are not finding the country too dull?'

She shook her head. 'I do not miss London. The conversation at the salons is not nearly as lively as in my young days. In fact, I have determined to spend more time here. There are more horses and really I find them much better company than most people.'

'Doubtless.'

She glanced at him, her blue eyes sharp. 'Do I detect a smile? Lud, I remember when you always had a joke and ready wit.'

'Those days are past,' he said.

Her rosy face puckered at his tone. 'Sorry, that was thoughtless. You have little to smile about. By the by, how is Elizabeth?'

He stiffened at this abrupt mention of his silent child. 'Physically well.'

'And the governesses?'

'Resigned or dismissed.'

'Oh, dear, was that wise?'

'Yes, when they think disciplining a frightened child will make her speak.' He spoke grimly and felt a tic flicker across his cheek.

'Maybe I should look for someone suitable? It's so hard for a man.'

'Thank you, but, no.' He spoke too curtly, he knew.

Lady Eavensham did not take umbrage. She reached forward, patting the arm of his chair with a plump hand, her rings flickering in the firelight. 'Be patient, dear. Heaven knows what the poor child endured in that dreadful prison or wherever he kept her.'

He flinched. The pain was physical, so sharp it winded

him. He shifted, needing to distance himself, to guard his emotions even from this kind well-meaning woman.

With relief, he saw the door swing open as Kit and several ladies entered.

Three ladies, in fact, although one slipped unobtrusively towards the back of the room. Indeed, her obvious desire to remain unnoticed caught his attention. Her appearance was so jarringly drab juxtaposed to the other ladies' finery, her hair mousy and her face kindly, but certainly not in the first flush of youth.

He felt a start of recognition. The rabbit girl, without the rabbit.

The light made the plainness of her face and gown all the more evident. Her hair was scraped into an unforgiving bun. She had high cheekbones, straight, dark eyebrows and a mouth too wide for fashion.

Lady Eavensham smiled in her direction. 'Ah, Miss Martin, let me present you to our guests. Miss Martin is the Crawfords' ward and lives nearby.'

The ladies turned, nodding and smiling, their movement so uniform as to appear choreographed.

'Mr Crawford's ward? Mr Leon Crawford, I presume. I never met him. Will he be here tonight?' the elder lady questioned.

'That would be difficult. He is deceased. I live with his widow, Mrs Crawford, now,' Miss Martin replied.

Her dress, a grey muslin, looked years out of date and hung loose as though it were second-hand and poorly altered.

Yet she had something, he thought. Poise—that was it— and a certain irrepressible quality as though, despite its hardship, she found life a humorous affair. There had been a time when he might have shared the philosophy.

'Delighted to make your acquaintance.' Sebastian bowed.

She looked up. Her gaze met his and he saw her blink in startled recognition. Her eyes were a grey-blue, not a flat shade, but deep and intense, framed with long dark lashes.

'Good evening, Lord Langford. I trust you have had a chance to enjoy the country air?' Her voice, pleasantly low, rippled with mirth.

Unaccountably, he smiled.

'Gracious, his lordship has only arrived. He is not likely to go out,' Lady Eavensham bellowed.

'I thought he might have been enticed for a stroll.'

'A pleasure postponed for another day,' Sebastian said.

'Watch out for burglars.' Merriment sparkled in her eyes. Her lips curved, a lopsided dimple denting her left cheek.

'Burglars? Good gracious, we are not so ill-bred as to have burglars. Oh, I do hope the weather will improve. Miss Martin, look outside and see if the sky looks promising.' Lady Eavensham waved her hands in the direction of the curtains. Her jewellery jangled.

Miss Martin complied, her head bent so demurely that Sebastian wondered if he'd imagined that look of devilment moments earlier.

'Windy, but I can see the moon.'

Sebastian could see it also, peeking through fast-moving clouds. The white orb silhouetted her profile, touching her pale skin with moonlight and giving it a luminescent quality.

He wondered now if he had been entirely accurate with his initial assessment of her looks. No beauty and yet—

'Good, we run with the hounds, you know,' Lady Eavensham said. 'Well, I don't with this foot, but Lord Eavensham loves a good hunt.'

The curtains swished into place as Miss Martin turned towards the room, the movement abrupt. A flicker of distaste flashed across her countenance and her shoulders tensed under the drab gown. Sebastian wondered if she now intended to denounce fox hunting. Given the rabbit incident, he presumed it possible.

Before he could comment, the younger of the two ladies claimed his attention, leaning towards him with a breathy gasp. 'Tell me about London. I long for it, you know, and have been so looking forward to the Season.'

Sebastian groaned inwardly. *Debutantes.* The curse of modern man. They hadn't a brain between them while having an excess of pastel muslin, pale skin and manipulative wiles. He glanced towards Miss Martin, half-expecting to see another flash of wry humour cross her features.

He didn't. Instead, her countenance held such wistful longing that he looked away. Of course, once she must have hoped for London and marriage, as did they all.

It was a sad life, he thought, then frowned. What foolishness. He had no time to worry about the emotions of country misses. With his meeting with Kit over, he should focus on how best to extricate himself from the monotony of a country weekend and return to his silent daughter.

And then there was the matter of his great-aunt's latest foolish insistence that he should remarry. Sebastian drummed his fingers against his leg. He did not have time for debutante balls. He cast a glance towards the simpering misses.

No, he must make his aunt understand that he could not and would not give up.

All his energy and resources must be focused towards his children.

Edwin would be found.

Chapter Two

The fox hunt was today.

That stark thought shot through Sarah's mind the moment her alarm sounded.

Shaking off the remnants of sleep, Sarah shifted in the decadent comfort of Lady Eavensham's guest bed and blinked blearily at the rose-print wallpaper and pink curtaining.

Of course, she'd stayed the night at Eavensham.

Getting up, Sarah padded across the rug's thick pile and pulled open the velvet curtains. Bother. Morning sunshine flooded the chamber, turning floating dust motes molten.

She'd hoped for rain. In the happy event of a deluge, the hunt would be cancelled and she could snooze in the unaccustomed luxury of that wonderful bed.

Indeed, she might even have had the opportunity to rescue Miss Petunia Hardcastle from the tower in which she currently languished.

Or she could have breakfasted with Lady Eavensham's guests and heard something of London. Of course, they were hardly likely to have stumbled upon Charlotte, but just hearing about the city made her feel closer to her sister—as though her quest were more possible.

Sarah sighed. It was not to be. Albert and Albertina

must be rescued. They were the only mating foxes within the area. Lord Eavensham seemed bent on extinguishing the local population.

With this thought, she pulled off her nightgown, stooping to pick up her dress. Blood still spotted the sleeve. Bother. She'd forgotten all about the rabbit.

Moving with greater urgency, Sarah splashed water across her face and pulled her hair into a bun. Then, scrawling a note of thanks to Lady Eavensham, she hurried down the stairs and towards the cellar door.

Fortunately, the stubby candle remained where they'd left it last year. She sighed. Animal rescues had been a good deal more fun when Kit had been a rebellious adolescent and they'd done this together.

She lit a match, putting it to the wick so that the candle flickered into reluctant life. Cautiously, she stepped down the stairs and into the murky darkness, her shadow undulating eerily against the casks of wine and gardening implements.

To her relief, the wicker baskets and leather gardening gloves remained and she grabbed both baskets and gloves, hauling them upstairs into the scullery. Fortunately, this room was empty save for Gladys, the scullery maid, who stood washing dishes at the sink. Likely, the other staff were occupied in the kitchen or serving breakfast.

'Morning, miss,' Gladys said.

'How's Orion?'

'Orion, miss?'

'The rabbit.' Sarah flushed. She had a foolish habit of naming her animal friends and had called him after the constellation.

'I near forgot. He's over there, miss. I give 'im some vegetables. The stuff what's wilted round the edges.' The girl's broad-boned, country face remained impassive as she scrubbed the plates, moving reddened hands with methodical rhythm.

'Um, could he stay a little longer? I promise I'll pick him up soon, but I have to do something.'

'I dunno what Mr Hudson'll say.'

'Not a word if he knows nothing. Besides, he'll be too busy preparing for the hunt. By the by, would you have any table scraps left from last night?'

The rhythmic movements stopped. 'Oh, miss. Mrs Crawford don't have you on starvation rations, does she?'

'What? Oh, no, nothing so drastic. I need them for another project.'

'To do with four-legged critters, I'm supposing. You are a one. Ain't you ever going to grow up?'

'Seems unlikely at this point.'

'Well, there's a bowl for the 'ounds in the larder. 'elp yourself.'

Sarah did so.

Within half an hour she had manoeuvred both baskets to the outskirts of the forest and set about propping up the traps.

The bugle sounded.

She started and, biting her lip, glanced about nervously, half-expecting the thunder of horses' hooves. She'd be lucky if she had time to capture both foxes now. Hurriedly, she pulled out the meat scraps from her handkerchief, placing them within the bottom of the baskets.

A flash of rust-brown fur skirted the periphery of her vision and she spotted two curious eyes, bright pinpoints of light, within the cover of the bushes. Sarah held her breath.

The fox stepped forward—a dainty movement like a cat on snow. Albertina. Her red tail had puffed into a brush, making her body appear ludicrously thin.

Sarah sat so still that each woodland sound was magnified. The woodpecker's tap-tap-tap, the drip from leaves wet from yesterday's rain, the rustle of an unseen bird or squirrel.

The fox edged closer.

Finally, with a burst of brave energy and a wild scrabble of claws, she darted into the basket.

Sarah pulled the string. The lid snapped shut.

She hated this part; the frightened yelps, the scratch of paws and the smell of fear and urine.

'It's going to be fine, Albertina. It's for your own well-being.' She spoke softly in the sing-song voice she always used with animals, throwing in French phrases while pulling the twine tight around the clasp. The basket rocked, creaking noisily with the animal's exertions.

She'd done this for years now, since she'd first arrived here. It had helped with the sick loneliness.

In those first weeks without either her mother or sister, animals had been her only friends. They'd populated her world, making her life as an unwanted child within a strange household bearable.

Her sister had so loved animals. Indeed, Charlotte had few accomplishments; she was not well educated and could not paint or play the piano, but she had always demonstrated this steady, undemanding kindness. Nor did she discriminate, somehow finding good in scrappy urchins or grumpy shopkeepers.

When Sarah had first come to the Crawfords, life without her sister had felt intolerable. Sarah would dread both sleeping and waking and her whole body had felt hollow and bruised as though she had been kicked.

Sighing, she refocused on the basket, still rocking with Albertina's exertions. This was not the time to reminisce. She must get the animal to the other side of the stream and, with luck, return to capture Albert. After that, she would go home and work on Miss Petunia's release and hope that, just maybe, this manuscript would sell and a trip to London might enter the world of possibility.

The blasted babbling brook did it. The memories hit, the pain dizzying in its intensity. For a second, Sebastian saw his children, real as the hounds and horses. He saw them paddling, laughing, carefree.

His hands tightened reflexively and, seeking solitude, he urged his horse up the hillside and away from the other riders. His mount stopped at its summit and he found himself looking into a picturesque valley, interrupted by a silver stream threading through its base.

Something—a flicker of movement—caught his attention. He stiffened. Some village idiot was wading through the water. Even worse, he saw that the stream looked more like a river and was in flood. It moved swiftly, almost overflowing its banks.

'Hey!' he shouted.

It was a woman.

He spurred his horse down the slope. 'Madam! Can I help?'

She did not turn and moved awkwardly, a massive basket propped against one hip. He shouted again. This time she turned, glancing over her shoulder.

'Lord Langford?'

He started, hearing his name, then felt a jolt of recognition.

'Miss Martin! What in heaven's name are you doing?' He jerked his horse to a standstill, dismounting.

'I cannot stop—'

She must have slipped and was caught off balance by the force of the rushing water. She lurched backwards, dropped the basket and, hands flailing, fell. She righted herself within the instant, lunged after the basket and tripped again. This time she fell face-first.

At this rate, the woman would drown herself in three feet of water.

Dropping the reins, Sebastian stepped into the stream and grabbed her hand. She straightened, regaining her foot-hold. Water streamed down her face and strands of hair fell forward in a dripping tangle.

'Albert—' she gulped, reaching for the basket.

'Leave it—'

'She'll drown.' She lunged again.

'Stay still! I'll get it.' He caught the basket, pulling it towards them.

He had meant to take her back to the bank, but the fool woman was already wading to the other side.

He followed, his feet squelching in the mud as he placed the basket on the bank. *What—*

He stared. The basket rocked as if possessed and a yip-ping, scratching noise emanated from the wicker slats.

'What on earth have you got in there?' he asked.

Miss Martin flushed. Sebastian bent, cautiously peering under the lid. He closed it quickly, stepping away.

'It's a fox,' he said.

'Albertina.'

'You have captured a fox?'

'They would have killed her,' she said.

'What?'

'The hounds.'

'That is the point. And what a fool thing to do. You could have been hurt. It could have bitten you,' he said.

'No. I wear gloves and follow a strict procedure to pre-vent injury. I do not approve of fox hunting.'

He saw no hint of apology or regret in the stubborn lines of her face.

'You ruined the hunt.'

'I saved Albertina's life. It is a cruel practice. Moreover, their population has been decimated.' She put her hands to her hips and thrust out a surprisingly full bottom lip. 'Albertina is a creature that wishes to do no harm.'

'Tell that to the chicken farmer.'

She opened her mouth as if to argue, hands still at her hips. 'But—'

'Enough, enough. I refuse to debate the merits of fox hunting while freezing to death on a riverbank.'

'I'm not cold.'

'I am.'

'If you are feeling the chill, there is no reason for you to remain. Indeed, I should go. I must get Albertina away before they spot us.' Miss Martin spoke quickly, already bending to pick up the basket.

'Leave it. I'll carry it wherever you are going.'

'I can manage.'

'So far you have managed only to half-drown yourself.'

'I was not in any danger. The stream is not deep, although faster than on previous occasions.'

'You make a habit of this?' He felt incredulity, irritation and an uncharacteristic desire to laugh.

'Not a habit exactly.'

'You've done it before?'

'Yes, but really there is no time for questions.' She frowned, giving a worried glance towards the ridge.

'Very well. Where to?' he asked, bending to pick up the basket.

'Just beyond those trees. We'll be hidden there. Oh…' She paused briefly. 'I just realised, you must have been part of the hunt. I hope you are not too disappointed?'

'A rather belated sentiment, but, no, not overly. I'll be able to get back to London sooner.'

'You do not enjoy country weekends?'

'Not particularly.'

'Are the others leaving as well?' she asked, a little wistfully.

'I do not know. Had you stayed for breakfast instead of embarking on this fool enterprise you might have ascertained this information in a civilised manner.'

'You think I am ill-mannered?'

'I think you are peculiar.'

A grin lit up her face. 'That is an established fact.'

He felt again a reluctant, unfamiliar tug at his lips. How Edwin would tease and even Elizabeth would giggle if they could see him squelching through mud, accompanied by this bedraggled woman while carting a fox within a basket.

Or they would have done.

Before.

Any desire to laugh deserted him, leaving behind that familiar dull, empty feeling. Forgetting always made remembering worse.

The wind blew cold. He shivered in his sodden clothing. Now he wanted only to see this woman was safe and waste no more time on foxes.

'Is this suitable?' he asked abruptly, placing the basket on the ground.

They'd entered a copse, darkly cool and scented with bark and moss and mushrooms.

'Indeed, and please do not trouble yourself further,' Miss Martin said. 'I'll take her to the barn, once I get Albert and the coast is clear.'

'You'll what? You are planning to capture a second fox and take them somewhere—'

'Yes, I have a basket back—'

'That is the most foolhardy plan!'

Sebastian made a sudden decision. Bending, he pulled loose the string of the basket. It rasped through the clasp as he tugged it free, kicking open the lid.

The fox scuttled out, disappearing within a second.

'Why did you do that?' Miss Martin turned on him,

her pale face suddenly flushed and her straight, thick eyebrows drawn.

Because it felt so damn good to *do* something! Because it was a hell of a lot better than waiting.

Of course, he did not say this. Instead, he spoke in calm, level tones. 'It is foolish to introduce a fox to a farm or wherever you live.'

'Of course, I do not introduce them. I release them once the hunt is done. I certainly do not wish them to become habituated to human interaction.'

'You could have fooled me.'

'I do not aim to keep them as pets if that is what you are thinking. I aim to save a species which we are likely to drive into extinction.'

She spoke with surprising dignity for someone dripping wet from head to toe. Tendrils of dark hair had loosened from her bun, dangling about her face. He saw also that, under the folds of clinging cloth, her figure was not as nondescript as he had imagined.

'Well, extinction is postponed for another day,' he said curtly. 'The hunt is likely done. Now, I will take you home or to Eavensham before you catch your death.'

'Your further assistance is entirely unnecessary.' She placed her hands on her hips.

'It is entirely necessary and I have every intention of delivering you to safety.' He whistled for Jester who immediately stepped across the stream and headed up the bank towards him.

'And I have absolutely no intention of being delivered anywhere. I am not a—a bolt of cloth or a bag of potatoes.'

'Then perhaps I should tell Lord Eavensham of today's exploits?'

'Blackmail? That's hardly honourable.'

'But expedient.' If the last year had taught him anything, it was that the honourable finished last.

'I will not give in to blackmail.'

'I can respect that.' He stepped forward, planning to put her on his horse by physical force, if necessary. He would waste no more time on cajoling or fancy words.

She must have read his intent because she raised two small fists, her well-marked brows drawing fiercely together. 'Don't even think of it. Kit taught me to box and I am not afraid to use every trick in the book.'

He stared. She sounded as though she'd swallowed the book or a bad script more suitable for the stage. And she looked such a funny, feisty scrap of thing with her wet clothes and dripping hair.

The unfamiliar urge to laugh returned. His lips twitched. He couldn't help it. The situation was so ludicrous; this diminutive woman was ready to wrestle him to the ground, provided she had sufficient time between rescuing vermin.

The laughter wouldn't be stopped. It burbled up, ending in a belly roar. He laughed as he hadn't laughed for a year, as he hadn't laughed since, well, since the beginning of this nightmare.

When he stopped, he saw that she had dropped her fists and no longer looked fierce, but stared at him as though fearful for his sanity.

'Do you know you've witnessed a miracle?' he asked, once he had regained the power of speech.

'I know Mrs Eagan in the village would advise Epsom salts and Mrs Crawford would arrange an exorcism.'

'Then I'll stay well away from both ladies.' His voice still shook with laughter. 'Truce?' He put out his hand.

She looked uncertain, but either good manners, good nature or a genuine fear for his sanity overcame her misgivings.

She took his hand. 'Truce.'

She smiled, the expression transforming her face. She had removed her heavy, leather gloves and he could feel the delicacy of her fingers within his grasp. For a second, it felt right, comfortable even, to have her hand nestled in his palm. He felt a half-forgotten stir of pleasure.

He released her hand and bent, picking up Jester's reins. 'Your steed awaits.'

'You're still planning to escort me home?'

'If I may,' he said, with pretended humility.

'He's rather big.' She looked at the animal with apprehension, surprising for a woman who forded rivers.

'He is a horse, Miss Martin.'

'A big horse.'

'Is it possible, Miss Martin, that despite your ability to capture wild animals, you're nervous of horses?'

'Big horses. I haven't ridden often,' she admitted.

'We'll go no faster than a walk.'

'A slow walk.'

'A slow walk,' he agreed and again felt that odd *frisson* of pleasure as she nodded, placing her hand in his own.

Sebastian positioned Miss Martin in front of him—no easy task given that she still clutched the basket. He urged Jester forward and they started down the incline, the quiet broken only by the crack of twigs under Jester's hooves.

Thankfully, Miss Martin did not seem a female addicted to chatter.

'Would you prefer to return to Eavensham or your own home?' Sebastian questioned as they stepped on to the country lane at the bottom of the hill.

'My home, if possible.'

'Entirely. If you give me directions.'

'I can. But—' she shifted and he was aware of her movement and her quick, nervous inhalation '—will you drop me at the barn and not the main door?'

'That would be unusual.'

She glanced back, her face again suffused with that slow,

transformative smile. 'I don't think anything about this morning could be considered usual.'

'Perhaps not, but I would still like to see you safe at your doorstep. I'll not mention your sabotage of the hunt to your parent or guardian, if that is your concern.'

'No. It's not that.' She paused and then continued. 'My guardian would find your presence without a chaperon exceptional. She worries about my—um—morals, not realising that I am past the age and lack the physical attributes that make concern necessary.'

She stopped speaking and it struck him sad that a woman, still youngish, should dismiss herself so completely.

'I quite like your attributes.' He spoke without thought.

Her reaction was immediate. Her back jerked ramrod straight and she twisted about almost violently, despite her apparent fear of large horses and the danger of dropping the basket.

'Lord Langford,' she snapped. 'You will not insult my intellect. I am no beauty, but I am not dim-witted and refuse to be treated as such. I have gumption, if nothing else.'

Good Lord, the woman sounded downright furious.

'You definitely have gumption.'

She twisted even more precariously. 'I hope you are not scoffing again.'

'No,' he said. 'I was only wishing that Elizabeth might meet you.'

Again he had spoken with an uncharacteristic lack of thought.

'Elizabeth?'

'My daughter.'

'Why?'

'I don't know exactly, but she needs—'

Heaven only knew what Elizabeth needed.

But, he realised with a start of surprise, he would tell Elizabeth about Miss Martin when he returned.

He might mention nothing else about this country week-end, but he would tell her about the rabbit, the fox, the mud, the basket and Miss Martin's gumption.

Elizabeth would not reply, of course, but he would tell her.

Chapter Three

The barn was a ramshackle structure of mossy stone with an uneven slate roof patterned with yellowed grass. Sebastian dismounted. As he turned, helping Sarah from the horse, he was aware of a peculiar narrowing of focus. It seemed as though the barn, the trees and everything else except this woman became inconsequential.

He was keenly aware of her proximity, the faint soapy smell of her hair, the long dark lashes outlining her grey-blue eyes and the oddly endearing way she bit one pink lip.

'I—um—' She swallowed. He watched the movement in her throat. 'There's water for your horse inside.'

Everything sprang to sudden life.

'Thank you.'

He followed her into the dimness of the barn's interior. Straw covered the floor and the air felt dusty and smelled of hay and animals.

At almost the same moment, a loud, boyish whistle broke through the quiet and Kit Eavensham strode into the barn from the opposite entrance. He drew to a halt immediately upon seeing Miss Martin.

'I knew it,' he said. 'As soon as the hunt proved unsuccessful I knew you were involved. When will you stop such nonsense?'

'Likely never. That is one advantage of my circumstances. Society expects little of me.'

'But it is not sensible. I mean, it was fine when we were young and rebellious, but you can't go round saving foxes all your life. Besides, you look like an undersized drowned rat.'

'I slipped.'

'But was fished out quite handily.' Sebastian stepped forward to make Kit aware of his presence.

Kit's mouth dropped to form a round 'O'.

'Morning, Eavensham,' Sebastian drawled.

'Good Lord, Langford helped you? Do you know who he is?'

'We were introduced. Last night, if you recall,' Miss Martin said in composed tones.

'No, I mean—did you know—I mean—well, Langford is well, good *ton*. Though he hasn't been about much this past year. Still, a diamond of the first water, don't you know.'

'Then I am honoured— Oh!' She gasped, her gaze drawn to the window. 'Mrs Crawford is coming. Kit, you must not let her see you or Langford, *please*. You can lecture me later.'

Then, before Sebastian could say goodbye or even complete his bow, Miss Martin had disappeared through the barn door, letting it rattle shut behind her.

Stepping around the basket which he had placed on the floor, Sebastian went to a small, dirty window. Through its pane, Sebastian could see an older woman approach the barn from a square, stone house set some fifty yards back. She was gaunt, her grey hair pulled tightly from her face and her dark clothes cut for economy, not fashion. Her movements had a nervous jerkiness.

'Mrs Crawford, I presume?' he said softly to Kit who had followed to the window.

'Yes.'

'She looks strict.'

'And religious. Extremely so. I mean, she always has been somewhat.' Kit shrugged.

'You've known her long?'

'Mrs Crawford. Unfortunately.'

'No, Miss Martin.'

'Since she came to live here from London. She is a couple of years older than I am and Mother did not want me to get any romantic notions since she is as poor as a church mouse. Anyhow, my parents decided that the best way to avoid this was to ensure that we spent considerable time together, you know, like brother and sister. It worked, actually.'

'Practical woman, your mother.'

'Lucky for Miss Martin or she would have starved, most like. She is quite the zealot.'

'Miss Martin?'

'No, no. Mrs Crawford. She wishes to save money for the heathen. Knits socks for them. A dreadful lot of socks. Although the heathen always seem to come from these dashed hot countries. Can't see 'em needing socks.'

'Which explains Miss Martin's lack of fashion.'

'Lack of fashion? She's lucky if she gets a decent meal. Not sure she's quite all there. Mrs Crawford, I mean. Miss Martin is all there, although a tad eccentric. But jolly. Tough life for a girl.'

Turning back to the window, Sebastian watched Miss Martin approach the older woman, taking her arm and leading her towards the house. It struck him as a gentle gesture.

'Well, I'd best get back home before Father notices my absence. Just wanted to make certain that Miss Martin hadn't been bitten or drowned. Thought she'd have given up such nonsense.' Kit sauntered towards the barn door. 'I think the coast's clear. You coming?'

'In a moment.'

'Righto.'

Sebastian heard the barn door shut and Kit's boots tap sharply on the cobbles.

Jester whinnied, eager to move again, but Sebastian remained, gazing through the window, his fingers drumming on the sill. He followed the two women's progress, watching as Miss Martin supported her elderly relative, her head bent as though in conversation.

'Gracious,' Sebastian muttered to no one in particular. His fingers stilled. 'I wonder.'

Sarah took Mrs Crawford's hand. It felt cold. Her guardian had lost weight and Sarah could feel the movement of the bones beneath the dry, parchment skin.

'Come,' she said gently, rubbing the thin fingers. 'We must get you inside. You're chilled.'

Mrs Crawford glanced about, her angular face furrowed. 'Molly?' she said. 'Molly, it is good of you to come.'

'Of course I came,' Sarah said.

Molly had been Mrs Crawford's sister. She'd died twenty years earlier, but Sarah never corrected her guardian when these moments of confusion hit.

''Tis good to see you, Molly. You're wet,' she said as if only now noticing Sarah's sodden clothes.

'A minor mishap, but let us visit in the warmth.' Sarah pushed open the front door. It creaked as they walked into the hall, dreary after the sunshine outside.

Warm was never an accurate description of the Crawford house, and had never been, not even prior to Mr Crawford's death and Mrs Crawford's fanatical economy.

To Sarah, its interior had a frigid stillness as though time had stopped and all within had ceased to live. Like Sleeping Beauty, but with no happy ending. Oh, how she and Charlotte had loved fairy tales.

She smiled sadly and then refocused her attention on the

drab hall. 'Let's go into the drawing room where we can sit,' she said gently.

Mrs Crawford allowed herself to be drawn forward. 'But no fires.' Her face puckered, her hands fluttering like fragile, useless birds.

'No fires. Now sit here and I'll fetch a blanket.' Sarah helped her guardian to sit, reaching for a crocheted blanket, fuzzy with wear.

Mrs Crawford huddled in the chair but, after a second, her expression cleared and her gaze sharpened. 'You're not Molly.'

'I'm Sarah.'

'I knew that. Have you said your morning prayers? You have much for which you must repent.' Mrs Crawford always sounded cross after moments of confusion. Unfortunately such moments were all too frequent.

'Yes.'

'You must save yourself from the eternal damnation of your parenthood—a child conceived out of wedlock. And I must help you. It is my duty.' Mrs Crawford's voice rose again, her tone fractious.

'You have done your duty admirably. How about a cup of tea?' Sarah looked at the clock. She must not forget the rabbit or Hudson would have him skinned and in the pot.

Plus she still needed to change her dress and collect eggs. Hopefully, Portia and Cleopatra had been milked by the lad up the lane.

'The dinner party at Eavensham. It was not sinful?' Mrs Crawford asked after a moment.

Sarah grinned. 'I do not think Lady Eavensham runs to sinful parties.'

'And you did not enjoy it overly much?'

'I made certain I was only moderately content.'

'And no gentlemen made any improper advances?'

'At six and twenty, such an event is highly unlikely. Now

let me put the kettle on and make you a little luncheon.'
Sarah stood, moving briskly.

'Do not waste food.'

'I will use the bare minimum to keep body and soul together.'

After settling Mrs Crawford, Sarah entered the kitchen's warmth, which still smelled pleasantly of the fresh bread Mrs Tuttle, their only domestic, had made earlier.

With the ease of familiarity, Sarah filled the kettle, hanging it on the arm iron to boil before slicing the bread and spreading it with Cleopatra's creamy butter.

Her knife scraped the pot. She'd have to make more soon. Always so much to do... Plus she'd accomplished nothing yesterday. Not that yesterday had been wasted. Sarah smiled—just hearing about London thrilled her as though being in earshot of the words 'Westminster' and 'Regent's Square' made finding her sister more possible.

One day, she promised herself. One day she would get to London and look for Charlotte, the half-sister who had been more of a mother to her than the woman who had given birth to them both.

And once in London, she would scour every street, knock on every door and pray that she was not too late.

Next morning, Sarah rose early, rushed through breakfast and hurried to feed the chickens in the hopes of escaping to Eavensham to collect the rabbit and her valise.

Yesterday had proved too busy despite her best efforts and she just had to hope that Eavensham's kitchen staff would have looked after the creature. Likely they would. They had an affection for her from the days when she and Kit had requested treats and other edibles.

'Miss! Miss!' Mrs Tuttle's shrieks interrupted her only seconds after she had started to scatter seed.

'What? Is Mrs Crawford ill?' Sarah threw the rest of the

grain at the birds and hurried towards the house where Mrs Tuttle stood at the kitchen entrance, her pink face puce as she flapped her arms with agitation.

'What is it?'

'Miss Sarah, Miss Sarah, you have a visitor.'

Sarah stopped abruptly. 'A visitor? Is that all? I thought something dreadful had happened. Is it Mr Kit?'

'It ain't Mr Kit.'

Sarah had reached the door now. 'The vicar?'

'It ain't the vicar neither.'

'Gracious, who is it? Or must I play a guessing game?'

''Tis Lord Langford.'

'His lordship? Why?' Her voice squeaked and she frowned.

'I'm sure I don't know, miss,' Mrs Tuttle said, her eyes round.

'You are certain he did not ask for Mrs Crawford?'

'Yourself, miss. Most specific, he was.'

'Where is Mrs Crawford anyway?' Sarah asked, walking into the kitchen.

'Resting. She felt tired and was confused after breakfast. Should I wake her?'

Sarah paused as she cleaned her hands under the chill water of the kitchen pump. Mrs Crawford would not approve of her meeting a gentleman without a chaperon. At the same time, Sarah had no wish for Mrs Crawford to know about yesterday's events. Doubtless she would see an acquaintance with his lordship as either the influence of evil or an inherited flaw from her mother.

'Don't wake her. I will see him,' Sarah said with decision.

'Very good, miss. But what do you think he wants?'

'I haven't the faintest idea and can think of only one way to find out,' Sarah said, tucking a strand of hair behind her ear and walking purposefully towards the drawing-room door.

* * *

Lord Langford had not had a pleasant day following the incident at the stream. His host was in a bad mood, likely brought about by the unsatisfactory hunt. Lady Eavensham's foot hurt and she had taken to her bed while the young ladies kept giggling and engaging him in conversation.

This would not have been such an irritation if he had not needed solitude to think. The idea, when it had first struck him, had seemed ludicrous, the far-fetched scheme of a desperate man.

And yet he could not reject it out of hand. He remembered those few words of fluent French he'd overheard and, more importantly, Miss Martin's kindness to her elderly guardian.

The idea would, he thought, solve a multitude of problems in an efficient manner. He liked efficiency. Indeed, in the management of his estate, he would never dismiss such a practical solution without consideration. Surely, his personal affairs deserved the same attention.

And so he had listened to Lady Eavensham's vapid guests while thoughts whirled and he veered between the alternating conclusions that he was mad and eminently sensible.

He had retired, slept poorly, only to have the problem brought to a head the next morning with Hudson's arrival in the library.

'A message, milord,' Hudson announced.

Sebastian took it. As always, he was conscious of that shiver of apprehension, excitement, hope…despair.

It was from his housekeeper. He recognised the script. He scanned the lines which were businesslike and succinct.

The governess had quit.

'Miss Elizabeth has taken to remaining on her rocking horse for hours. Indeed, it is hard to make her stop even for meals and Miss Grosvenor could not endure the constant creaking of the rockers combined with Miss Elizabeth's silence.'

Damn. Sebastian crumpled the note, throwing it towards the hearth where it ignited. He watched the flame lick the paper's edge, the fire growing in momentary strength before subsiding to ash.

Damn and blast. Did not one governess have any backbone or staying power? Did none of these women have the skills necessary to return Elizabeth to some semblance of normality?

And it was then, standing in Lord Eavensham's library and staring at the dying flame, that had Sebastian decided.

Sarah found Lord Langford in the drawing room standing beside the unlit hearth. Although not much taller than Kit, he dominated the room and dwarfed the shabby furniture in a way her childhood friend could not.

It was not only his physical size, but his presence and the cold, controlled force of his personality.

Like a volcano under snow.

'Lord Langford.' She stepped towards him.

'Good morning, Miss Martin.' He made his bow.

'Did you wish to see me? Or perhaps Mrs Tuttle misunderstood. I could fetch Mrs Crawford.'

'Indeed, no. I expressly asked for you.' He spoke in a crisp, authoritative tone.

'Oh.' A shiver of nervousness tingled through her. 'Pray be seated.'

They both sat. Sarah felt stiff, as if her arms and legs had lost fluidity. It had been easier to talk to him while rescuing Albert, as though the very oddness of their occupation had made social conventions unnecessary.

She rubbed her hands together. They made a chafing sandpaper sound, emphasising the chill silence of the room.

'May I offer you refreshment?' she asked belatedly.

'No, thank you. Indeed, I will get straight to the point.'

'Please do.' She exhaled with relief. 'I much prefer blunt speech.'

He straightened his shoulders and shifted to face her more squarely as though putting his mind to an unpleasant task.

'Miss Martin, I need— May I have the honour of your hand in marriage?'

Chapter Four

Sarah gaped. Her jaw hung loose. Her eyes widened and her breath left her body in a winded gasp.

For a moment, her brain could not make sense of his words as though he had spoken German or another foreign tongue.

Then she understood.

Anger flashed through her, hot and powerful. She bounded to her feet, her cheeks heated and her hands balled with fury. 'My lord, I am not without pride and I will not allow you to make sport of me.'

He stood also. 'Miss Martin, I am quite serious and never make sport.'

She stilled. 'Then you are mad.'

'I do not believe so. Lunacy does not run in my family.' He paused, his expression suddenly bleak. 'I hope.'

'You expect me to believe that you are serious?'

'I seldom have expectations, but I assure you that I am serious,' he said.

She stared at him, taking in his even features, the dark grey eyes flecked with green, the dark sweep of hair across his forehead and the firm jaw. There was nothing about him to hint at madness or jest.

Turning, she rubbed her fingers along the mantel, studying their outline against the wood's grain as she tried to marshal her thoughts.

The clock ticked.

'If you are neither mad nor making sport of me,' she said at length, 'you must have a reason.'

'I need someone to look after Elizabeth.'

'For which one employs a governess.'

'They have a habit of leaving,' he said.

'Marriage seems a somewhat extreme action to ensure continuity of staff.'

'It does,' he said.

She raised her brows.

'My daughter is…quiet.'

'A quality generally admired in children.'

He did not answer for a moment and when he did, his words were slow as though reluctantly drawn from him. 'She hasn't spoken a word in six months. They find Elizabeth's silence unnerving. She also rocks her body and, according to my housekeeper, has now taken to riding on the rocking horse in a compulsive manner.'

'I am sorry. Is she ill?'

'I have two children,' he answered, his voice still flat and drained of emotion. 'Their mother chose to leave for France with them and her lover. She was subsequently executed.'

'How awful.'

'I presume it was for her.'

Sarah shivered at the detached tone.

'Both children were held for ransom. I paid and my daughter, Elizabeth, was returned to me.'

'And your son?'

'I don't know.' A muscle rippled in his cheek.

Instinctively Sarah shifted towards him; the stark loneliness of his grief touched her. 'I'm sorry.'

He nodded. They fell quiet.

She broke the silence tentatively. 'But I still do not see why marrying me would help.'

He shrugged. 'It probably won't. But there is something about you—' He paused before stating in a firmer tone, 'You speak French.'

'Yes. My mother taught me, but why would it matter?'

'Elizabeth has been away from England for two years and I presume whoever cared for her spoke French.'

'And you thought she might be more conversant in that language.'

He shrugged. 'I don't know. She has always been oddly silent.'

He paused, before continuing.

'As well, my great-aunt Clara demands that I marry.'

'What?'

'My elderly aunt, who is also extremely wealthy, wants me to marry,' he said flatly.

'Why on earth would she want you to marry me?'

'I doubt she would choose you, but she insists that I marry someone.'

'But why?'

'She feels it would be better for Elizabeth and that it would help me to rally, to focus on my surviving child and give up on my son.'

'She would have you stop searching for her own nephew?'

'She feels the case is hopeless,' he said, his voice raw with pain. 'And wants me to look towards the future and rebuild my life.'

'I'm sorry,' she said inadequately. The silence fell again.

She broke it with an effort. 'But if you are so opposed to marriage, why even agree to your aunt's request?'

'The crass matter of finances. Between the ransom and the ongoing search for Edwin, my financial resources are not as I would like and I will not cripple my tenants for my own purpose.'

'So you chose me to comply, but in a way bound to anger your aunt?'

'No...' He paused, drumming his fingers against the mantel. 'I am not so petty. Nor am I cruel. And it would be cruel to tie a young girl with prospects to one such as myself.'

The clock struck the hour.

'But you would tie me?' she asked into the silence.

'It would seem that your life is difficult at present.'

'And I have nothing to lose.' It stung despite its truth. 'You did not consider that I, too, might have no interest in marriage?'

'Every woman has an interest in marriage.'

'I—' She frowned, thinking of Mr and Mrs Crawford's union and Lord and Lady Eavensham's for that matter. 'In my experience, marriage hardly seems conducive to happiness.'

'I would concur but, in your case, it might be preferable to living in a cold, bare house with an elderly and perhaps unbalanced recluse.'

'I...' She paused, angered by the blunt words. 'I would not marry anyone merely to improve my circumstance.'

'How unusual.'

She hated the switch to cold sarcasm more than his earlier bluntness.

'However, the offer remains if you wish to consider it,' he said.

It was crazy. One could not marry a man one had only met forty-eight hours earlier, a man one didn't even like never mind love. Indeed, a man who seemed bitter and angry from his own admission. But—

'Where would we live?'

'London for some of the time and—'

But Sarah was no longer listening.
She could think of only two things.
London.
And Charlotte.

Chapter Five

Langford left. Sarah heard his brisk stride along the passage, followed by the whine of the front door and the solid clunk as it closed.

She exhaled. Pressing her face against the window's cool pane, she watched as he mounted his horse; his hair so dark it looked black, his movements fluid and his figure innately masculine with broad shoulders and narrow hips.

She should have seen him out, she supposed. Or called Mrs Tuttle.

But the importance of social convention had been dwarfed beside the stark reality that this man, this peer, this Earl, had asked her, Miss Sarah Martin, to be his bride. It seemed unbelievable. It *was* unbelievable.

Could Kit have engineered the whole thing as a hoax? No, Kit was high-spirited, but never cruel. Besides, Lord Langford was not the sort to play the fool in someone else's joke.

No, the Earl had proposed and Sarah had no alternative but to believe the offer was real, however prosaic his motivation.

She glanced towards the mantel where her father, the late Mr Crawford, looked down at her. He'd been dead five years now. They'd never had a close relationship. He had been many years her mother's senior and had seemed more like an austere visitor than relation whenever he had come to the small London house where they'd lived.

But he had provided for her following her mother's death, when the occupants of the tiny house were disbanded. Charlotte had not been so lucky. She didn't even know her father's name and had had nowhere—

'Sarah? Is it luncheon soon?'

Sarah jumped as Mrs Crawford pushed open the door, her voice querulous.

'No. Yes. I'm sorry.'

'You appear to be daydreaming. I hope that socialising the other night did not put frivolous ideas into your head. Daydreaming interferes with serious thought.'

Sarah smiled wanly. 'I will keep my thoughts serious.'

'Sometimes I worry that I have failed in my rearing of you and that your natural disposition might yet win out.'

'Mrs Crawford, you have done everything possible to instruct me in goodness and quell any leaning towards frivolity,' Sarah said. 'Now, sit and I will fetch something to eat and some tea.'

'A little tea, although we must be frugal,' Mrs Crawford said as she suffered herself to be led to the chair.

'Of course.'

'Did we have a visitor? I heard voices.'

Sarah paused, her hand tightening against the threadbare back of the chair. A glib reply died on her lips. Honesty had been too strongly instilled.

'Yes, it was Lord Langford. He is visiting at Eavensham,' she said.

'A gentleman. I should have been called. It is not seemly that you entertain him alone. We do not wish people to think you sinful. And why would he visit you? This Lord Langford?'

'He was on an errand for Lady Eavensham.' Honesty only went so far.

Mrs Crawford nodded, a look of childlike confusion clouding her face.

'I'll get the tea. You'll be all right for the moment?' Sarah asked.

'I am not a child.'

'I know.' Impulsively, Sarah bent and pressed a kiss against the older woman's forehead. Mrs Crawford smelled of carbolic soap and her hair was sparse with the dryness of the elderly.

'Good gracious. What was that for? I do not hold with emotional displays.'

'Merely a thank you,' Sarah said.

'Humph, a hot cup of tea would suffice,' Mrs Crawford replied, with a return to lucidity.

'Which I will provide immediately.'

An hour later, Sarah trudged towards the barn. As always, she felt a sense of relief as she exited the house, but today the need for respite was immense.

She felt filled with high-strung, restless energy which made her movements abrupt and her thoughts whirl. Nothing could distract her, not the familiar fields, the soothing rustle of tree branches or even the homely dank scent of animals and manure.

Straightening, she opened the gate so that Portia and Cleopatra could enter, their bells clanging as they shifted with easy ambling movements.

If she married Langford, she could go to London.

That thought emblazoned itself across her mind like fireworks at Vauxhall.

It dominated her thoughts as she patted the cows' rumps, dragging forward the three-corner stool and placing her fingers with practised ease on Cleopatra's warm udder.

And in London, she might find her sister.

The words thudded through her consciousness with the regularity of her own heartbeat. Even the squirt of the milk seemed to echo with its rhythm.

Closing her eyes, Sarah visualised Charlotte as she had last seen her after their mother's death: a tall girl of fifteen, her blonde hair and white face starkly contrasted against the dense blackness of her mourning clothes.

Cleopatra shifted under Sarah's lax hands. The bell clanged.

'Sorry, sweetie, did I fall asleep on you? It's just I have an enormous decision to make—although truly I cannot believe I am even entertaining the notion. I mean, could I really *marry* him? What do I even know of him? He hardly seems pleasant or enjoyable company. And certainly not flattering.'

The cow swung her head around, blowing moist, grass-scented breath into Sarah's face.

'I'd miss you.' She stroked the animal.

A mouse scurried into the corner, burrowing into the straw. How did animals know instinctively what to do? How did they know to build a nest, burrow and find food?

Was it easier to lack intelligence and follow instinct? And what would she do if she had little intellect and only instinct?

But that was easy to answer. One need would supersede all else.

Sarah had not forgotten the rabbit or her few belongings which she had neglected to take when she had left so precipitously to rescue the foxes. Therefore, after milking the cows, she set out along the familiar route to Eavensham.

The path was unchanged from yesterday. It still smelled of grass and leaves, the earth was spongy and birds twittered, unseen, within the woods' greenery.

Irrationally, Sarah felt a confused anger that all could remain so unaltered while her world had been turned upside down and shaken like a child's toy.

She'd felt the same after her mother's death when the routines of London continued amidst her own tragedy. It was egotistical, she supposed, but we are all the hero of our own story.

Upon arrival at Eavensham, she found that Orion had escaped the cook pot, largely thanks to the scullery maids who had kept him in a crate under the sink which served as a makeshift hutch. Sarah cleaned this out. Then she wrapped the rabbit in a scarf, carefully keeping its hindquarters immobilised.

Normally, she would not have minded seeing Lady Eavensham or her guests, but today she found herself as eager to return to the Crawford home as she had been to flee it.

Therefore, she picked up both the rabbit and her valise, thanked the maids and exited into the park.

'Miss Martin!'

'My lord!' Sarah jerked to a stop.

She had been so engrossed she'd almost collided with the man, who appeared to be coming from the stables. 'You pop up at unexpected moments.'

'And apparently you always clutch an animal to your person. It has escaped the stew pot?'

'Yes.'

'May I escort you home or are you staying for dinner?'

'No, the vicar's wife is making up numbers, the vicar being away.' She clutched the rabbit more closely, shifting her weight awkwardly while trying to think of suitable conversation.

What did one say to one's suitor?

Of course, Miss Hardcastle and her lover had discussed Petunia's eyes at length. Or gazed wordlessly at each other.

She doubted Lord Langford wished to comment on her eyes and already the wordlessness had become uncomfortable.

'May I walk you home?' he repeated.

'I'm certain I can manage.' She sounded ungracious, Sarah realised belatedly.

'I'm certain you can as well, but this would give me the opportunity to know you better.'

'You might have been advised to do so before proposing to me,' Sarah said. Then bit her lip. She'd aimed for humour, but realised that had sounded even less gracious than her previous comment. So absolutely *not* what Miss Hardcastle would say.

'Indeed, but then I seldom take advice.' His lips twisted in a smile, suggesting that despite his brusque manner he was not devoid of humour.

They turned towards the woods, walking in silence across the spongy green lawn until Lord Langford ventured a question. 'So, Miss Martin, other than rescuing animals, might I enquire about your interests? Needlepoint or the pianoforte?'

'Neither, actually.'

'Watercolours?'

'No.' She stopped abruptly so that the animal jerked in her arms.

'Miss Martin?' He stopped also.

'Lord Langford, I cannot make polite conversation when your proposal lies between us like an elephant.'

'An elephant?' His eyebrows rose and this time the smile widened, reaching almost to his eyes.

'That's what my moth—a relative called any topic everyone is thinking about, but no one will mention.'

'Your relative has a descriptive turn of phrase. And what, do you suggest, is our elephant?'

'Your proposal of marriage and my response. Or perhaps you have realised that the idea is ludicrous and now would like to withdraw the suggestion—'

'No,' he said. 'I do not vacillate or retract an offer once made.'

'Of course,' she said. He would be honourable above all else.

'So you have considered my proposal?'

'I have.' She forced her voice to steady.

A bird twittered overhead and a hawk flew. The stillness was so complete that she heard the feathered movement of its wings.

'And?'

Chapter Six

'Yes,' Sarah said.

Sebastian's gut squeezed, although whether this was due to nerves or excitement he did not know. For the past year—both emotions—*any* emotion other than the leaden weight of despair had felt foreign to him.

'I am honoured.'

'Nonsense and poppycock,' she said with a sudden return to animation. 'If this arrangement has any hope of success, we must be honest. I doubt you're honoured. Relieved at best.'

'Are you always this outspoken?' The woman did not mince words.

'In general. But—' She looked at him, her forehead puckered. 'There is one other favour I must ask. I hate to do so as I know it will cost money.'

'Do not worry, Miss Martin, you will have your own funds for whatever jewellery or knick-knacks you desire.'

'Thank you, but that is not it. The favour… It is for my guardian, Mrs Crawford. I cannot leave her alone. She has become peculiar. I fear she will starve or freeze or both.'

'You want her to come with us?'

'No. I thought of that, but she's lived here for years. She needs familiar surroundings or I fear she will become more disorientated. I hoped we could arrange for a companion, if that would not be too awfully expensive. I know that your circumstances are straitened—'

'I can arrange for a companion,' he said.

'And you think someone would agree to such a position? She can be difficult.'

'Money is usually an excellent incentive,' he said, although it had not helped him retain a governess.

'I feel I am abandoning her, but I need…' She paused, as though uncertain.

'Yes?'

'Nothing. Only that I will visit her when I can.'

'Of course, you are at liberty to come here as often as you would like.'

They walked forward again, continuing down the tree-lined road in silence until Miss Martin spoke once more in her forthright way. 'When were you thinking this marriage should occur?'

'I will talk to the local vicar and arrange for a common licence. I expect we can be married Monday.'

'Monday? This Monday?'

'It would save the necessity of chaperons on our trip to London and allow us to expedite our plans. If that is convenient?'

'I have nothing planned for the day,' Miss Martin said.

He met her gaze and they both smiled in recognition of the ludicrous nature of the statement.

'I must also ask your guardian for your hand.'

'Yes, I suppose.' Her face creased into a frown as though she were more worried about this than getting married within the week. 'I do not know how she will react. Don't come today. It is too late. She is more alert during the mornings.'

'Very well. But do not worry. I see no reason for her to disapprove of the match. I will, by the way, set up an account at the local seamstress's establishment so that you can purchase a wedding gown.'

'Oh, I hadn't thought of that. I doubt poor Miss Simpson could make a dress so quickly.'

'Again, money is an excellent motivator.'

'You have a jaundiced view of human nature,' she said.

A smile tugged at his mouth. His whole life people had pussyfooted about him because of his position, money or, more recently, his temper.

'I would say realistic as opposed to jaundiced.'

'But people can also be caring and compassionate,' she said softly, glancing up.

She had long lashes—dark, delicate fans which formed pretty patterns against her pale cheeks. He stiffened. His sense of ease dissipated. He should not be noticing her eyes, her lashes or that her skin had a creamy smoothness that made him want to touch it…

'People tend to care only when it is in their interests to express the sentiment. Moreover, now we are on the subject of emotion and motivation, I must emphasise that this is a marriage based on sound business principles.'

'Business principles?' Her eyes widened, her brows rising with a trace of mockery.

'Indeed, I gain a mother for my child and access to my great-aunt's largesse and you escape the drudgery of your current life. There is no sentiment involved.'

'And you do not feel cheated?'

'Pardon?'

'Most men would wish to at least like their wife.'

'Most men have not witnessed their parents' infidelities only to have their wife run off with a Frenchman, taking his children with her. Romance is too fragile a base for a lifelong contract.'

He clenched his jaw, wishing the words unsaid. There was a vulnerability in such anger.

They had exited into the small clearing which marked the end of the woods and the beginning of the Crawford property. By mutual consent, they paused, facing each other.

Her clear gaze met his own. 'I will ensure that it is a marriage without sentiment. I could develop some annoying habits if that would help.' Her lips twisted wryly, amusement glinting in her clear, candid gaze.

Again he felt his own sense of humour awaken. His smile broadened.

They should move on, but he found himself loath to break the moment and, as though of its own volition, his hand touched the smooth satin of her cheek.

Her mouth opened. He saw the sheen of moisture on her bottom lip. He heard the quick exhalation as her gaze widened as if in surprise or awareness. He stepped closer. The top of her head brushed his chin. He leaned towards her. Her hair smelled of—

What in the name of—

Jumping back, he stared at the wriggling creature in her arms.

The rabbit.

Her grip must have loosened and the animal scrambled free, landing a few feet away.

'Orion, come back here!' Sarah called.

It loped in the opposite direction, its left foot dragging behind it.

Sarah squatted on the ground. She pulled a carrot from her pocket. Good God, the woman *would* have a carrot about her person—and pushed it towards the miserable creature.

'For goodness' sake, you'll get yourself filthy. I'll catch it,' Sebastian said.

'Don't frighten him and his name's Orion.'

'You've named him?' Sebastian took the vegetable and thrust it towards the animal.

'It makes one seem friendlier. Less likely to put him into a stew pot.'

'An excellent place for him.'

'Don't say that. He'll never come.'

'I don't believe Orion is conversant with the King's English,' Sebastian said irritably.

'Animals know more than we think.'

'Right. Well, Orion, you'd better come to Miss Martin promptly or you'll end up as fox fodder.'

The rabbit hopped again in the opposite direction. Sebastian pulled off his coat with difficulty and approached the animal.

Of course Orion zigged and zagged. Sebastian threw down his coat, hoping to entrap the creature. On the second attempt, he covered the rabbit and, in a move reminiscent of schoolboy rugby, scooped it up.

'Well done,' Miss Martin enthused.

'We'd best continue promptly before he gets out again,' Sebastian said.

'I can take him. Truly you do not need to walk me home.'

'If I am to reclaim my coat, I do.'

'We could unwrap him,' she suggested.

'Better not. I have no wish to repeat that performance.'

They continued forward. He said nothing and was glad of her silence. What had that moment been about? He hadn't had thoughts like that since he'd met Alicia at her debut. Not even the mistresses he'd sought after his wife's desertion had evoked such feeling. Lust, yes. But not this confused mix of desire, humour, irritation and something else he could not even identify.

And now, instead of relief that he'd solved his childcare and financial problems in one master stroke without

involving a single debutantes' ball, he felt fear—panic—
and a deep, growing conviction that he'd made one hell of
a mistake.

Next morning, Sebastian stood within the spartan confines of the Crawford drawing room. No fire warmed the
hearth and the walls were bare except for an amateurish
portrait of, he presumed, the deceased Mr Crawford. The
scent of lemon wax permeated the air.

'Lord Langford, Sarah said you would be calling and
wished to speak to me?' A crisp voice interrupted his mus-
ing and he turned, bowing.

Mrs Crawford stood tall, but her clothes hung loosely
from her angular frame as though she had recently lost
weight. She wore black, the shade relieved only by a silver cross. Her hair was scraped back into a bun and her
skin appeared sallow, stretched taut across her cheekbones.

'Mrs Crawford, it is delightful to meet you,' he said.

She nodded, advancing a few steps over the threshold,
but she neither sat nor invited him to sit.

'I must ask you to be brief. It is almost time for my
morning prayers.' She spoke quickly, her left hand already
touching the silver cross.

How different this was from his first courtship, from
Alicia's coy expression and her mother's avaricious joy.

Sebastian inhaled. 'Mrs Crawford, I wish to ask for Miss
Martin's hand in marriage.'

Shocked surprise flickered across the older woman's
face. Her intense gaze turned on him, her eyebrows drawing together almost fiercely. 'Did she do something inappropriate? Blood will out, you know.'

'I assure you, Miss Martin was entirely appropriate.' He
did not have to force the haughtiness into his tone. The indignation he felt on Sarah's behalf surprised him.

'She is not young.'

'Her age is immaterial.'

'She has no money and her background is dubious. Her mother—'

'Her background is immaterial.' He spoke quickly, cutting off her words, conscious of an almost physical aversion to the woman.

'Then I have done my Christian duty to warn you. You cannot say I have not.'

'Miss Martin cares for you. I am surprised you would speak ill of her.'

'I speak honestly as is my duty.' Mrs Crawford clutched at her cross, so tightly that he could see her knuckles through her parchment skin.

'You have certainly dispatched your duty thoroughly. Will you now give us your blessing?'

'You have my permission. I am no cleric and cannot give a blessing.'

'Of course not.' He paused, uncertain how best to broach the subject of a companion to this thin-lipped woman.

'Was there something else?'

'Miss Martin is worried.' His fingers drummed against his thigh. He stopped their movement. 'She doesn't like to leave you alone and I wondered if you'd allow me to arrange for a companion—'

'A companion? I cannot afford another mouth to feed or a room to heat.' The thin hands fluttered about the dark cloth of her dress. 'I need to save, for the missions, you know.'

'I will ensure that any financial difficulties are covered.'

'I am no charity case and you are too free with your money. I hope you give also to the Lord's work. It would do your soul more good to give to the heathen than to me.'

'It would do my bride's peace of mind more good to know that you are comfortable.'

'Her peace of mind would be better assured through prayer. Do you pray, Lord Langford?'

'I—' Then he remembered Elizabeth.

And Edwin.

'I have of late,' he said.

But even as he finished the sentence, he saw Mrs Crawford's face change. Her gaze altered, becoming vague.

She stepped back from him, her expression confused.

'Who are you?' Her tone was high and wavering whereas seconds earlier it had been firm and strong.

'Mrs Crawford?' He softened his voice.

'Where's Molly? I lost my doll. I want it. I want it back.'

'Your doll?'

'Molly will find it. Or Sarah. I feel stronger when she is around.'

'Sarah or Molly?'

'I don't know,' she said, the taut shoulders drooping. Sebastian shifted his weight uncertainly. He realised now why Sarah had said that Mrs Crawford would need a companion. He saw also that her acceptance was moot—she would soon be in no position to refuse.

'Are you good at finding things?' Mrs Crawford asked, her voice tremulous like that of an overtired child.

'I—' He thought again of Edwin. 'I pray to God I am.'

Sarah sat within her bedchamber.

Her betrothed—her mind stumbled over the word—had come and gone. She'd heard his footsteps in the front hall. She'd heard the door open and close. She'd heard the clip-clop of horses' hooves.

Permission granted, she presumed.

This thing, this marriage, was gathering momentum, moving and surging with the unstoppable power of an ocean's wave. They would be married Monday. She would marry a man she did not even know on Monday.

On Monday—the day repeated in her mind as though the idea would be less bizarre on a different day, a Tuesday or a Wednesday perhaps. Five days from now. One hundred and twenty hours.

Her fingers tightened about the locket her mother had given her. She opened it, touching the dry strands of her sister's hair she had treasured for so long.

It would be worth it. If she could find Charlotte, it would be worth it. Her sister, Charlotte, who had always been there, so much more motherly than the laughing, glamorous woman who had birthed them. She could not…must not fail her—not when this opportunity was within her grasp. Besides, countless women married for convenience or money or a title or because their parents told them to. She was no different.

Her solitude ended when Mrs Crawford appeared. She stood within the doorway, her body rigid and her fingers tightly clasped about the wooden frame as though needing its support.

'Lord Langford has asked for your hand in marriage. You have agreed to this?'

Sarah nodded.

'Then there is little more to be said. Apprise me of the arrangements and I will, of course, pray for you.' Mrs Crawford turned as if to go.

'Um—'

Mrs Crawford paused, her hand dropping to the doorknob. 'Yes?'

Doubts and questions weighed on Sarah like the oppressive mugginess of a thundery day. The region under her breastbone ached with that familiar pain, that suppressed longing for affection.

'I'll miss you,' she said softly.

'Then you must look to the Lord for comfort.'

And that was it. The conversation was finished before it had begun.

Sarah watched as her guardian turned and left, her progress marked by the brisk click of her footsteps. The ache deepened. She could not blame her. Sarah's arrival at the Crawfords' residence must have represented the older woman's worst nightmare. While Sarah and her mother remained in London, Mrs Crawford could ignore her husband's infidelity. She could pretend the tiny house in one of London's dubious neighbourhoods did not exist.

But then her mother had died. The house had been emptied and Mr Crawford had transported her here.

She shivered, remembering that chilly reception. Bending, Sarah pulled out an ancient hatbox from under the wooden bed frame. She lifted the lid, inhaling its familiar musty mix of perfume and ink.

Charlotte's letters.

She knew them by heart. She knew every ink blot and loop of her sister's childish hand. She should. She'd devoured them, reading and rereading them a hundred times a day. Sometimes she'd even placed them under her pillow, slipping her hand underneath to feel the edges against her fingers and hear their rustle, taking comfort in the knowledge that her sister had held them, folded them, mailed them.

A tangible reassurance that someone loved her.

Chapter Seven

Sarah went to Miss Simpson. She chose the cloth for her wedding gown and requested that the dress be ready within four days.

Miss Simpson agreed, but paused, fingering the grey material, as though uncertain. 'This is for your wedding?'

Sarah nodded.

'I know it is serviceable and of excellent quality, but wouldn't you care for something brighter for a wedding?'

Sarah looked about the tiny shop at the bolts of multi-oloured cloth haphazardly stacked. Her mother had worn such clothes.

'Bright colours do not suit me,' she said.

Her mother had told her that often enough, frowning with displeasure at Sarah's pale skin and unruly, mouse-brown hair.

'I am not suggesting you wear a rainbow, but what about this lilac?' Miss Simpson pulled down a bolt. 'The colour would work well on you. It would brighten your skin and bring out the chestnut in your hair.

Sarah hesitated. Violet would so help her feel like Petunia. And Petunia would cope so much better with a wedding than Miss Martin.

But this was a business arrangement. Her primary role

was that of governess and she refused to entertain notions which might suggest otherwise.

She was not Petunia.

'The grey is more serviceable,' she stated resolutely.

Sebastian, or rather his man of business, found a companion for Mrs Crawford with remarkable dispatch.

The individual, a Miss Sharples, was delivered by his lordship's groom the day before the wedding. She was a short, pleasantly dressed individual with a plump face and determined chin at odds with the general roundness of her physique.

'Did his lordship explain the matter to you?' Sarah asked after leading Miss Sharples through the drab hallway and settling her into a chair within the equally drab drawing room. If she ever had the chance to decorate a home she would colour it butter yellow, like sunshine.

'Indeed, and I am used to invalids.'

Sarah frowned. 'Mrs Crawford is not infirm, at least not physically. She gets confused and is determined that we must save money for the church.'

'Do not worry, miss. My last employer was interested in the paranormal and felt he had been a Roman emperor in a past life. He'd hide in his bed on the Ides of March. He did not, however, escape death, dying in his sleep in August. Though, despite his oddities, he was easier than his predecessor, who was forever catching the bed curtains alight. Eventually, I had to hide the matches.'

At that moment, Mrs Crawford's brisk footsteps could be heard down the hallway. By common accord, Sarah and Miss Sharples stood as Mrs Crawford stepped into the room.

'Mrs Crawford, this is Miss Sharples. She is to stay with you when I leave.'

'So I hear. A totally unnecessary expense. I hope you knit.'

'Very well,' Miss Sharples said.

'We knit for the heathen.'

Miss Sharples nodded. 'I always say many hands make light work.'

'Hardly original, but appropriate, I suppose.' Mrs Crawford grunted in what might have been approbation.

'This is a beautiful room,' Miss Sharples ventured. 'With excellent proportions.'

'The house has been in my husband's family for many years.'

Miss Sharples nodded. 'But it needs furniture.'

Sarah quaked at this bald statement.

'I sold it to send money for the heathens,' Mrs Crawford explained fitfully.

'But one cannot have the vicar to tea without proper furnishings and one needs to do so, that way one can properly direct him in the guidance of his flock.'

Sarah felt her lips twitch. Miss Sharples might just suit after all.

On her last evening, Sarah walked to the barn to bid her creatures farewell. She would miss them, particularly Portia and Cleopatra. She'd miss their animal smell, the warmth and understanding in their bovine eyes, the fact they did not know about mousey hair.

Or bastard daughters.

'I'm sure I won't find cows half as nice as you in London.' She stroked the scratchiness of their rounded sides. 'I've arranged for the boy next door to milk you and I am certain he will do a good job.'

On her return to the house, she had anticipated going straight to bed, but light shone from under the crack of the drawing-room door.

Pushing it open, she found Mrs Crawford sitting in an uncomfortably upright chair by the hearth. A small fire flickered, casting weird, elongated shadows.

'I am glad you've come in,' her guardian said. 'I suppose you were talking to those animals. One of these days you'll be saying they talk back.'

Sarah smiled. 'They do, after a fashion. Did you need something?'

'To talk to you,' Mrs Crawford said, her back more ramrod straight than usual and her hands for once unoccupied, tightly clasped.

'I would like that,' Sarah said, sitting on the seat opposite.

'I realised that I'm the closest thing you have to a mother now.'

'Yes, that's true.'

'And I recognise that somebody must speak to you and, given the situation, that person must be me.' Mrs Crawford's thin fingers unclasped to pick at a loose thread within her knitted shawl.

'You need to speak to me?'

'To warn you.'

'About?'

'A man's needs.'

'Oh.' Sarah's face flushed, as she suppressed a giggle. What a delightful scene this would make. But rather nicer to write than to live through.

'You don't need to—I mean, I understand a little. From the animals, of course.'

'Yes, yes, that's just it.' Mrs Crawford's hands worked at the wool with almost frenzied speed. 'It is a system of procreation meant for animals.'

Sarah had never heard it referred to as a 'system' before. Not, she thought wryly, that it was a topic discussed at her limited social engagements.

'Mrs Crawford, please do not upset yourself. Truly, I understand the basic concept and it appears most women survive. It will be no worse and no better with Lord Langford than with any other man, I suppose,' she said, with determined practicality.

'You mustn't enjoy it.' Her guardian spoke more strongly now as though, with the first awkwardness over, she had warmed to her task. 'Only women like your mother enjoy it and they lead good men astray. Promise me that you will not enjoy it.'

'I will do my—um—best not to enjoy it.' Sarah touched the agitated fingers, stilling their movement.

'It is a duty, that is all. A duty.'

'A duty,' Sarah repeated. 'And if it gets me a child, it will be worth it.'

A mix of emotions flickered across the older woman's face. 'I used to think that. I used to hope, you know. I let him do it when I thought it might result in a child. I wanted a child.'

'I'm sorry,' Sarah said, seeing, with sudden sympathy, the barrenness of this woman's life.

As though exhausted by the conversation, Mrs Crawford allowed her spine to bend. 'Yes, I hope…I hope you are luckier,' she said.

'Thank you. You are… You have been kind.'

'Well, I've done my Christian duty by you. I have never shirked my duty.'

'You have done more than anyone could expect,' Sarah said. It was easy to be gentle now.

'I tried.'

'And I will miss you. Perhaps, if you're feeling well enough, you and Miss Sharples can visit us in London?'

'London? I think not. It is an evil place.'

'Then I will visit here.'

'You will be welcome.' Mrs Crawford stood, a little

awkwardly. 'You are not an uncomfortable person to have around.'

It was as close to a compliment as Mrs Crawford had ever uttered and Sarah felt the prickle of tears.

But before she could respond, her guardian's expression had changed, the lucidity leaving as her gaze turned vague.

'Will Molly come tomorrow?' she asked, looking around the room as though expecting her sister to appear from the faded paper.

'Not tomorrow.'

'The next day?'

'Perhaps.'

'I will go to bed and pray for her safe arrival.'

'That is a good idea,' Sarah said and, taking the candle, helped her guardian ascend.

'Goodnight,' she whispered, stopping at the threshold of the bedchamber.

'Goodnight, Molly.'

Sarah woke on her wedding day to rain, a steady, drizzling rain. Through her window, she saw clouds so low they touched the barn's peaked roof and tangled in treetops.

Above her, the familiar white ceiling gleamed in the half-light.

When she'd first come here, she found the house cold and drear. Her mother had never economised on light or fire and there had been a vibrancy she missed. To compensate, she'd made up stories about going to Italy with a talking donkey. In this dream, she'd found Charlotte and they'd lived with the donkey in a vineyard, warmed by the heat of the Tuscan sun. She remembered imagining the heat, the heavy perfumed smell of flowers, the movement of a scented breeze and the taste of wine which she'd never had, but determined would be thick and sweet.

After today this chamber would no longer be her home

and privy to her dreams. Instead, she would wake up to an unfamiliar ceiling in an unfamiliar house.

Sarah gazed about the chamber, which seemed suddenly dear to her; the threadbare rug, the convex mirror which distorted one's face, even the embroidery sampler completed in Mrs Crawford's youth.

And the wedding gown, a practical, grey article...so different from that which she'd once imagined.

Still, she'd long since thrown any romantic notions into her manuscripts. Petunia wore lace.

Sarah's gaze went towards a second hatbox, also awaiting transport. It was foolish to take along her childish scribblings, yet to leave them behind would mean separation from something infinitely precious.

She stood, pulling off the lid and looking at the familiar pages. Each buddle was neatly tied with blue ribbon. Each had been sent to London and returned. Perhaps if they had been published she would not need to enter this marriage...

But the manuscripts had always been returned.

With sudden impatience, she grabbed her dressing gown, wrapping it about herself to keep out the morning chill. There was no point in dwelling on what might have been. She must focus on what *was*. And right now she was doing what she must to find her sister.

And it was the right thing to do. Sarah sighed. It was just that being bold and courageous would be so much easier with rich golden hair and a veritable riot of curls.

Sarah descended into the kitchen. She'd intended to make breakfast, but before she could do so, Miss Sharples knocked on her door and entered, carrying a tea tray.

'Here we are,' that lady continued briskly. 'I'll not have you doing chores on your wedding day. Not with me here. I'll bring a cup for Mrs Crawford as well!'

'It's not necessary.'

'You let me be the judge of that. I know my way around a kitchen right enough. And you'll have other things to do.'

Sarah returned to her bedchamber. Of course, she should have things to do. After all, Miss Petunia Hardcastle had required the whole morning to prepare for her nuptials and had utilised the services of several maids, a hairdresser and a seamstress.

In contrast, Sarah sipped her tea and nibbled her toast with the uncomfortable feeling of time hanging heavy over her. She washed herself thoroughly, pulled her hair into a respectable bun and slipped the cool grey dress over her head. Once in this ensemble, she donned new gloves and a bonnet, both of sensible design.

With her *toilette* completed, she studied herself in the oval mirror. She looked clean, neat, respectable and exceptionally sensible.

She frowned, oddly discontented with the result. It was ludicrous to wish now for one of the more frivolous fabrics Miss Simpson had suggested. Sense and respectability were more important than fashion or beauty, given the situation.

The hall clock chimed.

Ask not for whom the bell tolls.

The quotation flashed into her mind. She thrust it away.

Kit appeared promptly, his arrival heralded by the crunch of carriage wheels and the steady clip-clop of the horses' hooves.

Upon descending to the hall, she found Kit frowning at her portmanteau as if concentrating on an advanced mathematical equation.

He pushed a lock of hair from his forehead as he had done as a lad when in trouble. 'Mother told me not to make a fuss, but you're absolutely certain about this? You know, getting married and what not?'

She nodded.

'But you know nothing about the man.' He walked past her into the drawing room, throwing himself on to the chair.

'The *ton* generally do not, but it has never stopped any number of debutantes.'

'That's different. I mean—you're not the type to care about titles and jewels and frippery.'

'I've never had the chance before,' Sarah said wryly, sitting opposite.

'So you're marrying a man you know nothing about for money?' he asked incredulously.

'May I say pot and kettle? Aren't you under strict instructions to find a debutante who is well off?'

'Well, yes, but I will also find one that I like tolerably well.'

'Perhaps I like Lord Langford tolerably well. I mean, do you know something to the contrary? Is he a veritable Bluebeard? Will I find wives hanging in inconvenient places?'

'There, you see! You are anxious. You always joke when you're scared.'

'Nervous, perhaps,' she conceded. 'Which is only natural, on one's wedding day. But I am resolved. And don't worry. I'm not expecting flowers and violins, you know.'

He shifted, his brows drawing together in a frown. 'But you believe in love and romance, heroic knights and such.'

'I do?'

'Yes, I mean, you used to.'

'I also used to believe in the gold wedding band my mother wore and fairies. I may still rescue rabbits and foxes, but in other ways I'm all grown up. I know Langford doesn't care for me. I do not expect him to. I do not have any deep feelings for him either. It is a business arrangement.'

'But why? Nothing can be worth getting yourself shackled for.'

'Finding my sister is.' Sarah spoke so softly that Kit leaned forward to hear her.

'But the task might be impossible. London is large,' he said.

'I must try.'

'Does Langford know?'

She shook her head. 'And I can't tell him. If I do, he will know I am a bastard.' She spoke the ugly word without flinching.

'Is that wise? He does not like deceit.'

'And I am not deceitful. He has never asked about my parents. But he speaks with such contempt about his wife and his mother. I cannot tell him that I am the offspring from such an alliance. I mean he is already determined not to like his wife. I do not wish to give him reason to despise me.'

'And you still think this wedding is wise?'

'Charlotte was like a mother and sister to me. She would have done anything for me. Now I must do the same.'

Mrs Crawford, Kit and Sarah drove to the church in the Eavenshams' coach, borrowed for the occasion. The vehicle swayed over the rutted lane, twigs brushing against the vehicle's side. Sarah wished she could have walked. It would feel so much more natural. She could pretend for a few moments that they were only tramping through the countryside to attend Sunday service as they did every week.

Instead, everything seemed different: the carriage's mustiness laced with Lady Eavensham's perfume, Kit's face, for once serious, and the measured clip-clack of the horses' hooves.

Then the lurching stopped. The hooves became silent. The vehicle stopped. Kit helped Mrs Crawford out. Sarah watched her guardian descend. This was the instant before everything changed. Briefly, she longed to still time, to encapsulate the moment.

And then time resumed. Sarah got out, stepping through the grasses into the tiny entry. Lord Eavensham waited, shifting slightly as though ill at ease and Sarah took her place beside him as Mrs Crawford and Kit slipped into the church.

If only she could also pass into the pleasant, anonymous dimness of the church's interior.

But not today.

Today she waited with every muscle tensed like a violin's strings pulled taut. Today she strained to hear every sound.

'Ready, my lass,' Lord Eavensham boomed in her ear.

She nodded. Her eyes prickled, suddenly thankful for his familiar bulk, his slow grin and kindly, if obtuse, countenance.

'I'm sorry your fox hunt wasn't successful last weekend,' she said.

He looked surprised, his eyebrows rising above his flushed countenance. 'I wouldn't worry about that on your wedding day, my dear. I'm certain the next one will prove better sport.'

A tiny irrepressible giggle bubbled upward. 'I'm sure,' she said.

They stepped into the body of the church. It smelled, as usual, of a mix of wet shoe leather, flowers, candle wax and furniture polish.

Everyone turned. Familiar faces nodded, stamped with curiosity, envy, disapproval and even pity. She recognised Mrs Crawford, Lady Eavensham and even Miss Simpson.

Then she looked past them all and saw him—Sebastian.

He dwarfed the vicar as he stood, immaculate, but with a grimness of expression which did nothing to relieve the butterflies within her stomach.

Of course, she could hardly expect him to look like

Petunia Hardcastle's lovelorn suitor. After all, he was being forced into a marriage by a possibly crazed aunt in the remote hope that he would secure sufficient funds to find his son who might well be dead.

The wedding march began—off-key, of course. The usual organist Mr Tangent had been taken ill and Miss Plimco, a nervous-looking spinster, had volunteered to fill in for him.

'Forward march,' Lord Eavensham said, apparently his military service still a feature of his vocabulary.

Again that irrepressible giggle burbled up inside.

One step, two step…

As she neared Sebastian, she saw his expression more clearly. He looked no less grim. Yet within the harsh planes of his face she saw something more. She saw exhaustion. She saw lines of strain and sorrow so intense that she felt drawn to him, if only to comfort or to help.

And this feeling drew her inexorably forward.

What was the woman wearing? Sebastian looked at the drab figure approaching. Goodness, he had given her money enough to buy a dozen bridal gowns and she'd chosen to look like a martyr.

Nor should she wear grey, at least not that dismal shade. As for her hair—she could not have chosen a style less becoming. It was pulled back without so much as a curl to soften the effect.

Worse yet, she would not even raise her eyes and suddenly she looked so sad, like one of her beloved animals brought in for slaughter.

His shoulders tensed. He was not a cruel man and had no wish to force anyone into marriage. In fact, he'd chosen to go about the business in such a way as to ensure he did not steal the future from some romantic debutante.

Besides she had no cause for complaint. Surely life with

him would be preferable from her current impoverished life with an unbalanced relative?

Sarah reached him and stood, as always self-possessed. 'Good morning, my lord.'

Did one usually greet one's betrothed at the altar as though acknowledging an acquaintance on Bond Street?

Alicia had not, but then his first bride had been so hidden behind veils and ruffles, he could scarcely discern her features.

'Dearly beloved, we are gathered here together...' The vicar intoned the words, his Adam's apple bobbing. 'In the presence of God, and in the face of this company, to join together this Man and this Woman in holy Matrimony...'

And Sebastian found himself saying the timeless words to this neat, compact creature in her sensible grey dress who replied in calm businesslike tones.

Then, with surprising rapidity, it was over—done in less time than it would take to read the morning newspaper. The music started, loud with off-key jubilation, and Sebastian and his bride proceeded down the aisle between the pews and assembled congregation.

He noted with almost detached interest that Lady Eavensham smiled while dabbing her eyes with her handkerchief and that Mrs Crawford sat, rigid and dry eyed. As for Miss Martin, or rather, the new Countess, Lady Langford, Sebastian glanced towards her. As always, she appeared composed, her even features giving little away.

Then they stepped through the vestibule and into the brightness outside where villagers waited, throwing grains of rice in a white shower.

Thank goodness he had refused Lady Eavensham's offer of a wedding breakfast. She had disapproved, of course.

'It's highly irregular,' she'd said.

'I do not believe anything about this has been regular,' he had retorted.

The crowd grew quiet. Sebastian watched as Sarah stepped forward, taking Mrs Crawford's hand and looking briefly as though she might embrace her.

'Goodbye,' she said, pressing a kiss to the elder woman's face.

'I will pray for you. I will pray that you do not fall into wickedness. Town offers much temptation.'

'Thank you. Look—look after yourself.'

'We'll be fine, miss—I mean Lady Langford,' Miss Sharples said.

'Then I suppose that's it,' his wife said.

His wife. Sebastian practised the words in his head as a schoolboy might repeat Latin declensions.

'My portmanteau?' she asked as she climbed into the coach.

'I instructed the footmen to load your belongings.'

'Thank you,' she said, seating herself neatly, drab against the velvet splendour of the carriage. But, within seconds, she bolted upright.

'Orion! I almost forgot—where is he?'

Drab, maybe. Colourless, not so much. Good Lord, the woman was hanging out of the door, peering about as though expecting to see the rabbit strapped to the vehicle.

'The coachman has him,' Kit Eavensham advised, pointing towards Dobbs, who approached the carriage carrying a wicker basket.

'I take it Orion is accompanying us?' Sebastian commented, keenly conscious of the onlookers' curious expressions.

'Yes—um—I didn't quite know what else to do with him and I believe you've already met,' she said.

'Once or twice. Put him somewhere, Dobbs, and stop hovering.'

'Here would be fine,' Sarah directed.

'Inside the coach, my lord?'

'If her ladyship wishes,' Sebastian replied.

Dobbs put down the basket. The door closed and they were off, the vehicle lurching down the lane. Sarah waved from the window as the group dwarfed with the increasing distance. Then the carriage rounded the corner and the cluster of figures disappeared. Sarah's hand stilled, although she continued to peer through the window as though hoping for a last glimpse.

Finally, dropping her hand, she turned away and leaned back against the cushioning, her expression unreadable.

Sebastian looked out at the countryside. He supposed it was incumbent on him to converse, to do something to ease them through these first awkward moments. But on what topic? Other than her interest in animals, he knew little about the woman's likes or dislikes.

Perhaps for the first time, Sebastian considered the minutiae of marriage: the breakfasts, the dinners, the walks and excursions. They stretched in an endless trail of triviality and conversation.

'Tell me about your estate,' she said.

And so it began.

Chapter Eight

The hours passed slowly. Sarah slept off and on. They stopped at an inn both to change the horses and eat luncheon. Then they journeyed again, sometimes talking of trivialities much as strangers might.

But as afternoon merged into evening, Sarah became aware of an unpleasant feeling within her stomach. It felt both hollow and nauseous. Her head ached and the roads seemed circuitous as though traversing a huge, never-ending loop.

'My lord,' she asked when she could endure it no longer. 'Is it possible to be seasick on land?'

He turned, his expression concerned as, with surprising speed, he moved to the seat beside her.

'I am inconsiderate. You are not used to travel.' His hands were gentle as he supported her swaying body.

With one hand still about her, he rapped on the roof and, with equal swiftness, rolled down the window. A blast of cool air whistled inwards as the coach jolted to a stop.

'Breathe deeply,' he instructed, angling her body towards the window. 'The fresh air will do you good.'

Dobbs came to the side, his eyebrows raised in enquiry.

'My wife is feeling unwell,' Sebastian said. 'We will wait a few moments here. Nothing behind us?'

The man looked incuriously behind the vehicle. 'Not as yet, me lord.'

'Then we will pause and will stop for the night at the first convenient location.'

Sarah closed her eyes. She breathed, enjoying the sweetness of the country air and the welcome stillness of the carriage. Then, as her nausea lessened, she became conscious of other things: his arm about her, the hardness of his muscle, the warmth of his splayed fingers on her arm, the steady rhythmic thumping of his heart.

She'd never had such prolonged physical contact with any man—it seemed almost indecent to sit so close to him and yet she did not dislike it. Her body did not want to withdraw, quite the opposite. Instead, she felt a need to nestle closer and touch the firm line of his chin… She felt a tingling which was half-pleasant and half-frightening.

Sebastian broke the spell. 'Do you feel well enough for us to continue to the next village?' he asked, withdrawing his arm.

'Yes. Absolutely.' She scuttled away from him, acutely conscious of her burning cheeks and quickened breath.

They rode for only another half hour before reaching a village. It was a small place, the main building being an inn of Tudor design with red bricks, massive timber beams and leaded windows. She supposed the place would be picturesque in summer, but now was dull, its hedgerows wet and the eaves of its thatched cottages brown and dripping.

The footman opened the coach door as soon as they had stopped within the courtyard and Sarah unfolded her cramped body and stumbled out. It felt good to stand and feel the outside air, cool against her cheeks, and inhale that country scent of grass, manure and straw.

'Ah, here is the innkeeper.' Sebastian had also exited the carriage and stood beside her, nodding towards a portly gentleman with a bald head and fringed whiskers. This individual walked forward with a rolling, nautical gait more suited to a ship's deck than land. Two dogs followed, barking.

'It is honoured we are to see you, my lord. Honoured, I say. My wife will be delighted to provide all manner of delicious morsels, delicious morsels, I say.'

Sarah smiled, delightedly. What a lovely character he would make. Indeed, she must take note of his speech pattern and weave him into a story.

Strangely, this familiar impulse comforted as though, by its very oddity, it proved that her identity had not been lost.

Following the landlord while Sebastian instructed the groom, Sarah found that the inn had its own fascination. Flickering sconces lit a narrow corridor, tapestries lined the walls, the ceiling hung low while the flooring was constructed of uneven stone. People must have been thin and short in Tudor times—although Henry VIII was never depicted as such.

The private parlour was painted a drab beige and had brown horsehair furnishings. A small fire burned in the grate which the landlord soon set to revitalising, wielding the bellows between huge hams of hands.

'We'll get it going in no time—' he said as the flames reluctantly rekindled. 'And I'll get them vittles I promised.'

He departed and Sarah sat on the brown horsehair chair. But she had barely settled herself before the door opened and a woman entered. She carried a heavy jug, smelling delightfully of spice and apples.

'This'll warm you up, my lady,' the woman said with a curtsy.

She placed the tray on the table and poured Sarah a generous measure in a large tankard.

The golden liquid not only smelled good, but tasted wonderful. It was warming, as promised, and comforting in contrast to the room.

Her body relaxed. It was a relief to be still and to no longer have to converse with this stranger who was now her husband. She sipped the hot, warm sweetness of the cider, listening to the clock's methodical ticking.

'Lady Langford,' she said softly, under her breath. She was now 'Lady Langford'. Those moments in the chapel had changed everything—her name, her home and even the way people treated her...

She drank more deeply. Travelling made one dry.

Images from the morning flickered through her mind. She remembered the vicar's nervous face and the way he spoke without moving his lips as though his mouth was filled with marbles.

She remembered Miss Plimco's off-key notes, her furrowed forehead and flustered hands. Sarah smiled. But the joke was not Miss Plimco. The true joke was that she, Sarah Martin, bastard child, had been miraculously transformed into a lady.

A lady.

She giggled, straightening in her chair to pour herself a second tankard.

Then, with another giggle, she took several deep draughts. For fun, she extended her little finger as she and Charlotte had done at pretend tea parties with pretend ladies and gentlemen.

'Good afternoon, my lady. How do you do, my lady? Would you like tea, my lady?' She spoke mockingly, rolling the words about on her tongue and pausing for additional refreshment.

'Excuse me, my lady.' Sebastian entered the room from behind her. 'Were you saying something?'

Sarah smiled. He did not seem as intimidating as he had in the carriage.

'Just practising, my lord,' she said.

Rather than turning, she angled her head backwards which granted her an inverted view of her spouse. She laughed. 'Your face looks interesting from this angle—all chin.'

My but he was tall and broad.

He frowned. 'Are you feeling better, my lady?'

Sarah nodded, then, realising that she was lolling in her chair, straightened. In so doing, she knocked the mug to the floor with a bang. Fortunately, it was empty and, being made of pewter, did not break.

Sebastian stooped, picking it up.

'Thank you,' she said.

'Have you been drinking?'

'Drinking?' she repeated. 'Indeed, I have. This refreshment is delightful, delicious and delectable. Don't you love "d" words?'

He sniffed the empty tankard. 'Mulled and potent. I believe, my dear, you are drunk.'

'Drunk?' She straightened even more, attempting to look dignified, an effort ruined by a loud hiccup.

'How much have you had?'

'Two cups. I was thirsty.'

'And you ate little at lunch and doubtless little for breakfast?'

'Breakfast?' She couldn't actually remember eating anything for breakfast. Gracious, his body was undulating in a most fascinating yet perturbing fashion. She put her head on one side to better study the effect. Yes, definitely he undulated as though seen through a heat haze. She liked him better that way. Much less dignified and formidable. It was hard for an undulating individual to look dignified.

'The landlady has not brought food?'

'Not yet, but I am not very hungry. Indeed, I am more sleepy than hungry.' Sarah yawned. The room itself seemed to be moving. She closed her eyes which made it worse. 'This is a very odd place. It moves as though on an ocean. Not that I have ever been on an ocean.'

She reached for the jug, planning to refill the tankard, but he had moved both away.

'No more for you, my lady,' he said.

'But it is most tasty.'

'We will get you something equally tasty and less alcoholic.'

Before Sarah could reply, steps sounded in the corridor accompanied by the rattle of crockery.

Moments later the door swung open and the landlord appeared carrying a tray bearing several platters.

'I must say,' Sarah announced, blinking because her voice sounded inordinately loud, 'this also looks delicious and delectable.'

'I'll serve,' Sebastian said to the landlord. 'You may go. We will stay the night.'

'Of course, my lord.'

'Are you certain?' Sarah asked as soon as the door closed. 'You'd hoped to reach to London.'

'Which doesn't mean I would travel when you're unwell. Besides, London has been around for centuries. I imagine it will stay put for another day.'

'You are kind. No one before has cared whether I am ill or not,' she said.

'No one has accused me of being kind,' he said. 'At least not recently.'

'Doubtless, because you have been grumpy and irascible. Sorrow will do that.'

'I...' He paused, his look for once unsure.

Sarah giggled. 'I surprised you?'

'You constantly surprise me.'

'And I am also surprised because I note that you are able to look uncertain. I like that. It makes you much less formidable. And more likeable. Undulating does that, too. Although it is a tad peculiar.'

'Undulating?'

She nodded, glancing suspiciously about the room. 'It is this place. I think it is magical.'

'And I think you need to eat,' he said, placing a platter beside her.

Sarah sniffed appreciatively. Perhaps she was a trifle hungry after all, although the portion seemed spartan.

'Are we also saving for the heathens?' she asked.

'No, but we don't want to overload your stomach.'

'My stomach feels quite fine.'

'It won't.'

Sebastian watched his wife nod and smile like an affable idiot and cursed himself. The poor woman had likely never tasted wine. He'd noted that she'd drunk only water at Lady Eavensham's dinner and Mrs Crawford would hardly keep a stocked cellar.

Not that the alcohol seemed to be affecting her appetite. She had apparently recovered from her earlier nausea and ate eagerly, carefully licking each fingertip.

There was a sensuality to the movement. He watched as she closed her eyes, carefully licking a smidgeon of gravy from her index finger, her pink lips parted and glistening.

Her mouth was well shaped and with a natural inclination towards a smile. Her nature, he surmised, was not as prim and proper as her hair and dress would suggest.

Not that either her hair or dress looked entirely kempt any more. Her bun had loosened so that strands of hair fell into her face and the top button of the drab dress had fallen open, revealing a triangle of pale skin. The tiny triangle held a surprising appeal.

He wondered who had convinced her that she was not

physically attractive. Mrs Crawford, he supposed. A flash of protective anger flashed through him on her behalf.

'Have I a stain, my lord?'

'Pardon?'

'Dirt on my dress?'

'Your dress is fine. Or as fine as it ever was.'

'Then why you are staring at me?' Her speech slurred and her head tilted at an enquiring angle.

'A husband may not look at a wife?'

'I don't know,' she said. 'I have little experience in the married state, but your observations make me feel…odd.'

'Odd?'

'Tingly.'

His lips twitched. 'Actually, I was thinking you looked quite fetching.'

She laughed, shaking her head. 'I told you before—no codswallop. No, I'm afraid you'll have to suffer with a plain wife. Such is the price of expedience.'

He winced at her speech and blunt appraisal.

'I believe you underestimate yourself. If you were to dress your hair more fashionably, you could look well enough.'

'High praise. Although not quite up to the pretty speeches of Miss Hardcastle's fiancé.'

'Pardon? Who is that?'

'An acquaintance.' Again her lips curved generously as though privy to some inner joke and he felt a curious longing to know and share in her mirth.

Sebastian made no effort to wake her when Sarah fell asleep after dinner. Indeed, perhaps the solitude would help him decipher the confused muddle of his thoughts.

He was finding his new wife unsettling.

More to the point, he was finding his reaction to his new wife unsettling.

Good Lord, it was not as though he had been a monk since Alicia's departure. In those first months, he had enjoyed both wine and women to an extreme—seeking oblivion, however self-destructive.

Later, he'd drunk and socialised as cover for meeting the Lion's emissaries.

But this woman differed from any he had met previously. It was unnerving. He felt…he felt…

He felt like something in his ribcage was hurting and expanding while his throat stung. He stood, an abrupt movement so that the chair moved back, banging the wall.

'Sarah.' He spoke roughly.

She made no response.

'You cannot stay here all night.'

She did not rouse. Bending, he shook her shoulder more firmly. She murmured incoherently.

Damn.

He strode about the room with a pent-up energy. He needed to distance himself from her. He needed to regain some autonomy over his thoughts.

'If you will not move yourself, I will move you,' he said and scooped her up in his arms.

She was surprisingly light. The cloth of her gown shifted. Her hair, loosened from its bun, fell in long loose waves.

He had not realised it so long and thick.

She gave a sigh, cuddling against his chest in a peculiarly trusting motion. Her hair smelled not of heavy perfume but fresh.

Protective—that was it. He felt protective. As though she was something good or special which must be safeguarded.

Except his time, his energy, his every resource must go to his children. He couldn't weaken his resolve. He mustn't become distracted.

He remembered how his brain had slowed, like cold treacle, after Alicia had taken the children. It was as though his grief and anger hung like leaden weights upon his thoughts.

He could not, must not, risk a recurrence.

Miss Martin, or rather Lady Langford, still did not wake, even as he climbed the stairs and pushed open the door, placing her on the bed.

Now what? His fingers drummed against his thigh. He supposed he could summon the landlady, except she'd seemed a somewhat rough individual.

Besides, both landlord and landlady had retired.

The baleen creaked as he sat on the bed. Sarah had curled away from him so that he could see her spine and the row of tiny, cloth-covered buttons. Gently, he touched one. It opened with a minute rustle.

He undid each one, so that he could gently push down on the cloth of her dress and reveal… He chuckled. He should have guessed. Her undergarments, like her outerwear, were simplistic to the extreme and constructed of a stark, coarse cotton without lace or adornment.

She rolled back towards him so that she lay on her back, flopping one arm across the pillow with delightful abandon.

His breath caught.

Her breasts. Released from the confines of the bodice, her breasts were full and lush and creamy, scarcely contained within the prim cotton. The fullness of her flesh and the unconscious recklessness of her posture fascinated him. It was so at odds with her daytime practicality.

Unsettling. He muttered a curse. Standing quickly, he pulled up a blanket so that it covered her completely. Then he left, his movements brisk and purposeful.

Sarah blinked at the bright sunshine which spilled through the half-open curtains. She rubbed her forehead.

She had a headache. Her tongue felt thick and her eyelids heavy.

Propping herself on her elbow, she surveyed her surroundings. The bedchamber appeared pleasant enough, sparsely furnished but clean and with a warm fire. The whitewashed walls were interrupted only by a small chest of drawers and portraits of nameless individuals with unsmiling faces.

She frowned, peering at the image of a whiskered gentleman sporting a monocle. She had not noticed him last night.

In fact, she remembered little from the evening before.

At this thought, she straightened, thrusting a hand through her mop of loose hair. It wasn't braided. Nor still in her bun.

Good Lord, she wore her undergarments and no nightdress. She did not remember undressing. Except she must have done so because she could see the pewter-grey folds of her wedding dress laid upon the chair.

But who had removed them?

Had Sebastian...?

Sarah slid back under the blanket in one fluid, impulsive movement, pulling the cloth to her chin as though expecting him to be still in the room.

Heat washed into her cheeks.

And if her husband had removed her clothes—had they done more? Had they—

Someone rapped on her door.

'Er...come in,' Sarah said, her grasp tightening on the material.

'Good, you're awake.' Sebastian strode into the chamber.

As always, his presence filled the space, so that the very air vibrated with energy.

'I thought you were the maid,' Sarah said nervously.

'Not when I last checked. How are you feeling?'

'My head aches a little.'

'I should never have let you drink so much. I neglected to realise that Mrs Crawford probably does not permit wine in the house.'

'We lived quite simply.'

The blanket was now above her chin, but felt insufficient. She doubted she'd ever conversed with a male in this state of undress.

Indeed, no doubt about it. She knew she had not.

'Right.' He looked away from her towards the curtains as if he also suffered discomfort. 'I do not wish to rush you, but I have ordered breakfast and hot water. You should eat. It will settle your stomach.'

'Thank you. You are considerate.'

It was true. She couldn't remember another time when anyone had cared about the state of her stomach.

'I will give you privacy and wait for you in the sitting room.' He nodded and turned as though to leave.

'My lord?' Sarah blurted.

'Yes?'

'Who undressed me last night?'

'I did.' A hint of a smile touched his lips.

'Did anything happen? I—I need to know.' The words came out in a gabbled rush.

'Nothing occurred. I am not in the habit of making love to comatose women,' he said and, with a bow, stepped towards the door.

Pausing, he glanced back. 'By the way, my lady, when I do make love to you, you will be aware of the event.'

Chapter Nine

The door shut. Sarah exhaled. Her cheeks burned. She would not touch wine or mulled cider again for the rest of her God-given days.

Standing unsteadily, she went to the looking glass and grimaced. Except for the splotchy redness of her cheeks, her face looked pale, dark shadows ringed her eyes and her hair resembled a haystack.

No wonder Sebastian was not unduly disappointed that they had not consummated their marriage. Likely he dreaded the event.

Pity there was no other way to conceive a child. Mrs Crawford was right. It was a system designed by animals and one would have expected humans to have improved upon it by now.

Briefly, she pulled her hair forward, twisting the tendrils about her fingers to form curls. She wondered if ringlets might improve her looks. She recalled an article in Miss Simpson's periodical that ringlets were all the rage.

What twaddle!

Ringlets might be suitable for people with youth and beauty, but certainly not for those with neither. She would do well to remember that.

Determined, Sarah straightened her shoulders, picked

up her brush, dragging it through her tangled locks with efficient, if painful, strokes.

A second knock at the door made her drop the brush so that it clattered to the table. She turned, half-expecting her wedded lord, but it was only the landlady with fresh towels and hot water, followed by a younger woman bearing a mug of chocolate.

'That will be all, Bridget. Off with you,' the landlady said.

The girl placed the chocolate on the table and left, bobbing a curtsy and tossing her blonde ringlets with an air of impertinent excitement.

'Would there be anything else, my lady?'

'No, thank you.'

'Do be callin' me if there's owt you'd be needin'.'

The woman left. Again Sarah felt her shoulders sink with relief as the door shut. It would appear that the well-to-do lacked for nothing, except privacy.

Her husband sat within the private parlour, perusing a newspaper. Breakfast had been served and the smell of fresh toast perfumed the room.

'My lady.' Sebastian put the paper aside, rising.

'My lord.'

His face hardened as he looked at her. 'It would appear you are ready for another hard day of some sort.'

'Travelling, I presume.' She frowned, confused.

Her wedding dress had been travel-stained and so she had chosen her brown church dress.

'I was worried that you had volunteered to clean out the stable or milk the cows.'

'Pardon?'

He sighed. 'No matter. Sit down and have breakfast.'

Sarah sat on the chair opposite.

'Will we get to London today, my lord?' she asked, to promote conversation.

'That is my intent.'

'I am looking forward to seeing the capital.'

'Really?' he drawled and then, perhaps realising that she needed conversation, relented. 'What do you wish most to see?'

Charlotte. Joy bubbled. She squashed it.

'Um…museums,' she said.

'Museums? Good Lord!' This time his chuckle was genuine. 'You must be the only lady who comes to London for the museums.'

'I used to go…' She paused. 'I used to dream of going.'

'And why do museums interest you?'

'Stories, I think,' she said, remembering those occasional childhood excursions. 'Every object tells a story. History is the most fascinating story one could ever find.'

'You like stories?'

She nodded. 'I love them.'

'Elizabeth used to like stories,' he said.

'Likely she still does.'

'She gives no sign.'

'Sometimes,' Sarah said softly, 'sometimes we have to believe in that which we cannot see.'

He sighed, his expression troubled, his face lined with doubt. 'And sometimes it's hard to keep believing.'

'I know.'

She thought of that last brief letter from Charlotte followed by years of silence, of nothing. And yet she believed. She had to.

'So tell me something more about your daughter,' she said.

He hesitated, but complied.

'She is eight…' He paused, then added, 'Even before

going to France she was different. She was slow to speak
and often rocked or spent hours arranging her dolls—'

His dark gaze softened and his lips twisted in a surprisingly gentle smile.

'And now?'

'Nothing. She sits doing nothing. Her face is devoid of
expression. Or she'll twirl or rock, moving her hands with
agitated motions.'

'I'm sorry.'

'I know.

'And now I expect you to help, to do something which
neither I nor Miss Clarence, Miss Nugent and several other
worthy ladies could accomplish. Goodness knows why.'

'Because you have to hope. We all have to hope.'

Just as she had to hope that she would find her sister
within a city of millions.

Impulsively, she leaned forward, reaching her hand
across the table to touch his own. She started at the contact. 'It may not be me, but it will be someone. You just
have to keep hoping. She needs your hope.'

His gaze met hers.

'Somehow you have helped me to hold on to that hope.'

The moment stretched between them, a crystalline instant, separate and distinct. Then, as though struck by the
same thought, she lifted her hand as he shifted backwards,
withdrawing his own.

'Well,' he said, his face again that of polite interest. 'We
will ensure that you see the British Museum in a timely
fashion. But now we'd best resume our journey if we hope
to be in London by nightfall.'

'Yes, of course.' She stood suddenly, knocking the table,
conscious of an excitement that was half-fear.

They arrived in London that afternoon. Sebastian had
ridden outside for much of the journey. Sarah had not

minded the solitude. The journey had allowed her to study his strong, straight figure, his ebony hair touched by sunlight and his easy movements which made man and horse seem one.

A part of her still could not believe it—that this peer could be her spouse.

Once in town, Sebastian rejoined her in the carriage. Sarah pressed her face against the pane, fascinated by the congested, cobbled streets lined with houses and shops. It seemed both new and old and she was conscious of a stirring of familiarity, an awakening of childhood memory. It was in the rattle of carriage wheels over cobbled streets, the quick glimpses of the Thames's slow-moving waters and the sour smell seeping from the outdoors.

She wrinkled her nose.

'It is better at my house,' Sebastian said.

Sarah nodded. She remembered the smell of sewage which wafted from the river.

Then the carriage left the crowded dirtiness and the streets widened, the houses becoming larger and more prestigious. So many houses. So many streets. How could she have forgotten the city's size—its vastness?

Her stomach knotted as she pressed more closely to the carriage side. She had dreamed for so long about getting to London that she'd thought little about how to find Charlotte once she was here. How did one even approach such a task?

Of course, her husband would know how to do it. Her glance slid to him. There was a calm efficiency about him. But she could not confide in him. She was a bastard. Her sister was a bastard. She shivered silently, remembering his cold contempt for his first wife and his mother.

'Here we are.' He broke the silence as the carriage halted.

Startled, Sarah jerked upright, refocusing her attention. The journey had seemed so endless that its conclusion felt disconcertingly unexpected.

The coachman swung open the door so that air whistled into the carriage. Outside, Sarah saw a stone house with impressive front steps and a dark lacquered door flanked by pillars.

Gracious, but it was grand—grander than she had envisaged and it suddenly seemed impossible that this could be her home. Her eyes widened. She swallowed, her throat instantly dry.

'Welcome,' Sebastian said, gently.

'Thank you.'

Awkwardly, with her legs cramped from sitting, Sarah clambered down. Sebastian stood at her side, his hand at her elbow. She felt the warm, reassuring strength of his fingers through the cloth.

With perfect timing, the front door opened and a liveried servant bowed. They entered, stepping on to a black-and-white-tiled floor leading towards the wide sweep of the staircase. Her gaze followed it, stumbling over a line of uniformed individuals standing at the foot of the stairs.

'Ah, good day, Harding,' Sebastian said, allowing a servant to remove his great cloak. 'Harding is the butler.'

This individual, who seemed more formidable than Sebastian himself, bowed. 'May I introduce you to your staff, my lady?'

'Yes…Harding,' Sarah managed.

She could do this. After all, Petunia had experienced a similar situation, prior to her unfortunate imprisonment, and had managed most wonderfully. Indeed, the staff had adored her fragile, blonde perfection—

The butler moved forward and Sarah followed, keeping her back ramrod straight and her chin up, unpleasantly aware of her damp, sticky palms.

Petunia had not suffered sweaty palms.

'Er—her ladyship's rabbit, Mr Harding,' Dawson, the

groom, said from behind her. 'Should I—er—take it to the servants' quarters?'

Nor had Petunia owned a rabbit.

'He will go to my room,' Sarah said with sudden force, instinctively asserting herself. Although, goodness knows, she'd crumble like a pack of cards if anyone opposed the plan.

'Should someone perhaps clean out his cage first and provide the animal with food, my lady?' Harding asked, his voice devoid of judgement or expression.

'Yes, that would be excellent.'

'Very good, my lady.'

Sarah exhaled.

The groom solemnly handed the rabbit to a footman who promptly disappeared towards the servants' quarters, she presumed.

Harding continued with the introductions. The servants stepped forward, one at a time, bowing or curtsying, according to sex. At the end of this process, the butler stopped, turning towards her, as if expecting some response. Naturally, Petunia had risen to the occasion most wonderfully with a stirring speech which had immediately inspired all with a fierce loyalty to serve.

'I am pleased to meet you. I look forward to getting to know you,' Sarah said—an inadequate statement and unlikely to foster lifelong anything.

'Right, that's done.' Sebastian spoke briskly, eyeing the assembled company. 'For my part, I expect you to remember that service to your mistress is a service to me. Giles, take up the cases. Mrs Lorring, show her ladyship to her room.'

With these instructions, Sebastian nodded curtly and strode from the hall and down a narrow corridor, the sharp clack of his steps retreating into the distance.

All fell quiet, leaving that complete silence that brings

discomfort. Sarah shifted her weight uneasily and rubbed damp palms against her brown, travel-rumpled dress.

'Right—um—you're dismissed,' she said, her voice squeaky.

They turned like soldiers at drill, leaving only a tall woman with a thin angular frame behind.

'I am Mrs Lorring, the housekeeper. I will show you to your room. Please, follow me, your ladyship.' She wore a black dress, unadorned except for the long chain of keys dangling about her neck.

'Thank you.'

Sarah stepped after the woman who seemed to glide more than walk, her movements singularly silent, except for the jangling keys.

Everything about the house and its servants spoke of grace, elegance and power. When Sebastian had first proposed, Sarah had not fully understood his station, imagining him on par with the lower gentry like Lord and Lady Eavensham.

He was on a rung above.

And Elizabeth—where was the child in this vast mausoleum? And how would she react to this stranger who was to be her stepmother?

'Your chamber, my lady. It adjoins his lordship's dressing room which, naturally connects to his bedchamber.'

'Er...yes, thank you.' Sarah stepped into the chamber, halting abruptly.

She gaped.

Good Lord, it was quite dreadful. Creatively ghastly.

She blinked. The walls had been painted a lilac colour with gold-leaf work on the ceiling and around windows. The curtains were of a purple cloth with a satin sheen and cupids festooned the ceiling, nakedly resplendent on rose-coloured clouds.

A laugh bubbled upward in her throat. She must make

sure Mrs Crawford never, ever saw this room. The poor woman would have an apoplectic fit.

The bed stood in the centre, a massive structure on a raised dais, shrouded with gauzy violet bed curtains.

'Her ladyship, I mean, her former ladyship redecorated the entire room. It took her considerable time and much attention to detail. She had particular tastes.' Mrs Lorring spoke in crisp, haughty tones.

'I see.'

Her mother, Sarah remembered, had liked bright colours in her decor. Perhaps it spoke to her own plebeian tastes that she did not.

'Would you wish me to unpack your bags, my lady?'

'No.' Sarah spoke quickly. She did not want this woman touching her meagre belongings.

Mrs Lorring's back stiffened even more, if that was possible. 'Very well, my lady. Do not hesitate to call if you require assistance.'

'Thank you.'

The woman left. The door clicked shut with wonderful finality. Sarah exhaled with a soft, relieved whoosh of breath.

Alone, at last. She sank on to a chair of purple velvet and stared, wide-eyed, around the lilac room.

She did not belong here.

She did not belong in this house. And certainly not in this room. Sarah could almost believe that the chamber resented her and that the plump cupids bore her malice. She shivered, looking about her as though surveying an alien landscape.

She went to the window, conscious of that uncomfortable feeling of being observed. Hairs prickled at the base of her neck.

It was probably the cupids.

Then she saw her, a crouched figure huddled at the far side of the bed.

Sarah gasped, jerking back so that her hip hit the windowsill as she silenced a scream.

The child was female with fair hair and a pair of unblinking, unfocused eyes.

Elizabeth.

'Hello,' Sarah said softly.

The girl gave no response. She wore a simple dress and her appearance was well groomed. Her hair had been parted in the centre and neatly braided into plaits tied with white ribbons.

But her face…

There was an eerie blankness there, a sense that she looked but did not see.

And yet she was here—in this room. She must have entered with purpose. Had Sebastian told her about this sudden marriage? Did she understand? Or perhaps she knew nothing and came here routinely to feel closer to her dead mother.

But, instead, the child had found an interloper—a stranger in her mother's purple bedchamber.

'My name is Sarah. I am glad to meet you.'

Elizabeth still made no sign of interest or attention. Then, without words, the girl stood and walked away, her slippers padding softly. The chamber door swung shut.

Sarah sat down heavily. She stared at the closed door. How could she help? How could Sebastian even expect her to help? She knew nothing about children. Even normal children. She could heal a robin, but this…? She was totally unfit for this marriage. She could not help the child. Nor could she be the type of spouse who would fit into Sebastian's world and provide this new start his aunt desired for him. Indeed, if anyone could, it would be an accomplished beauty from his own class, not a nonentity like her.

She looked grimly at her ugly brown dress against the resplendent colourful room.

Again she did not belong. She never had. She had not been pretty enough in her mother's house nor good enough in her father's.

And here, in this lilac chamber, she was a desperate man's mistake.

Chapter Ten

Elizabeth sat at the small table in the nursery which over-looked the garden. The room had that unnatural quiet quality Sebastian had noted many times previously. The silence was broken only by the occasional crackle of the fire and the rustle of cloth as Doris, the nursemaid, sewed.

His wife stood by his side. She had changed for dinner into another nondescript grey gown.

'Elizabeth,' he said.

She made no move. Her face remained expressionless. Indeed, he might have suspected that she were deaf except that noise woke her from sleep and one of the governesses had reported that she had reacted to notes played on the pianoforte.

'I would like to introduce you to someone,' he said.

She gave no reaction.

'This is Sarah. I have married her. She is my wife and will try to be your mother.'

'Perhaps I will try to be a friend first,' Sarah said softly. 'Hello, Elizabeth. We met earlier. I am so glad to see you again.'

For a moment, he thought he saw Elizabeth's gaze flicker towards Sarah, but he was mistaken. Instead, her glance went to the rocking horse and, without words, she walked to the toy, starting to rock in a rhythmic repetitive motion.

'Elizabeth,' he said. 'That is rude.'

'I'm sorry, my lord,' the maid said, standing and letting the sewing fall. 'Really, Miss Elizabeth, could you not smile when your father visits and brings you a new mother?'

'Friend,' Sarah repeated, stepping forward, a flush touching her cheeks. 'And I have found in life that it is hard to smile to order.'

'Yes, my lady.'

Sarah crouched so that she was at the child's level, but remained several feet back. 'Elizabeth,' she said. 'I will never try to take your mother's place. I will only attempt to earn my own.'

'I am not certain if she understands, my lady.'

'Nor am I, but neither do I know that she does not understand. I think it better to assume understanding than the opposite.'

'Yes, my lady.' The nursemaid curtsied.

'Goodbye, Elizabeth, I will visit you tomorrow,' Sebastian said.

They turned to go but, almost impulsively, Sarah stepped back to his daughter.

'I like your horse,' she said. 'I am rather afraid of real horses, you know, but this size would be fine.'

And then they left, stepping away from the nursery's warmth and into the corridor's chill. Elizabeth had shown no more interest in Sarah than she had her numerous governesses.

But what had he expected? That Sarah would do something so eccentric that Elizabeth would laugh and, within seconds, become a normal child or as normal as she had ever been?

'Give her time,' Sarah said softly, perhaps hearing his

muted sigh. 'Think of her as a frightened wild animal. She will not trust quickly.'

'I have limited experience with frightened wild animals.'

'But I have.'

And in that moment, the hope flickered again into reluctant life.

Dinner was over. The time was occupied by polite discourse about the British Museum and giraffes, the latter topic only because the museum apparently had a life-size replica of the animal.

Now Dawson was preparing him to retire as he did every night. Sebastian watched the valet's pale hands with their scrupulously clean fingernails as he removed the lint from the cloth of his evening jacket. This activity usually didn't irritate him to such a great extent. Tonight it did.

At last, Dawson had finished and bowed, leaving the chamber with mincing steps. The door clicked shut as the clock struck the hour.

Sebastian knocked and entered the adjoining bedchamber and, for a moment, the purple colour overwhelmed him. He had forgotten the decor and wondered why he had not instructed the servants to prepare another apartment.

But he supposed Sarah probably liked it.

'Is something displeasing you, my lord?'

Sarah sat at her bedside table, attired in a voluminous white cotton garment which covered her more completely than any number of day dresses. She was brushing her hair which, now released from its daily bondage, fell down her back in surprisingly lush waves. The lamp and firelight flickered across her pale skin, giving it that luminous quality he had first noted at Eavensham.

She looked up and their gazes met within the looking glass. That look—that mutual revelation of loneliness, desire and apprehension—sliced into him. Within it, he was conscious of that surprising, unsettling lurch of attraction—need, almost.

'If it were done when 'tis done, then 'twere well It were done quickly...'

The quotation flickered across his mind. Although to compare the bedding of his wife to the assassination of a Scottish king hardly seemed romantic or logical. Again he wondered why he felt this combination of desire and something akin to reluctance.

Without conscious thought, his fingers touched the heavy thickness of her hair. She started. He saw the movement in her throat as she swallowed. He pressed a kiss to her cheek. Her skin had a dewy softness. Moving aside the thick curtain of hair, he kissed the nape of her neck, the tiny, damp tendrils of hair.

She smelled of— He chortled. She smelled of lard soap.

'My lord?'

'You are a constant source of surprise.'

'Is that good?' she asked.

'I don't know.' Which was true enough. She made him feel off-kilter, as though the world had shifted on its axis and nothing was as it had been.

He saw her uncertainty. 'It is good,' he said, seeking to comfort where he had hurt.

She bit her lip and her hands twisted at the blue belt of her dressing gown.

'Sarah?'

She looked up, meeting his glance openly, but he saw the genuine fear lurking in those grey depths.

'You need not fear me,' he said, gently. 'I will not hurt you. At least, no more than I can help.'

'I do not. I mean, I do not fear you as an individual. I have met very few gentlemen, but you seem quite nice. It's just…somewhat discomforting to transform from spinster to married woman in less than a week.'

Again he felt his lips twitch, a smile lurking at her characteristic understatement. 'It must be,' he said. 'It is somewhat disconcerting to transform from widower to married man in so short a time.'

He stood, pacing to the window and staring out at the darkening London scene. He pressed his fingertips against the glass, feeling its coolness.

'But you know I—I am ready.'

He paused for another second, before turning slowly. 'It would seem that the haste in our marriage may require some adjustment in our lovemaking.'

'It may?'

'We hardly know each other. We have skipped the courtship and I cannot expect you to feel at ease with me within mere days. So I think tonight we will focus on kissing.'

'Kissing?'

'Yes, kissing.'

'And nothing else?' Relief threaded through her voice.

'Nothing else.'

'You're certain?'

'Yes.' He felt no regret, even as desire pulsed through him. It was suddenly incredibly important to him, more important than his own need and his own pleasure, that this woman want him, not out of duty but—

He pulled his thoughts away.

With gentle fingers, he stroked her neck and the delicate line of her chin.

'Kissing can be fun,' he said, bending to kiss her forehead, her nose, her chin, the indent on her bare neck where he could feel her quickened pulse.

Then, tipping her chin, he claimed her mouth. She stiffened. He felt her instinctive resistance. Gently, he teased her lips, tasting her sweetness.

She stood. Her hands clutched his shoulders and his own encircled her waist. Under his fingers he felt her ease towards him, her body relaxing into him so that he could feel the full softness of her breasts against him.

A need he had not anticipated burst into sudden life. Without thought, he wound his arms more tightly about her, pulling her closer.

She did not resist. Tentatively, she reached up for him, her fingers winding through his hair, her body swaying against him.

'Sarah,' he muttered, the word dragged from him, the longing more overwhelming than any he had ever felt.

He groaned. His hands went to the thick cloth of the dressing gown. He pushed it off her shoulders, his hands no longer so gentle. He pulled at the coarse fabric of her nightgown, tugging it down. His heart beat, a thudding thundering in his chest. He needed her. He needed this woman. He needed to explore every inch of her, to satiate himself within her, to bury his pain, to find hope—

The sensations grew, igniting her core, pulsating waves of heat. Sarah felt herself push towards him without conscious thought. Her hands roamed under the cloth of his robe, feeling the lean hardness of his muscles and pulling him closer.

Her skin tingled with the touch of his lips as he trailed kisses over her neck and along the line of her chin. As his mouth touched her own, it seemed as though a flame had ignited, driving into the core of her. She pressed closer and closer, aware of something wild, untamed and untameable unleashed within her. Darts of feeling; half-pain and half-pleasure, pulsed through her. She clung to him, her body demanding something which was foreign to her, but in a heady, wonderful way.

Sebastian groaned. The primal sound mingled with the wild thumping rhythm of her heart.

He lay her back on to the bed. She sprawled on it as he

lowered himself so that his body covered her own. She arched towards him, wanting to feel him, his bulk, his weight, his hard, muscled strength. Her hands clung to his shoulders.

She wanted—*needed*—

'Only women like your mother enjoy it.'

Mrs Crawford's words flashed, unbidden and unwanted, through her mind.

'Only women like your mother enjoy it.'

Her body froze.

She should not be feeling heat or desire or driving need. She should not be reaching for him or arching into him or enjoying the sensation of his muscles under her hands or his warm skin damp with sweat.

He must have felt her stillness.

He stiffened. She heard his breath. It came in raw, ragged gulps. One hand gripped reflexively at the bed linen. His hand tightened so that his knuckles shone white.

He cursed. 'I—will—keep—my—word.' He spoke haltingly. 'Unless you choose different.'

She swallowed. 'I—'

She wanted him. She wanted everything. Her mouth was dry. She did not fear him. She feared herself. She feared that part of herself that wanted a physical coupling and might react to him in a way that would disgust.

'No, I—'

She had been unworthy all her life. Now she must make a choice that would prove her a lady and not a whore.

He sat up, his breathing still irregular, but his expression was once again controlled. She felt bereft as the coolness of the night air washed across her nakedness.

Gently, he pulled up the shoulders of her gown. 'I will give you privacy and let you rest, my lady.'

'Thank you,' she stuttered, which seemed inane. But it

felt imperative to say something to reach for some form of normality.

Lying still, she stared at the purple ceiling as he stepped from the chamber. She could hear the pad of his feet, the rustle of cloth and the gentle click of the door. She shivered, cold despite her flannel gown.

Sebastian poured himself a cognac, welcoming its burn.

He desired his practical, surprising little wife with a driving need he had in no way anticipated.

It had taken him everything and more to keep his promise and even now he felt that insistent, pulsing longing.

For a moment, he had thought she'd felt a similar passion. He'd wanted her to feel it.

But that had all changed, had been swallowed in fear.

He sat in the plush comfort of his armchair. Perhaps he should be glad she showed this lack of physical desire. At least she'd be less likely to indulge in affairs as his mother had or to run off with a French lover having criminal intent.

He stared sullenly at the empty hearth, his fingers tightening about the glass.

No, what bothered him was not so much her reaction, but his own. He had wanted her too much. For that moment, he had wanted not only to pleasure her physically but to hold her close, to feel her warmth, to taste her lips, to bury himself within her as though the act would connect him to another soul.

As if he wanted or needed this connection.

But he was no callow, lovelorn bridegroom who believed that the physical act of lovemaking could in any way touch one's soul. Or that connection with another could empower.

This was a marriage of expedience. He must not care for his new wife. He would respect her. He would do his duty by her, but there would be nothing more.

He had once believed in unbroken bonds and promises.
But no more.
Reliance on human frailty led to weakness.
And for his children's sake, he must be strong.

Chapter Eleven

A knock announced her morning chocolate and, peering from under heavy eyelids, Sarah saw a maid opening the purple mass of curtaining.

'I brought you chocolate, my lady. And would there be anything else, my lady?' the girl asked, bobbing a curtsy.

'Hot water. And your name?'

'Alice, your ladyship.'

The girl spoke with a different accent than the country folk Sarah had known. It was more like her mother's maid's voice—cockney, that was it.

'It is nice to meet you, Alice.'

'Thank you, my lady.' She curtsied again. 'And will you be having breakfast?'

'No, I do not think so, only toast.'

The girl set about lighting the fire.

'How long have you worked for his lordship?' Sarah asked.

'Not long, and I'm not really a lady's maid, but Mrs Lorring said as how I'd have to do until you'd got someone proper like.' She stood up from the hearth, her reddened hands twisting at her apron.

'I'm sure you'll do admirably.'

'Yes, my lady.' Alice bobbed a third time and hurried from the room.

Alone, Sarah pondered both her upcoming agenda and yesterday's events. She was too honest not to recognise that she had enjoyed Sebastian's kisses in a way she had not anticipated.

She also knew that respectable women did not enjoy a man's attention. Even her mother had said so.

She remembered once riding with her mother in Hyde Park and all the fashionable ladies had looked the other way and her mother had laughed. 'They pretend they do not see me, but they need me and my kind as much as their husbands do. I save them the bother of entertaining their men.'

At the time, she had not understood, of course. But now—

Now it lent credence to Mrs Crawford's words. All of which made her confused and oddly tearful—which would not do.

'You had best develop a practical disposition as you do not have the looks to make weeping an attractive attribute.'

Her mother's words. And wise ones. Besides, she must take comfort in the fact that she had controlled that base part of her. And she was in London. The hunt for Charlotte was possible.

With this thought, she stood abruptly, focusing on the upcoming day. She must see Elizabeth. It was her duty and an integral aspect of the marriage contract. Besides, the memory of that still figure with her bleak gaze haunted her.

And then there was Charlotte.

An eagerness coursed through her—an energy all the more vital after its long years of containment. She couldn't wait. She wanted to be outside, following every clue, interviewing every person, banging on doors and standing on doorsteps.

Grabbing one of her dresses, Sarah splashed water on her face and then started to dress, imbued with new urgency.

Elizabeth sat on the rocking horse, moving it rhythmically. The girl's two impeccable braids swung back and forth, bright blonde stripes against her dark clothes.

The maid sat by the fire sewing.

'Good morning.' Sarah spoke softly, feeling a foolish need to match the child's silence.

'Good morning, my lady. Would you be needing anything?' the maid questioned.

'No.'

Other than insight, inspiration, a miracle.

The maid curtsied and returned to her sewing. The room felt quiet, the stillness broken only by the creak of the rocking horse, the fire's crackle and the rustle of needle through cloth.

Uncertain, Sarah went to a low table. It had two chairs and was close to both the rocking horse and a window.

'Do you mind if I sit?' she asked.

Elizabeth made no reply so Sarah sat, her knees uncomfortably angled for the small furniture.

'Hello,' she said.

Elizabeth did not look at her, but kept her gaze downcast as though concentrating on the horse's tufted straw mane and her own rhythmic movements. From this angle Sarah could see her pale face washing into the equally pale hair.

Sarah looked about the room's white walls, blank except for three pictures of squirrels and the nearby window. Through the pane, she could see a large chestnut tree with thick spreading branches. It reminded her of home—or rather the Crawford residence.

'You like animals?'

Elizabeth made no reply.

'I do.'

Nothing.

Sarah swallowed. She looked down, rubbing her finger against the grain of the wooden table. A sheet of paper and a stubby pencil lay on the table as though in a hopeful invitation that Elizabeth would abandon her constant motion and draw.

Outside, a branch touched the pane with a muted tap. It had rained the night before and water clung to the undersides of the leaves in glistening drops.

A movement caught Sarah's attention as a brown squirrel scrambled along the branch, moving jerkily and then freezing into stillness.

'I used to feed the squirrels when I was in London. I mean when I lived in London before,' Sarah said.

Elizabeth made no sign that she had heard the words.

Acting on impulse, Sarah pulled the paper towards her, picking up the pencil. Although she had no great talent, she had a certain knack at sketching and she used this now.

With quick strokes, she sketched the squirrel, exaggerating its bright eyes and adding cheeks puffed full of nuts and a thick plume of a tail.

Of course, the animal's limbs were out of proportion and its ears more closely resembled those of a rabbit. Shrugging, she added whiskers, a waistcoat and top hat.

Briefly, Elizabeth glanced at it, her pale gaze sliding over the paper and then skittering away. She made no response and Sarah felt a surge of unexpected embarrassment at the girl's expressionless reaction. What had she expected—instant appreciation of her childish art?

'Perhaps I could—um—draw in a rabbit later,' Sarah said, to fill the silence which was becoming uncomfortable. 'I have one, you see. In my room. He was injured in the country. I'm not certain if he was there when you visited yesterday.'

Had the movement of the rocking horse slowed?

At that moment, she heard a soft knock and her husband stepped into the room.

His unguarded expression held great gentleness as he stepped towards his daughter, but then he stiffened, registering Sarah's presence.

'My lady, I did not expect you to be here. I trust you slept well.'

'Yes, thank you.' Heat flushed into her cheeks.

Elizabeth continued to rock. Sebastian stepped towards her, crouching and slowing the horse while still allowing its movement.

'Good morning, Elizabeth. I am happy to see you. Now that I am back, I thought perhaps you could ride on a real horse. Remember Annabelle? You always called her Bella and loved her. She is very slow and likely has not moved much faster than an amble.'

Elizabeth made no response.

The nursemaid curtsied. 'We'll be looking forward to it.'

'Don't,' Sebastian said.

'Pardon, my lord.'

'Don't speak for her. Miss Elizabeth will find her own words. Indeed, she may not be looking forward to it.'

'Yes, my lord.'

'But thank you for your care of her,' he said, perhaps feeling the need to soften his words.

Sarah stood and left with her husband, stepping into the comparative coolness of the passageway.

'Thank you also,' he said.

'What for?'

'Visiting. Drawing a rabbit in a suit; or was that some other rodent?'

He was observant.

'A squirrel. But, you know, it is entirely possible that the maid was responsible for the art.'

He shook his head. 'Doris is a treasure and may be an

artist, for all I know, but she hasn't a spark of imagination. No animal drawn by her hand would ever wear a top hat.'

Sarah smiled. 'Sadly, Elizabeth didn't seem impressed by my efforts.'

'You tried.'

They had paused on the top landing and he lifted his hand to gently tuck a stray curl behind her ear. She startled at the contact, at the warm, slightly rough feel of his fingertip and how this caress made her breath quicken and her cheeks warm.

She stepped away. He dropped his hand.

'I thought you might find time heavy on your hands and have made an appointment for you,' he said.

'You have?'

'The dressmaker will be coming this afternoon.'

'The dressmaker? But I have several dresses which are quite serviceable. And I don't know if I'll have time.'

'Time? Good Lord, you no longer milk the cows or collect eggs. What else would you do?'

'Um…' Sarah paused. She could hardly say that she had planned to search the city for her illegitimate sister about whom he knew nothing.

'Unpack.'

'Gracious, you have nothing to unpack. Or get a maid to do so. Besides, you need some decent clothes.'

'These are perfectly decent.'

'For Miss Martin maybe,' he said, turning to go. 'I will see you at luncheon.'

Sarah frowned, rubbing the cloth of her dress between her fingers while listening to his retreating footsteps.

'But I am still Miss Martin,' she whispered as his steps retreated down the hallway.

Indeed, he could dress her in any number of fancy dresses and she would still be Miss Martin, the odd little child the Crawfords had adopted whose origins had always been the subject of rumour and innuendo.

That familiar sense of inadequacy cloaked her, enfolding her in its weight.

Walking back to her chamber, she recognised that it would be more prudent to delay the search for Charlotte until another day.

But she could not. She would not. She was not yet ready for Lady Langford to give up the freedom she had enjoyed as Miss Martin.

And Miss Martin was imbued with one purpose.

Half an hour later, having retrieved her reticule and cloak, Sarah descended to the front hall where she was greeted by the footman.

'Would you require the carriage, my lady?' His face registered surprise.

Goodness, she hadn't considered that option. She was so used to travelling on foot. She bit her lip. A carriage would get her to her destination more expediently. But, no, it wouldn't do. The coachman might gossip.

She shook her head. 'No, thank you. I am merely getting some air.'

'I could send for the groom, my lady,' the servant suggested.

Bother. She frowned again. Ladies were probably not supposed to take the air unaccompanied.

'Um—no,' she said.

The servant looked doubtful. At this rate, egress would be blocked by her own servants. She must summon Lady Pamplemousse. Lady Pamplemousse was one of her favourite characters and featured in all of her manuscripts.

'I prefer to walk alone,' Sarah said in autocratic tones.

Thankfully, the Pamplemousse voice did the trick. The

servant opened the door and Sarah stepped into the cool morning air, feeling much like an escaping fugitive.

She allowed herself only a moment of indecision, before turning down the street and walking briskly, as though fully cognizant of her whereabouts. Fortunately, she did not have to carry on this farce for long as she found several hackney cabs immediately upon rounding the corner.

Quickly hailing a vehicle, she clambered inside, stepping gingerly on the grimy floor. The old, dried leather of the seat crackled as she moved on it, leaning forward to provide her sister's last known address.

It was somewhere to start, if nothing else.

As the hackney gained momentum, Sarah took in her surroundings with renewed interest. London had once been her home and she found she had missed the city. It had such energy, with the newsboys shouting from the kerb, pedestrians bustling into shops and vehicles clattering through the streets.

As the cab rounded a corner, Sarah saw that the houses appeared considerably less grand than those on Sebastian's street. Rather they had a square, solid sense of determined middle-class respectability. The cab lurched to a stop, the horses' hooves clip-clopped into silence.

'Could you stay here?' Sarah asked as she descended from the cab, passing the driver a coin from her reticule.

The man eyed it with such suspicion that she half-expected him to bite it like a pirate. Instead, he shrugged, pocketing the coin and giving his grunting ascent.

Sarah eyed the square structure before her. In her haste to arrive, she had given little thought about how she intended to pursue her enquiries. Of course, she could go directly to the front door, but presenting herself as Lady Langford would cause no end of gossip.

Moreover, the mistress of the house would likely not

remember a servant who had left several years earlier, yet another servant might.

The decision made, she approached a flight of stairs descending below street level. Thankfully, her garb was quite suitable for this visit.

At the bottom of the steps, she knocked on the door.

'And what would you be wanting?'

The door opened and a sizable lady filled the space, so large and well corseted that she had an air of immovability.

'I came in search of employment. I was wondering if Mrs Rogers might wish for a companion,' Sarah said, uncertainly.

'Can't see as she would. She got three unwed daughters which fill that capacity.'

'Oh.' Sarah felt her face fall in crestfallen lines—so much for that excuse.

The woman opposite must have seen her disappointment. Her expression became sympathetic. 'Someone give you a wrong tip, eh?'

'Yes, I—some time ago I met a young lady...um... Charlotte Martin, I think. Yes, that was her name. She spoke kindly of this place. She used to work here. Do you remember her?' Sarah's fingers twisted through the ribbons of her reticule.

The woman frowned, her dark, slightly bushy eyebrows drawing together. 'I haven't heard that name in years and I very much doubt as you just ran into her yesterday. You're after something and I'm not going to stand here while you attempt to bamboozle me.'

The woman made to close the door.

'No, no, please wait.' Sarah spoke with a quick tumble of words. 'You're right. I should have told you the truth from the start. She's my sister. I need to find her. Would you know her current address? Or anything about her?'

The woman's face softened and she released her hold

on the door, shaking her head so that her multiple chins jiggled. ''Fraid not, dearie. They sent her off some years since. Without a reference, which wasn't right in my mind.'

'Why?'

'The usual reason with a young girl and a middle-aged gentleman. Charlotte caught Mr Roberts's eye, you see. Mrs Roberts was none too pleased.'

Sarah shuddered. She knew too well what a dismissal with no reference might mean to a young girl, particularly one with no other contacts, money or skills. 'Did she leave any forwarding address?'

'Forwarding address? That sounds mighty proper. We ain't the Queen, nor yet the Prince Regent.'

'I'm sorry. I was just hoping…' Sarah turned, ignoring the smart of tears in her eyes.

'Come back, come back. My bark's worse than my bite, as they say. I'll make us tea. Who knows, she might have sent me something although that was a good many years ago.'

Hope bubbled inside. 'Thank you. Thank you, so very much, Mrs…?'

'Crooks, dearie. I've been here for ever. Come this way.'

Mrs Crooks swung open the door and Sarah followed her along a narrow corridor, which seemed all the narrower because of her companion's impressive size.

'Make yourself comfy, dearie,' Mrs Crooks offered, waving her arm expansively.

The kitchen was spacious and warm, pleasant after the oppressive narrowness of the hall. It was scrupulously clean with a long trestle table, a large hearth and shining pots hanging from the ceiling. A soup pot bubbled on the stove and the air felt damp and pleasantly perfumed with beef and onions.

Sarah sat at the table while Mrs Crooks pumped water into the kettle and set it to boil.

'Now tell us about yourself. How come you're in London?' The older woman settled herself within a chair and rested her round arms upon the table.

For a moment, Sarah was tongue-tied. She could hardly share that she was Lady Langford and had recently moved to London with her husband, an earl. Besides, she doubted she would be believed.

'Um…' Sarah paused before continuing with greater confidence. 'My sister and I were separated after the death of our parents, but I recently received a small inheritance which has allowed me to journey to London to find my sister.'

'You look different from Charlotte, I must say. Although it was a few years back and I might not be remembering quite right.'

'We are half-sisters. My sister's father was my mother's first husband. He died and my mother remarried.' Sarah twisted her hands within the strings of her reticule, but managed the lie.

The kettle's whistle pierced the kitchen's quiet and Mrs Crooks levered herself out of the chair and set about making tea.

Sarah moved, glancing at the clock as Mrs Crooks produced a pound cake from the pantry and then settled back in her chair with the air of one getting herself comfortable for the duration.

'I—um—don't mean to rush you,' Sarah said, some time after finishing her second cup of tea. 'But I must leave soon. Would it be possible for you to look for the address?'

'Gracious child, where has the time gone? I'm lucky the family's out and it's the other servants' half-day.' Mrs Crooks pushed herself upright and walked to the sideboard where she rummaged through a drawer overflowing with paperwork.

Sarah's heart sank. It seemed unlikely that anything could have survived more than a decade in such chaos.

'Aha.' Mrs Crooks held up a crinkled sheet like a trophy. 'And from the face on you, you doubted I'd ever find it. There's something to be said for a one-drawer filing system. There you go.' The woman pushed the remaining papers back into the drawer and handed Sarah the sheet.

'Thank you.' Sarah's fingers folded tightly against the paper. It was written by Charlotte. Even at a glance, she recognised the round childish hand and could almost visualise her sister writing it, her fair brows drawn together in concentration.'

'No trouble, dearie. I always keep everything. And I wish you luck. She were a nice girl.'

'Yes,' Sarah said, repressing a shudder at the housekeeper's unconscious use of the past tense.

Chapter Twelve

Sebastian frowned.

He sat alone at the vast dining table, chewing methodically on the succulent roast beef. The dressmaker waited in the upper apartments. The cook kept Sarah's food warm in the kitchen.

His wife was absent.

Annoyance mixed with growing concern gnawed at him. Where was she? She had only just arrived in London so she could hardly have anyone to visit. She certainly did not have suitable clothes for visiting.

Besides, the servants had said that she'd left at an unfashionably early hour.

Alone and on foot.

He glanced towards the window which looked out on to the street.

Perhaps she'd suffered an accident? Or got lost and now wandered London's streets alone? Was he destined to mislay wives as others misplaced socks? And why was she wandering off? And saying nothing of her activities in the first place?

He stabbed his fork into another piece of beef.

A rattle of wheels interrupted his thoughts as a hackney

cab pulled up in front of the house. Seconds later, his wife emerged, descending into the street from the drab vehicle.

His relief was fast chased by irritation.

Sarah marched briskly up the steps in an odious brown dress. She looked neither frightened nor lost.

Sebastian stood and strode into the front hall. 'I wish to talk to you in the study—now, if that is convenient.' He added the latter phrase for the benefit of the footmen.

Sarah jumped, her mouth opening as to speak.

'In private.' Forget the servants. Harding could think what he damn well pleased.

After removing her pelisse, Sarah followed him to his study.

Sebastian opened the door. 'Sit,' he said.

'Should I roll over and fetch also?'

'Pardon?'

'I thought perhaps I had assumed the role of *canine domesticus.*'

Humour flickered inside him even as that pulse of anger grew. 'My wife,' he said, 'does not ride in a hackney cab. I have a coach which is at your disposal. My wife does not go out without a suitable escort of footman and maid. My wife does not leave without even telling me where she is going and my wife does not arrive late for luncheon, keeping the dressmaker waiting.'

'Perhaps you should tell me what I *can* do. It would be a shorter list.'

'You can arrive on time for any appointment as is only courteous.'

'If I am consulted in the arrangement of said appointments, which is also only courteous,' she retorted.

He was reminded of her blunt, fearless honesty as she'd stood in that stream after ruining Eavensham's fox hunt.

He frowned. 'Consult? There is no need to consult. It

is obvious you need to see Madame Aimée. You can't go traipsing around in…in clothes more suited to a governess.'

'I thought that was my primary function?'

'No, I—' He found himself unusually stuck for words. 'Your clothes are not the main issue. It is that you absented yourself without explanation.'

He paced to the window, looking through the glass and drumming his fingers against the sill.

'And what did you do this morning?' Sarah asked.

'Pardon?'

'I was merely enquiring after your own activities. Or is it only I who must account for my movements?'

'No, I—' He frowned. Since his father's death ten years earlier, no one had questioned him. His mother and Alicia had not cared sufficiently and likely he'd scared everyone else away.

Immediately after Alicia's departure, he'd been like a bear with a sore head—too often drunk. Then the revolution had broken out and while his drinking had lessened, his bad temper had not.

'I am not an unescorted female unused to London's dangers and traffic,' he said at last.

'You were worried for me?' Genuine surprise laced her tone.

'Yes, I have no wish to bury another wife,' he said at length, turning from the window.

'On that we agree. I have no wish to be buried.' She smiled, flashing that delightful tomboyish grin that he'd not seen since the country. For some reason it delighted him, even as it irritated.

'Good. Then let us continue this uncommon accord over lunch.'

'Are you certain? I can go to Madame Aimée immediately.'

'She will ensure she is well paid whether she is making

you clothes or gossiping with her feet up. I will not have you hungry.'

He escorted her back to the dining room and nodded to the footman to bring in the food. As they entered the room, a look of apparent delight lit up her face.

'It's beautiful. I had not properly realised it last night and, of course, the sun was not up.'

He followed her gaze. Truth to tell, long familiarity had made him oblivious to the room, but now he saw it with fresh eyes.

It *was* beautiful, with a solid, old-style charm.

A stone fireplace took up one wall and several mirrors lined the other. Outside, a ray of sun pierced heavy clouds and shone through the window, striking the chandelier which hung low over the table. A myriad of shimmering rainbows patterned the walls mixed with the diamond sparkles of the cut glass.

Sarah stood, her eyes shining, looking more like a child than a grown woman.

'I supposed it is attractive,' he said, conscious of an unusual pride. Again she both annoyed and appealed to him with this ability to live within the moment.

She went to the table, then paused, punctuating her words with a throaty chuckle. 'Gracious, I thought we might be less formal at lunch. I shall require a foghorn to talk to you. Surely, I could sit to your left when we are alone.'

'I—it has always been this way.'

'Which does not mean it must always be so.'

'As you wish, my lady, although I do not enjoy change for the sake of change.' Still he nodded to the footman who complied, shifting the table setting.

'And what do you enjoy, my lord?' Sarah asked in that straightforward, blunt way of hers.

'Pardon?'

'You do not enjoy change for change's sake so I wondered what you do enjoy,' she repeated.

Country walks with Edwin and Elizabeth, teaching them to play chess, seeing their faces light up with excitement when fishing... Hearing Elizabeth talk...seeing her rare smiles...

'My club, I suppose. Politics.'

'Really?' Surprisingly, she appeared interested. 'I didn't know you liked politics. Are you a Whig or a Tory?'

How did she even know such terms? 'I am in favour of any party that can improve living conditions and reduce poverty.'

'I thought landowners were mainly Tory and in favour of the Corn Laws and the status quo.'

'What do you know about the Corn Laws?'

She flushed. 'I used to talk to Kit when he debated the point with his father. I liked to listen.'

'More than most politicians do.'

'And you? What is your interest?'

'Through birth I am a member of the House of Lords,' he explained. 'But, as you correctly mention, I am somewhat unusual in that I oppose tariffs and the Corn Laws. I want to avoid the English seeking a radical solution.'

'You mean revolution. Like in France?'

She *was* quick.

'Yes.' His jaw tightened, tension twisting across his shoulders.

'I like that about you,' she said.

'Pardon?'

'That you recognise inequality and want to make it better. That is the way I feel about my animals.'

He couldn't help but laugh, the sound unfamiliar to his own ears. 'Well, that rather puts things in perspective.'

'I did not mean to insult—'

'You didn't,' he said. 'You made me laugh...again.'

And again she had made him feel jarringly off-kilter.

Having finished the soup course, she laid down her spoon, placed her elbows on the table so that she could prop her head on her hands in an almost childlike gesture. 'Do you think England could go the way of France?'

'Not immediately, but if we don't change our ways, we might. We need to learn from France's experience, but most Englishmen are reluctant to do so.'

She nodded, as the footman served her the roast beef. 'It is not that people do not want to learn, but rather they take away different lessons. For example, Lord Eavensham felt that England should impose harsher sentences for any crime, however petty. He thought such a policy would prevent revolution. Kit believed such action would provoke it.'

'I am with young Eavensham in the matter.'

Sarah did not reply as she had her mouth full. She took an open delight in her food, her expression one of concentration as though to better discern the flavours. There was an openness there, an absence of pretence and an almost sensual pleasure.

Again he felt a quick, hard rush of desire.

He frowned. Lust and desire were all very well—unless they became a distraction. And there was something about this woman: her intelligence, her bluntness, her oddly engaging peculiarities which threatened to distract.

Yes, he could tolerate the physical distraction of lust, but he could not permit her to impact his mental faculties or his clarity of thinking.

Twice women had derailed his life. It could not happen again.

Sarah could think of nothing except the crumpled paper Mrs Crooks had given her. She almost vibrated with tension as she stood in enforced stillness so that Madame Aimée could take her measurements.

Madame Aimée was a short, plump lady with salt-and-pepper hair. She moved with painstaking slowness, each movement precise as she measured and draped the fabric. Every so often she would pause, stare at Sarah, her head slightly cocked with pins clenched between her teeth, saying little other than, *'Tsk...tsk...tsk...'*

The mantel clock ticked away slow seconds. Sarah shifted. The cloth rustled.

'Stand still, *madame*!'

What an abysmal waste of time. At home she'd have cooked, cleaned, milked and done any number of useful activities.

No, not at home. The Crawfords' residence was no longer her home. This overwhelming purple chamber was her home.

Of course, even without the appointment, she could hardly have dashed out again without arousing Sebastian's suspicion.

Moreover, she knew that this urgency was illogical. Sarah had waited fourteen years to find her sister. A few more days should not matter.

Except it did.

Sarah ventured to roll her shoulder, hoping that the diminutive seamstress would not notice the motion. As she did so, she had that peculiar feeling of being observed she'd felt on her first day here. Her gaze flickered over the purple bedchamber. It was empty except for herself, the dressmaker and Orion the rabbit.

'My lady,' Madame Aimée grumbled through the pins still clenched between her teeth.

The feeling persisted. Then, with a jolt of recognition, she saw Elizabeth's pale face, visible within the dark aperture of the doorway. Sarah stifled a cry, knowing instinctively that she must not attract Madame Aimée's attention to the girl.

If she had hoped for recognition or response in Elizabeth's expression, she was disappointed. The girl's countenance didn't change and there was an eerie vacancy to her gaze.

'Eek!' Madame Aimée suddenly screamed, jumping back, the pins falling from her mouth in a tinkling cascade.

'What! What is it?'

The seamstress shrieked. 'A rat!'

'What? Where?'

Sarah scanned the room. She was not particularly afraid of rats but knew they could carry disease. She followed the direction of Madame Aimée's outstretched hand, then laughed. 'Oh, that's Orion. He's a rabbit, not a rat. You hadn't noticed him earlier?'

'A rabbit! A rabbit! You expect me, Madame Aimée, to work with a rabbit?' Madame Aimée said, the decibels and pitch of her voice increasing with each agitated syllable.

'No, I—'

'I do not work with rabbits. That is a-abominable. I will not stand for it.'

It was on the tip of Sarah's tongue to say, *Then sit*, but she was not rude by nature.

'He is in his hutch,' Sarah said in consoling tones.

'Ugh! He will sniffer me!'

'But he can't get out. Look, if he bothers you, I'll remove the hutch into the dressing room or something.'

But before Sarah could step forward Elizabeth entered, walking with an economy of movement as she crossed the floor. With no further comment, she stooped, picking up the hutch and carrying it away.

'Um—thank you,' Sarah said, but as she'd expected the only response was the smack of the bedchamber door and the muted pad of feet.

* * *

Ascending to the nursery later, Sarah was aware of a tentative hope. Elizabeth had entered her chamber. She had responded with both sense and empathy by removing the rabbit. Surely that was a good sign, an indication that there was understanding and intelligence beneath that vacant gaze.

The scene, as she entered, was identical to this morning. A fire crackled in the hearth, the maid sewed while Elizabeth rocked rhythmically. The only difference was the rabbit hutch standing against the opposing wall.

Sarah walked towards Elizabeth and bent, as Sebastian had, so that she was on the child's level. 'Hello, um, thank you for looking after my rabbit, Orion, and saving Madame Aimée from the vapours.'

Elizabeth's face remained expressionless.

'Right…um…' It was surprisingly hard to carry on a one-sided conversation. 'Anyhow, I wanted to thank you for both their sakes. I am certain they were both petrified.'

A glowing coal disintegrated in the hearth with a hiss and crackle. Elizabeth had stopped riding the horse and sat quite still.

'Um, I don't know what you like to do. I mean other than riding horses. But—um—I could read you a story if you would like?' Sarah added tentatively. 'Or tell you one?'

Elizabeth said nothing, but slowly and with deliberate movements stood and approached the round table. She sat in front of the picture Sarah had sketched earlier.

'I can tell you more about Mr Rabbit and Mr Squirrel.'

Elizabeth's head moved slightly. Or Sarah thought it did. She pulled forward a second sheet of paper and smoothed it out, the vellum dry against her fingers. Licking her pencil, she drew a female rabbit complete with the large hooped skirts of the decade earlier.

'Mr Rabbit has a wife,' she explained. 'They live in a

burrow in the shade of an old chestnut tree, like the one outside your window.'

Elizabeth watched and while she did not smile, Sarah thought she detected a softening of the girl's expression. Encouraged, she added a tiny rabbit with an oversized chequered tablecloth draped over his shoulders.

'They have two children. This one is Oswald, Ozzie for short. Ozzie was so impressed with his parents' clothes that he decided to make his own with his mother's best tablecloth. He aimed for a cloak, such as a knight might wear. He was happy with the result, but his mother was cross. Indeed, as punishment he had to stay home and write "I will not cut up my mother's tablecloth". This was a tough punishment as writing is particularly difficult when you only have paws.'

Sarah added a final image depicting the rabbit hunched over a table, beads of perspiration visible on his brow.

At the story's conclusion, Elizabeth got up, retreating to the rocking horse and again starting her rhythmic motions.

Sarah stood also, rubbing her hands against the cloth of her skirt. 'I'll leave the pictures here. You could add to them if you like. Perhaps we might be able to make a story together. Did you want Orion to stay here with you? He can if you would like.'

Elizabeth's face remained expressionless. Everything about her thin body seemed folded in on itself as though it were a barricade against any external influence.

Sarah held her breath, unsure if she should repeat the offer or pick up the hutch and leave.

Then, very slowly, Elizabeth nodded her head.

Chapter Thirteen

'I will be at my club,' Sebastian announced the next day at breakfast.

He had received a terse note the day before, which he presumed to be from the Lion. As always he felt that mix of hope and worry. He did not enjoy the long hours of waiting, all the while pretending he was not waiting, but merely wanting to fritter away his entire day at the club.

Sarah must have seen his expression. Her forehead puckered in concern as she placed her elbows on the table, eyeing him anxiously. Not exactly good etiquette, but damned appealing.

'You would tell me if I could help in any way?' she asked.

He glanced at her sharply, glad no servants were present. The woman was too quick for her own good.

'It seems unlikely that I would require your assistance at my club,' he said.

'No—I meant—' She let the sentence hang.

He knew what she meant.

'I hope you will not find things too dull here.'

'No,' she said.

Sebastian studied her, aware of a certain eagerness in her expression. He couldn't blame her. He had not been entirely attentive, having been out most of yesterday, securing funding from his great-aunt. Besides, their marriage still occupied a no man's land and he was reluctant to change that situation until he had regained full emotional control.

'And now you are doing it again,' Sarah said. 'Looking at me as though I have a smudge or a stain.'

'I'm sorry,' he said.

'No matter. Mrs Crawford often looked that way, particularly if I forgot to knit socks.'

'Well, I can promise you that I do not expect you to knit.'

'That's good because I am a dreadful knitter. My socks never looked as though they were meant for human feet. They always seemed to stretch most dreadfully. They might fit a giraffe.'

'Talking of which—didn't you want to meet a giraffe at the museum?'

'Definitely. If it is still there.'

'I'm sure it is. We should go some time, if you would like.'

'I would,' she said.

As he stood from the breakfast table, he found himself thinking of the giraffe and the marble statues within the museum and whether she would smile and make a comment which was both eminently sensible and completely ludicrous at the same time.

He frowned and ordered his carriage in curt tones. He needed to connect with the Lion. He needed to be alert. He needed to save his son, not dwell on his wife's improbable comments.

As soon as breakfast ended, Sarah returned to her bedchamber and opened a map which she had requested earlier from the butler.

With nervous hands, she unfolded it. Then, picking up the crinkled paper provided by Mrs Crooks, she smoothed it out, discerning the numbers written in Charlotte's rounded hand.

Twenty-one Dobcroft Avenue. She bent over the map, tapping a nail against the thin black line of ink. It intersected Oxford Street and while a second solo walking excursion would cause comment, a shopping expedition would not...

Sarah tugged on the bell cord. On Alice's arrival, she briskly ordered a carriage to be brought to the front. Then, dressing quickly, she hurried down the stairs and instructed the coachman to transport her to Oxford Street immediately.

Oxford Street was largely as she remembered it from childhood: busy, bright and colourful. Young men in their foolishly stiff collars strolled lazily, debutantes and formidable mothers hurried in and out of shops while newsboys and flower girls hawked their wares with sing-song voices.

Sarah instructed the groom to wait with the coach and then, gripping her reticule, exited the carriage and strolled down the street as though having nothing more pressing to do than the purchase of a new bonnet.

As she surveyed the busy thoroughfare, she was sorry that this was not the case. She would have enjoyed observing the scene. She loved the country, but the city offered vibrancy, colour, noise and busy bustle. Shop bells clanged. Carriages passed by with a whine of wheels while the air was heavy with the smell of coffee from the coffee houses and the fleeting wisp of lady's perfume...

It would be nice to record all the details and use them in a story with Petunia. A bookshop looked particularly inviting. Instinctively Sarah's steps slowed and her body swayed towards its entranceway. The few novels she'd read had belonged to her mother and were decades old. How lovely it would be to purchase a new one, to smell the printer's ink and feel the softness of the leather binding.

Sarah drew away. Novels would not help find her sister.

After ensuring that she was no longer visible from the coach, Sarah hailed a hackney cab. Seconds later, she was ensconced within the cab's confines, rattling away from Oxford Street.

Surprisingly, given the short distance, the surroundings changed dramatically and Sarah quickly realised that while the neighbourhood might be geographically close to London's west end, it was an entirely different world.

The streets were narrow, bordered with low buildings so tight-packed their eaves touched. The smell of coffee no longer tainted the air, but instead coal smoke hung heavy. The people did not wear fine clothes or bright colours, but seemed garbed in uniform greys and brown.

''Ere we are, ma'am,' the cockney driver called down, stopping in front of an unprepossessing brick façade. 'You sure you 'ave the right address?'

'I hope so. Here is a guinea. Make sure you're here when I return and you'll be suitably rewarded.' Sarah said, adopting Lady Pamplemousse's tones.

Lady Pamplemousse always achieved her ends and Sarah had no wish to be stranded in this neighbourhood.

Straightening her back and quelling a lurch of unease, she descended into the street. The air felt cooler here, tinged with a damp bleakness as if close to the river. The uneven cobbles hurt her feet and two street urchins watched from the pavement, their eyes large in their thin, grime-streaked faces.

She knocked at the door and heard a woman's shout and shuffling footsteps. The door swung open and a wizened individual appeared within the aperture.

'Yes?' the woman said, her voice loud for so frail a being.

'Good morning.'

'If you says so.' Obviously, the ancient held this in some doubt.

'I am hoping you could help me,' Sarah started, then frowned. The redoubtable Pamplemousse would be less tentative. 'I require information.'

'And what's in it for me?' A wrinkled hand stretched from the frayed sleeve.

Sarah took the hint and produced a coin. The hand closed, claw-like on the piece, retracting rapidly.

'I understand that a lady, a girl, Charlotte Martin, stayed here a few years back. I'm looking for her. Did you know her?'

'I did.'

Sarah gulped. Her stomach dropped with a nauseous lurch. 'Did? She's…not dead, is she?'

'Not that I knows of. But she's been gone from here for a good many a years.'

'Oh—would you know where she is?'

'I might.' The crone waited, hand delicately outstretched, palm up.

Sarah extracted another coin. 'Where is she?'

'I don't know.' The woman took the coin, the gnarled fingers bending and enfolding it.

'But you said—'

'That I might.'

'And you don't know anything?' Sarah asked, disappointment heavy in her chest.

'I still knows my name and address.'

'No—I mean—'

The Lady Pamplemousse persona had escaped her.

'I knows what you mean, but as I don't like talking at doorways, you'd best come in. My pins get cranky standing. I'm Mrs Neville, by the way.'

The door widened and Mrs Neville retreated into a

narrow corridor which felt damp and smelled of boiled cabbage.

Sarah followed the landlady into a small parlour. It was also cold with no fire lighting the hearth. Faded flowered wallpaper decorated the wall and damp circles rose from the skirting boards.

'Make yourself at home.'

'Thank you.' Sarah perched awkwardly on the horse-hair sofa. 'If you know anything about Charlotte Martin, I would appreciate it. Any memory which could help me.'

'A pretty girl. Down on her luck, as I recall. Soon went through her money.'

'She didn't get a job?'

'Turned out with no reference at her last place. I let her stay as long as I could. I am not a cruel woman. The girl tried to get a position as a housemaid or scullery maid, if I remember right, but nothing doing. I kept her as long as I could.'

'And then?'

'Had to turn her out, didn't I?' Mrs Neville said with a shrug.

Sarah felt a flash of anger, although not entirely at this woman. Indeed, if Mrs Neville had allowed Charlotte to stay rent-free for any length of time she had done more than most. 'Where did she go?'

'She figured she had a choice of the street corner, a brothel or the stage. I figured it was probably the same difference, but the clientele might be better. Dunno in which place, though.' The woman gave a cackle at her witticism.

Sarah's stomach turned. She swallowed. 'Do you know where she went? The—the name of the establishment?'

'Establishment, is it? La-di-da. I dunno about that, but I was chatting with another girl in the same line of business, so to speak, and she said as how Charlotte had become the concubine of some Lord Whatsit.'

Sarah caught her breath. 'Recently—I mean might she still be there? Do you—would you happen to know his name?' Her fingers worked nervously at the fabric of her gown.

'I might.' The wrinkled hand reached forward again and Sarah placed another coin on the outstretched palm. The woman's skin was cold, the bones visible under translucent skin. 'What is it?' Sarah asked.

'Lord Wintergreen, he was, like the mint.' Mrs Neville laughed again. 'It was a few years back, mind.'

'Would you have an address?'

'Sorry, dearie.'

'Well, at least I have somewhere to start.' Sarah said, feeling her mouth curve slightly. 'Thank you.'

She stood from the horsehair sofa and impulsively pressed another coin into the gnarled hand.

'You didn't want tea or any other refreshment?' Mrs Neville asked as though suddenly reluctant to let her visitor go.

Sarah shook her head. Indeed, it took conscious effort to walk and not run from the place. The house with its smell of cabbage and its atmosphere of hopelessness repulsed her. She longed to escape, to burst outside and gulp great draughts of fresh air.

And yet her sister had not even been able to afford this sad place.

She and Mrs Neville walked back down the passage to the front door which the old lady opened with a whine of hinges. Sarah stepped out, thankful for the light, the space and even the rubbish-tainted air.

The hackney waited. Thank goodness for Pamplemousse.

'Where to, ma'am?' The man hurried forward.

'Have you ever heard of Lord Wintergreen?'

'Lord Wintergreen? Why, yes,' he said.

'Good. Take me to him.'

'But, ma'am, I can't do that,' the man said, touching his forelock.

'Why not? I'll pay you well enough.'

'He's dead, ma'am.'

Chapter Fourteen

Sebastian walked into the carpeted comfort of his club. The air was warm from the fire and a hushed quiet filled the place.

Seating himself within the familiar cushions of an armchair, Sebastian stretched his legs towards the hearth, nodding for brandy.

He'd done this often, enacting a façade, a repetitious play with only one act—and likely an audience of none. He would sit here, mimicking the man he had once been— a gentleman of leisure.

But today was different.

Today was the real thing, the climax, the reason for the charade. Sebastian sipped the brandy a waiter brought over, barely conscious of its taste. Then he settled back.

Through lazy, half-closed eyes he surveyed the room. A group of gentlemen played cards at the far end and one man, half-hidden behind his newspaper, dozed in a corner.

The card game progressed and was punctuated with chuckles, a soft oath and the steady thwack of cards. The sounds mingled with the fire's crackle and the occasional rustle of the newspaper.

How long had it been since he'd had nothing more on his

mind than the roll of the dice or the ingestion of fine rump roast? How hard it was to sit in forced repose.

Lord Palmer arrived with a loud, convivial entry typical of country gentlemen with a love of fresh air and sport.

Sebastian stiffened, every nerve and muscle tautening, even as he forced himself to relax.

'Greetings, old chap.' Palmer's jovial tones boomed in his usual 'hail fellow well met' way as, grunting, he sat in the armchair opposite him.

'Good to see you, Palmer.' Sebastian kept to the script. 'Care for a brandy?' He signalled for a second glass.

'Lovely, lovely, warm the cockles, don't you know. I hear felicitations are in order, what?'

Sebastian nodded. 'And how are things going in your part of the world?'

'Well enough. Well enough. Can't complain. Been in Yorkshire for a while. Good place Yorkshire.'

Palmer recited the doings of his estate, the hunter that had twisted its left ankle and his own ill fortune at the track—a barrage of the inconsequential in which to hide the consequential.

'Of course, I like the country, but it's good to be in town, what. Missed the old place.' He nodded, his gaze wandering over the club's dark wooden furnishings and plush curtains. 'Thought I'd go to Carlton House this evening. You planning to go? I'd love to meet your new wife, eh? Certain she'd enjoy it. Women always enjoy these flim-flam outings, don't you know.'

'We should be able to make it.' Sebastian said, removing his snuffbox from his breast pocket and flicking it open with a whine of minute hinges.

'I'll be there about twelve. Hope it won't be too much of a crush, mind. A fresh air man, myself.'

'Nothing like the fresh air,' Sebastian agreed.

Done.

That which mattered had been relayed.

Sebastian relaxed, his muscles easing as Palmer continued with the inconsequential conversation—chickens which wouldn't lay, dogs which wouldn't hunt, cows which wouldn't calve.

At last, Palmer raised himself from the chair, stood as though momentarily off balance and then approached another acquaintance with his rolling, lumbering gait.

Ten minutes later, Sebastian also left. He needed to get home. He needed to tell his wife that tonight she would be presented to a prince.

'She's gone? Again?'

'Took the carriage, my lord.' Harding's lugubrious face fell into heavy lines as though the removal of the carriage worsened the situation one hundredfold.

'Where to?'

'Oxford Street, my lord. She's been gone several hours. She did not return for luncheon.'

'Hours? But she still doesn't know anyone.'

'Women like to shop, my lord,' his butler suggested.

'Not—' He shrugged, leaving the sentence unfinished.

Irritation snaked through him. Sarah had never seemed disposed to shop. He'd virtually had to force Madame Aimée's services on her and now she was spending hours in that pursuit.

Why couldn't he keep tabs on his own wives?

'Tell me as soon as she returns,' he said, turning sharply and striding to his study.

Roughly half an hour later, he heard the rattle of the front door.

'About time!'

He stood, ready to go to the hall, but paused. He refused to chase after his own wife. With an irritated tug of the bell pull, he summoned the butler, requesting that her ladyship come immediately to the study.

Then he sat behind his desk, glowering.

'What time do you call this?' he asked abruptly, the moment Sarah entered.

She glanced at the mantel clock. 'Six,' she said, looking vaguely about the room as if distracted.

His irritation increased. 'Rather late as you still need to change for dinner. Is it impossible for you to be prompt?'

'Oh, um, yes, I am sorry.' She spoke flatly, a crease puckering her forehead.

'What is it?' he asked, worry softening his tone.

He noted now that she looked pale. Her mouth was turned down and shadows circled her eyes.

'I—' Her hands made an uncharacteristic flutter.

Apprehension gripped him. 'Is Elizabeth all right?'

She looked startled, as though coming out of a reverie. 'Yes, yes. Absolutely. Please, it is nothing to do with her and I had no wish to alarm you.'

'But it is something.' He stepped from behind his desk and, bending, tipped her chin with his hand, the better to study her expression. 'You are worried.'

She bit her lip, her teeth white against the pink flesh.

'Is it Mrs Crawford? Have you heard something?'

'No. Please do not concern yourself.'

'I am your husband,' he said, his thumb gently grazing her jaw. He allowed himself briefly to enjoy the touch of her skin. 'I will always concern myself with your welfare and help you if it is within my power.'

'Really?' Her grey eyes widened, confused doubt and uncertainty tangling in the dark depths.

'Yes.' Gently, he stepped closer to her.

He should stop. Any intimacy should be in its place, within the bedchamber, as though by containing the physical location, he could contain its impact upon him.

Her lips parted with an exhalation and that tiny breath weakened all resolve.

He pressed a kiss against the warm, yielding softness of her mouth. His kiss deepened. She swayed slightly towards him and desire pulsed huge within him. His arms tightened, his fingers tangling within her hair and down to her shoulders and waist. He felt the pounding of his heart and heard the thumping of his pulse against his eardrums.

He edged her back towards the desk, his kisses becoming more demanding as his fingers roamed over the unyielding fabric of her gown.

A knock and the creak of the door jerked him back to reality. He swung around.

'Yes,' he snapped at the hapless Dawson.

'A message, my lord, and what time were you wanting the carriage?'

'What? Nine, I suppose.' He took the envelope.

Dawson left. Sebastian scanned the missive, a demand from his great-aunt that he introduce this wife *if*, she had added in her bold hand, the woman was real.

He glanced towards his flushed bride. Yes, she was real enough.

Too real. Too tempting. Too distracting.

'We eat in an hour. You'd best change. And we are going out this evening. A formal event. The Prince Regent will attend.'

'What? Must we?'

The irritation, which had been simmering inside him, flared.

'Yes,' he said. 'Yes, we must go. Most women would be delighted to dine with royalty. Or perhaps you'd prefer to stay in with the rabbit.'

'I would, actually,' she retorted.

He inhaled, walking to the hearth. Despite his frustration, he had to admire her total disregard both for his distemper and for the Prince Regent's company. And underneath it all, more dangerous than either feeling, he wanted to hold her and kiss her and reassure her that whatever her worry, he would help.

Except he couldn't. He couldn't even help himself, or his daughter or son.

'Well, you get the prince, not the rabbit,' he said shortly. 'And I have arranged for Madame Aimée to come. She will help with your hair and provide a suitable dress.'

'I'm sure that isn't necessary.'

'I will not have my wife looking unsuitable.'

'Then perhaps you should have chosen a different wife. But I will channel my inner Petunia.'

And with that incomprehensible statement, she left the study.

Sarah sat amongst the parcels littering her bedchamber. If she'd known any curses she would have sworn.

She'd come to a dead end in both a literal and figurative sense. She was no closer to finding her sister than she had been with the Crawfords. She now wondered why she had been so foolish to assume she could find Charlotte within London's sprawling vastness.

And what was next? Wintergreen was dead and she could scarcely go to his next of kin and ask if he'd ever had a mistress named Charlotte.

Bother. She glared at the ostrich feather attached to a ludicrous hat that Madame Aimée had sent earlier. Why would one even want to wear an ostrich feather? Wasn't it a risk to public safety, at least for anyone taller than oneself which, for Sarah, represented the majority of the population?

Nor was she making headway with Elizabeth. Orion remained in the nursery, but the child seldom interacted with him and still rocked or sat with an unusual stillness for a child.

And now Sebastian demanded that she appear at an event where she would look sorely out of place. Moreover, she would have to put up with Madame Aimée's doubtless futile attempts to improve her looks.

And then there was Sebastian.

Worse, there was her reaction to Sebastian. And that moment when she had come so close to confiding in him, when she had felt that he would understand and could help.

But how could she expect that? How could she expect him to understand that the woman he had married largely to care for his vulnerable child was, herself, illegitimate?

'I hope that dreadful animal is not around,' Madame Aimée said immediately upon entering the bedchamber, her brows fiercely drawn over darting beetle-black eyes.

'No, he is in the nursery.'

'Good. Madame Aimée does not work with animals, *non*. Now, let me show you the creation that I propose you wear this evening, *oui*? I must say this is dreadfully short notice. Madame Aimée is not used to such demands.'

'I—um—am sorry,' Sarah said, aware that some reply was required.

'Humph, no matter. I will show you my creation now, *oui*. Alice, you will help, *s'il vous plaît*,' she directed, pronouncing the girl's name 'Aleese'.

With careful, almost reverent movements, Alice complied, taking the gown and laying it carefully upon the bed.

Sarah gasped. It was beautiful. Truly beautiful. The silk's sheen made the brilliant emerald-green luminous and tiny pearls had been sewn about the neck in an intricate design. Sarah touched the cloth, her fingers sliding over its softness.

'I've never had anything half as lovely,' she said. A

lump formed in her throat and tears prickled in her eyes. It seemed impossible that such a dress could be for her.

'Try it on, my lady.'

Sarah allowed them to undress her and place the shimmering waterfall of a gown over her head. It had no corset, but followed a newer style which Madame Aimée assured her was 'all the rage'. The neck was low, the bust tight while the rest of the gown cascaded in loose folds to the floor.

Almost shyly, Sarah glanced into the looking glass. Gracious, Mrs Crawford would be shocked. Her hand automatically went to cover her bare chest. Lud, it was cut so low she feared her breasts would burst from the fragile bodice.

'It looks a trifle—um—revealing.' She fingered the cloth. 'Will I be wearing a kerchief?'

'A kerchief? *A kerchief?* At a formal event with one of Madame Aimée's creations? Never! Never would I permit such a thing.'

Sarah felt her lips twitch and had a vision of herself sneaking out with the aforementioned article. That would make another good scene in a book.

'And you must acquire a proper lady's maid. To wear my clothes a maid is required. You will get one *immediatement, oui*?' The seamstress continued, nodding her head to emphasise this directive.

'Yes,' Sarah said.

Apparently, Madame Aimée had rather strict rules regarding her customers' conduct and appearance.

'I will make a few minor alternations. Alice, you are performing the tasks of maid until someone more suitable can be found?' Madame Aimée questioned, looking in the girl's direction while taking out a box of pins and placing several between her teeth.

'Yes, *madame*.' Alice bobbed a curtsy.

'Are you good at hair?' Madame Aimée asked, her voice muffled by the pins.

'I try, *madame*,' the girl said, looking nervous and rubbing her hands together.

'Try?' The pins were removed. 'I do not like this "try". Although her ladyship's hair cannot look worse than it does now.'

Fortunately, Alice did not disappoint. Indeed, she proved to have a natural talent. Under Madame Aimée's direction, she cut a delicate fringe across Sarah's forehead which she later curled. Bunches of curls were also carefully placed at Sarah's ears with tendrils falling from a loose bun.

Initially, Sarah had opposed both the fringe and curls. 'Won't it look dreadfully untidy? I like to have my hair pulled back and out of the way.'

'Fiddlesticks. We do not aspire to be tidy, but to be beautiful.'

'Tidy might be slightly more attainable,' Sarah said.

Both Alice and Madame Aimée worked diligently, refusing to allow Sarah to peek at her reflection until they announced the transformation complete.

'It is not bad,' Madame Aimée said with a sniff, stepping back with a satisfied expression.

'You're beautiful, my lady,' Alice said.

'And you need spectacles,' Sarah chortled.

She doubted very much she looked even close to beautiful and only hoped she did not look too odd. Like a mutton dressed as lamb, or any other barnyard animal.

'Do not be grimacing until you have the opportunity to look at yourself,' Madame Aimée said. 'Which we will not permit until we get you back into your gown. And then you will see a miracle.'

Sarah acquiesced, allowing them to dress her, place ribbons in her hair and complete a number of finishing touches.

'Ta-da!' Madame Aimée announced, swinging the oval mirror about.

Sarah gasped, her mouth dropping open. The improvement was amazing, indeed almost miraculous. The fringe covered her high forehead, softening her face and making it less angular. The delicately curled tendrils furthered this effect, framing her face and cheeks. Even her eyes looked better, bigger and brighter, while excitement had touched her cheeks pink.

'I look nice,' she whispered.

'You look well. A credit to Madame Aimée and I can give no higher, how do you say, compliment.'

'You and Alice have done wonders.'

'Wonders! We have performed a miracle, a veritable miracle. I will bid you adieu and return to fit the other dresses soon, *oui*? As for the lady's maid, I think perhaps this Alice will do. Sometimes, it is better to get them young and teach them. I bid you adieu.'

'Um—goodbye and...and thank you.'

With an imperious nod, Madame Aimée left, sweeping from the chamber. The door shut.

'Seems like you've passed muster,' Sarah said to the maid with a chuckle. 'Now I will have to see if I have equal success at Carlton House.'

'My lady, I know you will,' Alice said, happy excitement suffusing her face. 'You look beautiful. Truly you do.'

'Thank you,' Sarah said, suddenly appreciative of the girl's company and steadfast confidence. Only now was she realising just how lonely her life had been in the country.

A knock sounded and Sebastian entered. He looked... He looked immaculate, amazing—handsome in a hard-edged, dangerous way. His raven-black hair, chiselled nose and jaw gave him the look of a classical statue and made her ache somewhere beneath her breastbone.

For a brief second, she thought she detected a reaction, a flicker in his gaze as he took in her new hair and gown. Indeed, there was a flash in his eyes and a flaring of his nostrils but he merely said laconically, 'Good, you are ready.'

She detected no other change in his expression and felt foolishly disappointed. Although why she anticipated that he would fall to her feet merely because she'd changed her hair, she did not know. Such a reaction might occur in the realm of imagination, but not in Sarah Martin's prosaic reality.

'Right.' She crossed the floor with a swish of silk. 'We'd best get this done with.'

Chapter Fifteen

Nothing in Sarah's previous life had prepared her for Carlton House. Black-and-white marble tiled the entrance hall. A wide staircase swept upward towards the upper floor. Nymphs and cupids decorated every inch of the ceiling and even the door frames glittered with gold leaf. Perfume scented the air while huge candle-laden chandeliers hung low, creating a mix of golden light and shadows.

'It's glorious,' she whispered.

Apprehension slithered down her spine as her gaze skittered between the august guests and even more august servants. She had a numb, nebulous feeling that nothing was real. How could it be? How could she—the illegitimate child of a country gentleman—be here?

'It is not fashionable to gawp,' Sebastian said in a terse whisper.

'I have never been accused of fashion,' Sarah muttered, but jerked herself out of her reverie and started her ascent.

She caught a glimpse of her reflection in a huge gilt-framed mirror and looked nervously away. Her dress, which had felt splendid in the house, paled in comparison to the other ladies' gowns. The profusion of ringlets clustered over her forehead no longer looked as stylish as she had thought. Indeed, they were likely unsuitable.

'It would so much be easier if I were blonde,' she said, then flushed, realising that she had spoken out loud.

Sebastian looked at her. 'I like brown hair. Particularly yours.'

She felt her face grow warm, but there was no time to reply or consider his response. Already they were halfway up the staircase, the noise of music and chatter spilling from the ballroom and into the hall.

Sarah stood at the top of the stairs and looked around in disbelief. The ballroom surpassed the entrance tenfold. It was Oberon's palace peopled with fairies. Gowns of every hue danced in dazzling, mesmeric patterns and huge bouquets of flowers decorated the room with splashes of pink and purple, their fragrance mixing with the ladies' heavy perfumes so that the air was redolent with scent.

'Lord and Lady Langford,' the footman intoned.

Was it her imagination or did hundreds of curious eyes peer at her in blatant curiosity?

Her fingers tightened against the cloth of Sebastian's sleeve and her stomach lurched. For an awful moment she feared she could not do it, that she must turn and push through the people behind her in a desperate escape.

She didn't, stumbling forward instead.

'I'll get you a drink and introduce you to a few people and, for goodness' sake, stick with lemonade,' Sebastian said as they reached the floor.

'I am no fool.'

But before they could go towards the refreshments, an elderly woman approached with a determined step and, despite a stooped back, an autocratic bearing. She wore an old-fashioned gown of black brocade, nipped at the waist, and had an impressively high, powdered wig on her head, which had grown out of fashion many years ago.

'Sebastian,' the lady said, her voice so loud it trumpeted over the music. 'Apparently, she exists. Although I must say, I do not like being introduced in a ballroom like any Tom, Dick or Harry.'

'Great-Aunt, you're better? I called yesterday, but the servants said you were not to be disturbed.' Sebastian bowed low over her outstretched hand. Diamonds glittered, huge on fingers swollen and twisted with arthritis.

'The servants fuss over me, egged on by that foolish doctor. He thinks there is something wrong with my heart. However, I have never believed him before and will not take up bad habits now.'

'Of course, not. Aunt Clara allow me to introduce my wife. Lady Langford, this is my favourite great-aunt, Lady Harrington.'

'*Only* great-aunt, more like. My sisters died. Didn't have my stamina. So you married the boy, eh?'

'I did,' Sarah said.

'Well, I will give you both credit for efficiency.' Lady Harrington stared at Sarah, making no attempt to hide her scrutiny.

'It is pleasant to meet you,' Sarah said, feeling a need to respond.

'That is only because you don't know me well. My friends never find me pleasant.' Lady Harrington paused, turning to Sebastian. 'I take it you married the first female you found to annoy me, but I refuse to be annoyed. I like to be contrary.'

Sarah felt her lips tweak into a smile.

'Moreover,' Lady Harrington added, 'she has a sense of humour and could be intelligent, which is more than I can say for your last marital attempt.'

Sarah winced at the callous mention of Sebastian's former wife, but he showed no emotion.

'So you approve?' he asked.

'That might be putting it too strongly and is a question

I can better answer once I am acquainted with my new niece. You may remove yourself now so that I can do so.'

Sarah stiffened and Sebastian must have felt her anxiety. 'That is kind of you, but don't overtire yourself.'

'Nonsense, I am not like to keel over on the spot, if that is what you mean. Indeed, I have every intention of dying in bed in a civilised manner. Now, take yourself off.'

'As you wish, but be nice and introduce her to any French *émigrés* you know. She speaks French like a native.'

'Really? Dreadful language. I have forgotten most of what I learned which wasn't much despite my governesses' best efforts. Well, off with you.'

Sebastian acquiesced at last, sauntering away with fluid grace.

Sarah suppressed an urge to cling to him and could not deny a nervous gasp as Lady Harrington put a surprisingly firm hand at her elbow, propelling her towards a row of chairs lining the wall.

Lady Pamplemousse in the flesh.

'I need to sit. My underpinnings are aching and my feet hurt.' Lady Harrington promptly sat on a chair behind a rubber plant. 'It's my bunions. Dreadful curse. I am glad the boy has gone. It will allow me to get to know you better. How do you find Elizabeth?'

The question came abruptly and, glancing towards her companion, Sarah saw her worry, a crack in the elder woman's invincible façade. Her knotted fingers worked at the beading of her reticule.

'Sad,' she replied.

'Has she taken to you? Sebastian wrote that he thought she would.'

'I don't know.'

'Don't know? What sort of an answer is that? Has she smiled or looked at you?'

'Not exactly, but she took my rabbit—'

'Rabbit?' Lady Harrington interrupted.

'I—um—have a habit of rescuing stray animals.'

'Where did she take the rabbit?'

'To the nursery. He was in my bedchamber, you see, and Madame Aimée didn't appreciate his presence.'

'Hmm…' Lady Harrington said, narrowing her eyes. 'Stray animals now? I thought the marriage foolish and I can't say I have changed my opinion.'

'Is it not Elizabeth's opinion we were discussing?' Sarah said, stung.

'Good Lord—the cheek of you!' Lady Harrington exclaimed, but did not seem unduly affronted. 'I could almost like you except Sebastian makes awful choices with women and I find men are dreadful creatures of habit.'

Lady Harrington fell silent and Sarah, stumped for any suitable response, said nothing also.

Then, with visible effort, the older lady straightened her bent back, shifting uncomfortably in her chair. 'However, I did not come here to sit all night. We have much to do. I would like the *ton* to think Sebastian has an attachment for you. That it was a love match.'

'He hasn't. It wasn't.'

Lady Harrington chuckled. 'Blunt.'

'And why would you want people to think he is attached to me?' Sarah asked.

Lady Harrington said nothing for a moment while she accepted a drink from a waiter.

'I am not quite the monster he no doubt has described.'

'He hasn't—'

Again Lady Harrington silenced her with an autocratic wave. 'France is a country in turmoil. Naturally, I want him to look for Edwin, but I worry. I think it would be better if the rest of the world thinks he has moved on, made a fresh start, abandoned the search and immersed himself in a new family.'

'You're worried for Sebastian's safety?'

It was a new thought. There was such an aura of invulnerability about the man that Sarah had not considered that his single-minded search for Edwin might place him in jeopardy.

Again the elderly woman shrugged. 'Somewhat. The French will stop at nothing to find this Lion and anyone so open in his search for a loved one might prove a target. Regardless, Sebastian needs balance. He always was a single-minded lad. At this rate, his obsession to find his first child will undermine his ability to care for his second.'

'Elizabeth,' Sarah said softly.

'Indeed. Anyway, enough chatter.' Lady Harrington stood stiffly, leaning uncomfortably on her stick. 'Let me introduce you. Find you some *émigrés* on which to practise your French although personally I avoid 'em like the plague. They like me, of course, because of my title. They put a lot of stock in title and lineage.'

Lady Harrington peered around the ballroom as though expecting them to pop out from the walls.

'I hope they'll want to talk to me,' Sarah said doubtfully.

'Of course they will.'

'They will?'

'Naturally. I am your relative.'

'Of course,' Sarah said, squashing her amusement at the imperious tone.

Lady Harrington gave her a sharp look before starting to walk towards the refreshments, her slow movements painful. Then she stopped, looking back at Sarah, her blue eyes bright within their wrinkled pockets of skin.

'I do not expect you to care for a man or child you hardly know. Doing your duty is sufficient. I am a great believer in duty. But if you lead them to think that you do care when you do not, then I will curse you from this side of the grave and beyond.'

'I—'

'Shall we proceed to refreshments and introductions?' Lady Harrington said.

Two hours later, Sarah felt she'd met every individual with any social standing within the perimeter of London. Names and titles blurred in the hubbub of laughter and music. Her head ached and her ringlets stuck damply to both forehead and neck.

Lady Harrington also looked tired although she denied this even as she allowed Sebastian to escort her from the ballroom.

'I am as right as rain and do not let that quack of a doctor tell you otherwise,' she said, leaning heavily on Sebastian's arm. 'Besides we haven't introduced your wife to the prince yet.'

'Apparently he is not coming tonight and Sarah prefers the companionship of rabbits,' Sebastian said, moving towards the exit.

'They do cause considerably less trouble,' Lady Harrington agreed.

Sarah watched their departure. She'd liked the old lady for all her bluntness. Still, she was not sorry to see her go. For the first time in hours, she allowed her countenance to relax. Lud, what she would give for fifteen minutes in the peace and quiet of Mrs Crawford's spartan home with no need to dance, converse or curtsy.

She was unused to socialising or to this crush of people. It felt as though the ballroom had grown smaller with the curtained walls, the music, the hot air and brightly dressed people pressing in upon her. Even the air felt too thick to breathe, with its sludge of smells.

In the last sixty minutes, she had met more people than

she had in her whole life and their names and faces swam about her in a jumbled, nauseous whirl.

The need for solitude overwhelmed her. She had to get away from this hot place, clogged with humanity, and find quiet, if only for a moment. Like a fugitive, Sarah sidled along the back wall, slipping from the ballroom into a narrow corridor.

Exhaling, she leaned against the wall and closed her eyes. Here it was cooler, thank goodness, and the music was softened by distance.

Paradise was the peace in which to think one's own thoughts.

But even as she formed the thought, she heard voices and footsteps. She stiffened. Could she not get two minutes alone?

Sarah crossed the hall and, like a fox entering its lair, pushed open another door. She stepped into what appeared to be a library. The air felt almost chill and the ceiling was high, matched by tall windows and shelves lined with books. Two wall sconces provided puddles of light and the fire was low, the coals barely glinting.

Sarah sank into the deep, creaking, leathery depths of the armchair. She'd not stay long, of course. Just a few moments—

Damn.

She muttered Kit's expletive and would not even edit the word. With a mix of desperation, anger and amusement, Sarah saw the brass doorknob turn.

On impulse, Sarah bolted from the chair to the window, sliding behind the velvet curtaining so that she was hidden behind the soft, musty folds.

Within the instant, she regretted the action. It was immature and foolish. If she'd stayed put, she could have explained her presence. Now what could she do? She could hardly reveal herself as there could be no reasonable excuse for subterfuge behind the curtains.

Bother. She would have to wait them out and hope she did not sneeze.

'This should do. There's no one here.' It was a masculine voice, cold with the infinitesimal trace of a foreign accent. Indeed, it was less an accent but more a too-perfect enunciation of the English language. 'Did you find out who he is?' the same voice asked.

'I kept Lord Palmer under observation as you requested,' a second voice, also masculine, stated.

Thankfully this was no lovers' tryst.

'Yes?'

'I have a list of all his contacts. As you thought, Langford was among them. Although there were several others.'

Langford? Her Langford? Sarah stiffened. Her breath caught.

'Relay the conversation.' The first man's tone was harsh, as though he was well used to respect.

'All of it?'

'Yes. What am I paying you for?' the other snapped. He sat down or at least Sarah thought he did. She heard the wheeze of cushioning.

'Lord Palmer spent time complaining about his ankle and his estate. Then he said as how he was going to Carlton House this evening and Langford said he would come too and bring his wife who likes flim-flam things.'

'And that is it? Every word?'

'Um…' Paper crackled as though the man might be referring to his notes. 'He did say as how he was a fresh-air man and would be here at midnight.'

'Fresh air—*mon Dieu*!'

Thwack. A fist banged on the table and Sarah jumped, her every nerve taut as a violin string strung too tight. She bit her lip, desperately suppressing a sneeze, triggered by the curtains' dust.

'The terrace!'

She heard the hurried scuffle of someone standing. Peering through the slit in the fabric, she discerned a man's bulk.

'You are satisfied, sir?'

'What? Yes, yes, but out of my way now. Langford is going to meet this damned English Lion and I'll miss it if I don't hurry.'

'But what about my money?'

'Not now.' A door slammed.

Sarah waited, her ears straining for any sound that might indicate the presence of either man. She heard nothing except the thumping of her own heart and the rasp of her quickened exhalations.

Nervously, she eased herself from behind the curtains and stepped into the empty room. She sat, sinking on to the sofa and staring blankly at the furnishings as though expecting that they might provide some clue.

What did it mean? How was Sebastian involved? What could, or should, she do?

She rubbed her temples to better clear her thoughts. Then, unable to remain seated, she paced the floor, striding in front of the hearth, before circling back. Instinctively, she knew the men were a threat.

But what could she do?

She had to do something. She could not let Sebastian walk into a trap. She hurried to the door, but paused, hand resting on the handle. Mrs Crawford had always said that the devil's work was done by impetuous hands.

She stood still, briefly frozen. The mantel clock ticked. She looked back at it. Almost midnight. Those men, whoever they were, thought that Sebastian was going to meet the English Lion in mere minutes.

Devil's work or not—she had to do something.

Chapter Sixteen

Heat and noise met her the second she entered the ballroom. She scanned her surroundings for Sebastian, her gaze roving over both the swirling dancers and those individuals clustered about the other refreshment table.

There…she'd spotted him. He was halfway across the room and talking with several other gentlemen. She started towards him but, getting to there was no easy task. Indeed, by the time she'd arrived, he'd gone again.

A whisper of cool air touched her and she saw that the terrace doors stood ajar, the turquoise curtaining undulating in the breeze.

She stared at the moving cloth. He must be out there already. Her gaze moved to the wall sconces and mirrors as though they could provide some answer or solution.

She had no talent for espionage.

But she could not do nothing and allow these men, whoever they were, to jeopardise Sebastian, the work of the Lion and the rescue of a child.

Straightening her spine and squaring her shoulders, Sarah stepped swiftly outside. The air felt cold to her overheated skin. Goosebumps prickled and she could discern little in the gloom, save for the lumpy outline of the shrubbery and balustrade. Gradually, her eyes adjusted and she saw a tall, male figure.

'Sebastian.' She made her voice light and flirtatious. 'How romantic. I love moonlight.'

He made his bow, glancing at the darkened sky. 'My lady, did you need me?'

'Yes, I—I wanted to dance,' she said, walking to him.

'Naturally, I would be delighted to dance with you. If you will give me a moment in this cooler air, I will join you on the floor presently.'

'No, I—' She reached forward and grabbed his hand, conscious that her own were warm and sweaty. 'Humour me, my lord, I am absolutely desperate to dance now. I cannot wait.'

'It will be my pleasure, in a few moments.' She heard the iron in his voice, but met his gaze, willing him to understand.

Swaying into him, she stood on tiptoe so that her head rested on his shoulder.

'Please, it is my very favourite melody.' She brushed her lips against his ear as though in affection while whispering fiercely, 'Come in. It's not safe.'

She felt his body stiffen imperceptibly, but he gave no outward sign that he had heard. Leaning against him, she listened to the steady thump of his heart as she counted the long seconds.

At last he nodded. 'If you wish to dance, I will be delighted to oblige.'

Her body felt weak with relief and her knees shook as they crossed the terrace and moved back into the crowded room.

Sebastian led her out to the floor, his face impassive and his manners impeccable. He placed his hand against hers as the music for the minuet started.

'What are you playing at?' he asked as they met.

A nervous tingle shot through her. 'I had to. Sebastian—'

'Smile, for goodness' sake. You look as though you were enduring medieval torture.'

Because I'm dancing with a caged tiger.

But he was right—about the smile that was. She forced her lips to twist upwards, her feet keeping perfect time.

Thank goodness she'd been forced into endless hours helping Kit learn these dances.

'You are being watched. They know about the meeting with—'

She paused as they stepped away.

'How do you know this?' Sebastian smiled lazily, leaning towards her as though whispering compliments.

'By chance, I was—'

'You are certain?'

'Yes.'

They turned and then turned again.

'Very well and thank you.'

The sudden heat in his eyes made her heart quicken. She was conscious of his proximity, his size, the raven blackness of his hair and the angry, raw energy which emanated from him like a physical force.

The music stopped. Sebastian made his bow, bending over her hand.

'Go to the ladies' retiring room. Pretend you have a headache so we can leave,' he said.

An hour later, Sebastian stood at the hearth in his study, staring at the miniature.

He did not need to look. He knew the image. He saw it waking and sleeping. He might have escaped a trap and for this he was thankful, but he'd also missed a meeting.

Rescue was no nearer. Indeed, with the Lion's enemies circling, it would seem to be more and more remote.

Sebastian shivered. It was cold. The fire was dead and he had not ordered it to be relit.

The door opened. He heard its whine and her footsteps across the room as she came up behind him.

'Is that him?' she asked, her voice a soft whisper. 'Edwin?'

'Yes.'

He stared at the lad's face. He would be older now, of course. He touched the painting with his fingertip, tracing the outline of his son's cheek. What news had the Lion hoped to impart? All day he had been torn between elated hope and fear.

Now nothing.

Nothing.

'I'm sorry,' she said.

His finger moved to the frame, the jewels and enamel uneven under the tip. Edwin was not dead. He would— he *must* believe—that his son lived. A father would know otherwise. He would feel it within the depth of his being.

But then, perhaps, he did. Perhaps that was why he dreamt, night after night, of the guillotine's blade descending. Perhaps that was why he heard the rasp of the rope pulling up the blade and the high, whining whirr as the knife descended. And why he smelled the blood and saw the basket of severed heads.

He turned, a violent movement.

'Tell me everything. Everything you heard or saw,' he said, almost harshly.

She nodded. 'There were two of them. I never saw either face. One had a French accent, but it was very slight. I think he was well educated. Really, it was more that his English was too perfect.'

'And the other?'

'I did not recognise the voice, but he was of a lower class and English.'

'What did he say?'

'That he had kept Lord Palmer under observation and that you'd met him, Palmer, I mean. At your club.'

Sebastian fists clenched. 'They'd heard our conversation?'

'Yes, he said that Lord Palmer spent a lot of time complaining about his ankle and his estate. Then Palmer said he was going to Carlton House that evening and you said you'd come, too.'

'Is that all?'

'Palmer mentioned he was a "fresh air" man and something about midnight.'

'Damn.' Sebastian paced in front of the hearth. 'The only people that were there were some fellows playing cards. But they were young, no older than Kit Eavensham, and very loud. I doubt a member of their party could have overheard.'

'Maybe he was a servant,' she said. 'You would be less likely to notice a servant and he sounded of a lower class.'

He nodded, considering her words. She was right. It was true that his class tended to forget that those who served also had ears.

'So will he contact you again? The Lion?'

He frowned. 'What do you know of the Lion?'

'Very little. Only what everyone knows—that he is a hero. The men just said that you were meeting him and I guessed he is trying to rescue Edwin. I would like to help.'

Help?

No one could help and yet, as he glanced into those grey eyes, he felt comforted.

'I know.' He touched one of Sarah's newly minted curls. It twisted slightly about his finger. 'I feel—'

The sentence hung in the air.

'I like the hair,' he said instead.

She flushed, the pink touching the fine porcelain of her

skin with a rosy glow. 'Madame Aimée and Alice worked hard to make me presentable—no easy task.'

'Don't.' He stepped even closer to her so that they were only inches apart. 'Don't put yourself down. You have your own beauty.'

The flush deepened. 'No, I—don't. I am not fishing for compliments, but I am fully aware that I am on the plain side.'

She bit her lip, glancing down so that the dim glow of the lamp light touched her lashes, forming intriguing shadows against her cheeks. He wanted to tell her about the many forms of beauty, the gaudy and the subtle, and how there was something about her—

Again he couldn't find the words. Almost without thought, he cupped her chin and lifted it so he could look into her steady grey gaze. 'You have beauty,' he said huskily.

His lips touched her mouth. He tasted her soft sweetness and felt her start of surprise and then the surrender as her lips opened. His hand reached for hers. Her fingers were warm with a slight, tingling roughness at their tips. His other hand still cupped her chin and he brushed his thumb against the silky softness of her skin.

She smelled of lemons.

His kiss deepened, want and need flickering into flame. His hand moved from her chin to twist through her hair while the other reached to touch her back.

He pulled her closer, enjoying the feel of her curves and the full softness of her body pressed flush to him. He felt her quickened breath and a wonderful quiescent swaying.

Then she stiffened with sudden rigidity and withdrew.

'What—what is it?' he muttered, his need for her trebling.

'I'm sorry. I—I am trying not—not to feel.'

'What?' He lifted his head, releasing her so suddenly that she slumped against the desk. 'What—in the name—what do you mean?'

'Not to allow my base instincts to show. I don't want to disgust you,' she whispered, looking down, her cheeks now bright red patches of colour.

'Disgust? What the…?' He paused, biting back his temper. He did not want to frighten her. Grasping for control, he said more gently, 'What are you talking about?'

'That a gentleman wouldn't want his wife to—to enjoy—that only women like—like—p-people that are not good enjoy—'

'Mrs Crawford told you that.' It wasn't a question. He spoke with heavy certainty.

She nodded.

Ludicrous woman. He should string her up by her own apron strings.

'Sarah.' He moved from her, certain he could not speak logically or with control while she looked at him with her hair undone, a glistening sheen of moisture visible on her parted lips and unshed tears brightening her eyes.

'Listen,' he said, seeking the right words. 'Mrs Crawford is wrong about so many things. She is a hurt, angry woman. There is nothing you could do that would disgust me. I want to hold you. I want to pleasure you. I want to feel your response. I want you.'

She glanced at him with endearing surprise. 'You do?'

'Yes.' He stepped to her now, again lifting her chin so that he could look in her eyes and show his sincerity. 'And I want to consummate this marriage.'

'That is a relief. I—I think I do, too. And I find the pretence greatly exhausting.'

He chuckled. 'And I do not want you exhausted, my lady. At least not at the beginning of the night.'

* * *

His bedchamber was spacious and decorated in muted colours of beige and brown. She had not seen it before.

'I like this. It is peaceful.'

'I needed a place that was mine.'

'A sanctuary. My room at Mrs Crawford's was like that—'

'Hmm...' He nuzzled her neck. 'You talk too much.'

He pressed kisses along her collarbone as his hands clasped the small of her back, pulling her closer. As though of their own volition, her hands reached for him, gripping his shoulders. She swayed, needing the support, because her knees felt wobbly and her body seemed as though liquefied, hot and molten.

'So very desirable,' he murmured.

Petunia maybe, never me—she thought, or maybe she spoke the words out loud.

And then she stopped thinking as thought and words slid into the fog of desire.

Sebastian lifted his head, catching her mouth. With intuitive knowledge, she pressed her tongue to his own, as his body edged her backwards.

She felt the mattress against her knees and tumbled on to the bed. He followed and she almost laughed because it seemed altogether wanton, fun and wonderful to be sprawling with this man in the softness of the immense bed.

'There is no shame in our loving,' he whispered, his lips brushing ear. 'Whatever nonsense Mrs Crawford has fed you with.'

With gentle hands he stroked her, tracing her face, her shoulder bones, his fingers dipping under the silk of the low neckline of her dress. She shivered at the tingling sensation of his touch against her skin.

'Too many clothes,' he muttered.

But he did not remove her gown, as she expected. Instead, he slipped free of his own linen shirt.

'Your turn,' he whispered.

She looked confused. Gently, he took her hand and, after kissing the palm and each finger, placed it flat against his chest.

'I—'

'Don't talk. Feel.'

Tentatively, she moved, pressing her palms to him, sliding her fingers across his shoulders, feeling the muscles and sinews, hard and strong under the warm skin.

With growing confidence, she sought the small, male nipples and ran her hands over his ribbed abdomen. He exhaled at her touch, the muscles tensing under the skin.

'Never be ashamed of what you feel and what you do to me,' he said huskily.

Then he took off his breeches, sliding free of the cloth. Her eyes widened at his nakedness.

'And now,' he murmured, 'you are most definitely over-dressed.'

'Then I must remedy that,' she said, sitting up and pulling off her gown, in a way that was daring, exhilarating and oddly freeing. She threw it so that it rustled to the ground with a soft swish of silk. She watched his face. She saw his gaze roam her body. She saw his breathing quicken as he noticed her nipples hardening against the cloth of her chemise.

He wanted her. At least in this second, he wanted her.

Slowly, instinctively, she undid the bodice, untying the ribbons at her waist and letting the cloth fall forward. His expression changed, passion flaring, and she felt neither fear nor shame, but a wonderful heady mix of desire and power.

And then he was on top of her, his warm, hard body covering her. He smelled of soap combined with a musky, masculine scent. He kissed her hair, her cheeks, her lips and the column of her neck. She arched against the long, lean length of him.

With a groan, his lips roamed and this time she knew no reluctance and no constraint. Desire and something else, something more tender, filled her.

She raised her hips to him and he thrust into her, taking her fully, swiftly and completely.

And, as she clung to him and welcomed him, she felt a sense of completeness.

Of coming home.

Chapter Seventeen

Sebastian had left when she awoke the next morning and she was alone within the huge bed. A mix of emotions touched her at his absence—both regret and a certain relief. She flushed when she thought of the night before. How did one discuss trivia over morning toast after...that?

She rose quickly, slipping hurriedly into her own room before Alice came with chocolate. The lack of privacy afforded the aristocracy still felt odd to her.

Later, she would visit Elizabeth, she decided. After all, there was little she could do to find Charlotte this morning and it was only through frequent contact that she could hope to develop a rapport with the child.

And now, the concept of a family was so much more real than before. That one thing which Sarah had never had and had always wanted.

The nursery, as always, seemed unchanged with the nursemaid, the silent child and flickering fire.

'I came in to see Orion,' Sarah said tentatively, pausing on the threshold.

Elizabeth continued rocking. The nursemaid stood, curtsying, while Orion clawed at the cage. Closing the bedroom door, Sarah stepped into the room, and, crouching, opened the cage door. A bad idea, no doubt. Orion was still largely wild and would hide under the bed and prove difficult to recapture.

Surprisingly, the animal hopped out, but did not dive for cover as she had anticipated.

'He is less wild,' she said softly. 'You are taming him.'

She watched as the animal hopped about the room, aware that Elizabeth had slowed her movement on the horse. Hardly daring to breathe, she studied the child as she stiffly removed herself from the toy and picked up a chunk of carrot from on top of the dresser.

Crouching, Elizabeth pushed the carrot forward and waited as Orion approached, ears cocked and nose twitching. He took the carrot, then, with hurried movements, went into his hutch to enjoy the treat.

'Thank you for looking after Orion so well,' Sarah said. 'It is always hard for a wild animal to get used to captivity. Um—may I?'

Taking silence as assent, Sarah sat at the small table, letting her gaze roam over the earlier sketches.

She bent forward, the movement jerky. Elizabeth had added to them. Pain squeezed her chest as she looked at the harsh lines on the paper. The sketch depicted the rabbit and was well drawn, but the raw talent was not what had captured her attention. It was the mood and atmosphere. Elizabeth had used charcoal and employed thick heavy strokes which gave the image the appearance of darkness and gloom.

One drawing was realistic, but the others were caricatures, personified with clothes and near-human facial expressions, similar to those Sarah had made except awfully different at the same time.

Two young rabbits held hands and stood close together, their eyes wide, their fear evident.

'They are afraid,' Sarah whispered.

Elizabeth still stood by the rabbit's hutch.

'Why? Why are they so scared?'

Elizabeth said nothing. Sarah hesitated, unwilling to turn the page without the child's consent.

'May I?'

But Elizabeth stepped to the table. She shook her head and, with an almost darting movement, removed the papers, crunching them into a tight, crinkled ball.

Sebastian sat astride his mount. It was not Jester, but a pretty mare which he hoped would be suitable for Sarah. So far, the animal was proving satisfactory. Her movements were good and she seemed to have an easy temperament.

Therefore, he had no reason for his sour mood. Pale sunbeams peaked though the clouds, splashing colour and warmth so that Rotten Row seemed almost springlike, despite the calendar.

He rolled his shoulders. They felt tight. His own bad temper irritated. What man suffered from distemper because making love to his wife had been better than anticipated?

His fingers tightened on the reins as he urged the horse into a trot. She moved easily, responsive to the lightest touch, which was well as he doubted Sarah could be anything but gentle to an animal.

How did one stay whole, he wondered, when his entire being had been split open and his careful reconstruction after Alicia's treachery cast asunder? Because making love with Sarah had felt wonderful and awful, as though his heart could no longer be contained within his chest and now lay exposed.

And he couldn't afford such vulnerability.

Not now. Not again. Never again.

When he had married Alicia he had loved her with his mind, body and soul. Indeed, he hadn't even fought the feeling, but had revelled in its depth and ferocity. It was as if all his affections from his lonely childhood had been stored, waiting for her.

Then his children had been born. In those first years, he had felt a joyful contentment. At last, he had the family, the sense of belonging, for which he had always searched.

Nudging the mare, he pushed her into a gallop as though with sufficient speed he might escape the memories. Her hooves beat the turf, a constant rhythmic drumming. The wind blew cold in his face, tugging at his hair.

Alicia's death and the kidnapping of his children by Beaumont had both killed and saved him. When Alicia had first left he'd engaged in self-pity. He'd gambled and drank, like his father before him.

But their danger galvanised him as though struck by the energy of a thousand lightning bolts. That blur of self-pity and cognac had dissipated and he had done everything to save them. He was still doing everything.

And he must not, *would* not, allow anything—or anyone—to distract or make him vulnerable again.

Sarah's efforts to find Charlotte had stalled like a wind-still ship. Her tentative enquiries about Wintergreen and his estate had led nowhere. She'd even asked Sebastian's great-aunt, who had had shaken her head reprovingly.

'Wintergreen was never quite the thing. Best not to talk about him in polite company.'

Briefly, in her desperation she contemplated telling Sebastian about Charlotte, but remembered the cold look on his face when he'd spoken about both Alicia and his mother's affairs.

Besides, the consummation of their marriage had not brought the closeness she had hoped it might. Making love to him had touched her to the inner core; it continued to touch her and fuse her to him. Yet during daytime hours

Sebastian was frequently out or hidden behind his newspaper or he would talk about the doings of people she did not know and had never met.

Sometimes she thought that this forced restraint in the day compensated for their night-time passion. Perhaps, for all his assurances, Mrs Crawford had been right about respectable women.

She shook her head. She could not tell him of Charlotte, and risk exposing her own illegitimacy. This was a secret she must keep.

Being in town himself, Kit arrived promptly following her summons. He accepted a cup of coffee and flung himself into a wing chair, his legs stretched towards the hearth and his eyes heavy as though only reluctantly awake.

'Why,' he grumbled, 'why did you get me here at this ungodly hour? Terribly early for a social call and I was at White's until dawn.'

'Yes, but I knew Sebastian would be exercising his horse.' She poured herself coffee, added sugar and stirred. 'And, Kit, I—um—need your help most desperately.'

Kit rubbed his chin, a gesture well remembered from childhood days, 'What about? Rescuing some manner of animal, I suppose.'

'No. I need to know what happened to Wintergreen's mistresses after he died.'

'You what?' His cup cluttered on to the saucer and he jerked his body upright in his chair. 'You're...you're not even supposed to know about mistresses.'

'I'm the daughter of a mistress. Of course I know about mistresses. Just because I am a lady doesn't mean you have to tiptoe around me.'

Kit shifted as though uncomfortable. 'Still shouldn't talk about 'em. Really not the thing. Anyhow, why do you want to know about—um—Wintergreen's mistresses in particular?'

'Because my sister was his mistress and I haven't been able to find out what happened to her after he died. I thought she might be in a brothel and that maybe you could make enquiries.'

'My God, what do you know about brothels?'

He stood up, looking so outraged that Sarah giggled.

'Not much. That's the problem.'

'This is no laughing matter. You should not even know that such places exist. You want me to comb London brothels for your sister?'

'I am sure you could do so ever so tactfully.'

'No.' He paced to the window. 'You'll not get me with flattery.'

'Then desperation.' Sarah stood also, approaching him. 'I cannot abandon my search, you know that. And if you do not help, I'll have to do it myself.'

'Good gracious, you must do nothing of the sort!'

'Then you will help me? Please.' She dragged out the last syllable.

Kit thrust a hand though his hair, quite ruining its style. 'You have a husband. Couldn't you send him on this errand?'

She shook her head. 'He does not even know I have a sister.'

'That's easily enough remedied.' Kit turned from the window, an irritable frown creasing his face.

'Kit, how can I share information about my sister without explaining that I am a bastard?' She spat out the word.

'Maybe you should level—'

'No! I cannot. If you will not make enquiries for me, then truly I must, I will, make them myself.'

'That is blackmail.'

'I have no choice.'

He paced the length of the floor. 'How is it...?' he said, stopping momentarily to glare at her before continuing to pace. 'How is it that I always get embroiled in your tom-fool ideas?'

'You'll do it?'

'Yes. Yes. I'll do it. I only hope this whole thing doesn't cause some ungodly mess.' He turned to the door. 'I'll do it, but in my own time so that it doesn't cause unnecessary comment. Is that all, your ladyship?'

'Yes,' Sarah said, then stood, stepping forward and touching his arm. 'Thank you.'

Chapter Eighteen

'You told her to draw?' Sebastian almost shouted, entering her bedchamber.

Sarah jumped, turning towards him. His face was bleak and his jaw tight. He threw some papers down upon the bedside table, the impact loud within the room's quiet.

'I—yes,' she said. 'I thought it might help.'

'It does not appear to have done so.'

Her gaze fell to the sketches piled on the table top. She gave a muted gasp. The picture depicted an owl flying to its nest, the tiny bodies of the squirrels dangling in its talons. In the foreground, the mother squirrel lay dead, its head severed from its body.

'She drew that?' she asked, realising too late that it was a foolish question.

'I have not taken to drawing decapitated animals,' he said.

She picked up the sheets, studying the graphic details and the stark images. She could understand why her husband was angered and shocked and yet…

'I don't know if it is a bad sign,' she said at last.

'You what? You think it is healthy for a child to draw murdered animals?' he snapped, bristling with anger.

'No,' Sarah said quite calmly, choosing her words with care. 'But we know Elizabeth is not emotionally healthy.'

'And this—' He picked up the pages, shaking them. 'This is not helping.'

Sarah remembered her mother's sudden death. She was ill only a few days before she'd died. She remembered her own removal to the Crawfords' house, sent adrift without her sister, her mother or even the servants she had known previously.

She would have gone mad or sunk into depression if she had not had the outlet of her writing. It had comforted her and made sense of that which was incomprehensible.

'I think everything she has seen and endured is bottled within her. She is unable or unwilling to speak about it. Surely it is better to draw, to communicate in her own fashion, than not?'

Sebastian paced between the small hearth and window, the tension and energy visible in his abrupt movement and clenched jaw. He picked up the sketches, again studying the harsh images.

She saw his conflict; his need to protect his daughter even from her own memories and the slow recognition of a different perspective.

'You have a point,' he said at last. 'I hadn't thought of it like that. I was angry. Shocked.'

She nodded. The images were shocking.

'You really think it will help?' he asked.

'I don't know. I have no expertise. I only know that this feels better than silence. I know that I found—find writing helpful.'

He nodded again before walking to stare out of the window, placing his hands upon the frame, his shoulders hunched.

'My father drank. When he found out about my mother's

first affair, he drank. Then he died. She had more affairs and then she died, too.'

'How old were you?'

'Eight when she had her first affair. Or the first my father found out about. Eighteen when she died. They were dead within a year of each other.'

'I'm sorry.'

'We were all silent.'

'The Crawfords' was also a silent house,' she said.

Her father and Mrs Crawford had spoken about minutiae, details about the village, the farm, the village... And all the while, Sarah could feel their anger, their hurt made all the worse by her own presence.

'I took the pictures away. Should I return them?' he asked at last.

Pain threaded his voice, but she heard also a confused humbleness in his tone and was touched by it.

'I do not know,' she said. 'But I think so. They are her story. I think she needs to decide what to do with them.'

He nodded. 'You will come with me?'

'Yes,' she said.

Elizabeth sat in her usual chair, but glanced up upon their entrance. Orion had been released from his cage and hopped about the room. His paws made a soft intermittent sound. The maid was picking something up and started as she saw them. She stood, curtsying quickly.

'Hello,' Sarah said softly.

Moving slowly, as she might approach a wild animal, she crossed the floor and touched the chair next to the girl. 'May I?' she asked.

Elizabeth made no response, but did not flinch or look away as Sarah tentatively sat beside her. Sebastian sat on the other side, endearingly oversized within the tiny chair, his knees angled uncomfortably.

'I brought these back,' he said awkwardly, placing the vellum sheets in front of his daughter. 'Um—you have talent.'

Elizabeth reached for them, placing them beside the pile of other drawings.

'May I?' Sarah asked again.

This time Elizabeth made no effort to remove them and, taking this as tacit consent, Sarah pulled each page towards her and studied the images. The uppermost drawing depicted an owl in flight. Each feather had been carefully drawn, the painstaking detail evident and its size grossly out of proportion to everything else within the scene, particularly the two baby rabbits dangling in its claws.

'It must be hard for them to be so small and alone and… and so scared,' she said.

Elizabeth made no comment.

Sarah looked at Sebastian and saw his mute appeal. Playing for time, she bent, reaching to touch Orion's silky fur, as he hopped about her feet. Startled, the animal scuttled away with a burst of frenetic energy.

Wordlessly, Elizabeth slid to the floor. She made no move towards him, but waited for the animal's return with apparent patience.

Acting on instinct, Sarah pulled a blank sheet towards her, grasping the pencil with nervous fingers.

'Elizabeth, I think we need to help these rabbits,' she said, starting to sketch. 'We cannot leave them hurt and scared and alone.'

For a few moments, the chamber was quiet, save for the noise of her pencil passing over the page. She paused, conscious that Elizabeth was now standing, looking over her shoulder with her still unnatural gaze.

Thrusting a hand nervously through the curls Alice now created daily, Sarah swallowed, biting her lip before speaking in husky tones. 'You see, when Mr Rabbit saw that his children were in danger, he knew he had to save them. He knew that his love was so strong that he would think of something, a way to bring them back. So Mr Rabbit ran to his burrow. He rummaged through the leaves and grass to find something which might help. And that's when he found a—a—um—spool of string which the housemaid had dropped.'

Picking up the pencil again, Sarah sketched the rabbit, including a ball of string and showing the animal carefully placing the end in his mouth.

'Carrying it, he raced to a wall. The wall was very high, but there was a bench beside it. Using his powerful hind-quarters, he leapt on to the bench and then up to the wall.'

As she sketched the animal scrambling up the wall, she warmed to her task. '"I'm coming! I'm coming!" he shouted. Then he tied one end of the thread to the branch and the other about his waist. Very carefully, he positioned himself so that he could jump to the owl's nest, grab both of his children and leap to the safety of the ground below.'

Sarah drew a final picture showing Mr Rabbit and the two young children sliding safely down the length of string.

Sarah stopped, conscious of the fixed attention of both Sebastian and Elizabeth. She held her breath, waiting for something, some reaction.

Elizabeth continued to stand, staring at the picture with single-minded, unnerving concentration. With deliberate movements she picked up a spare piece of charcoal. Holding it so tightly that the tips of her fingers whitened with pressure, Elizabeth slowly and deliberately blackened out the image of the second baby rabbit.

Found.
Meet me at side door.
Eleven p.m.

Sarah read and reread the simple note, clutching it tightly. It had been delivered to her shortly after she and Sebastian had left the nursery and Sarah had been wandering around in a state of dazed wonder ever since.

Found... Did that mean that her sister had been found or was Kit merely referring to something else connected to Wintergreen? The brothel maybe...

Why did he have to be so cryptic?

She reread Kit's words, her heart beating like a drum. She paced her purple bedchamber, her body filled with restless energy which made her want to run, to shout, to act.

And, even if her sister had been found, was she alive? Sick? Imprisoned?

Why couldn't Kit visit at a reasonable hour? Why did he insist on such cloak-and-dagger subterfuge and that she sneak out under cover of darkness?

Surely Charlotte must be alive. Kit would not be so cruel as to raise her hopes falsely. Yes, she would believe that. Charlotte had been found. Sarah laughed, a little wildly, conscious that her cheeks were wet from tears she hadn't known she'd shed.

Charlotte had been found.

Nothing else mattered.

But as the afternoon dragged on with an unrelenting slowness, Sarah wished desperately she could share her news with someone. If Sebastian had stayed, she might have—

Those moments with Elizabeth had brought back an emotional closeness and sense of family. She remembered how he'd stood outside the nursery, leaning against the wall and exhaling with a long whoosh of breath 'Thank you,' he'd said and touched the curve of her cheek. 'Thank you.'

But at lunch their conversation was so stilted and formal that she thought they had walked into a scripted play.

Then he had left for his club and Sarah remained with her own thoughts, a confused mush of anxiety for Elizabeth, hope and fear for her own marriage combined with the half-fearful elation that she might find her sister the next day.

Several visitors arrived, apparently with the sole purpose of driving her to further distraction. There was the Duchess of Marleau, who insisted on discussing her deceased relatives. The moment the duchess departed, Mrs Armstrong arrived and, although less morbid, her chatter was no more convivial, as she only talked bonnets.

Sarah knew little about bonnets and wished to know even less.

However, the afternoon's conclusion brought little relief. Sebastian did not return so she ate a solitary dinner and set about filling the interminable hours until eleven.

It was time.

At ten to eleven, Sarah pushed open her chamber door and tiptoed through the silent house to the servants' exit. She felt excited, scared, anxious and a little foolish. She was too old to be tiptoeing in the dead of night like a child playing pirates or spies.

Sebastian had returned, but she had not seen him as he had gone immediately to his study. Shivering, Sarah tiptoed down the unfamiliar stairs and pushed open on the bolt until it released with a snap, loud as a poacher's musket. She stepped into the night. The sky had cleared and she could discern the shapes of the shrubbery and carriage house. Nervously, she pulled her cloak tighter.

'Kit?' she whispered.

Nothing.

'Kit.'

'Here. Shh.' He spoke into her ear. She jumped, feeling the tickling warmth of his breath.

She twisted about. 'You scared me.'

His head and shoulders appeared from the shrubbery, the leaves releasing a cascading shower of cold water from that afternoon's rainfall.

'Sorry,' he mumbled, extricating himself from the bush and stepping on to the lawn.

'Kit! Tell me everything. Have you seen her? Is she well?'

'I haven't. I don't know.'

'But you have found her? You are certain?'

'I think so,' he said.

'Think? Oh, I wish you were certain. I cannot believe it. My mind can't take it in.'

'If you could disbelieve more quietly,' Kit muttered. 'Let's get away from the house. We can talk behind the coach house.'

They crossed damp grass, slipping behind the brick structure and inhaling the scent of moss, manure and garden damp.

'Where is she?'

'I believe she is the current mistress of a Mr Owens,' Kit said.

'Owens? You have the address? Can we go to find her? Now?' Sarah asked, her words tumbling out.

'Of course we can't go now,' Kit said, his tones so scandalised Sarah giggled, aware that her laughter was touched by hysteria.

'Why not? Please. We must. It would be like our childhood adventures.'

'With rather more at stake. Your reputation for one thing.'

'What do I care about reputation when I might actually see my sister?' Her laughter died, muted by need and desperation.

'Your husband might care,' Kit said. 'Besides, any such enterprise needs to be thought through. We are adults now.'

'So tell me more so I can think it through,' she demanded, ignoring his last comment. 'Tell me about this Mr Owens. At least, it is good news that she is the mistress of one man and not in a brothel.'

'For goodness' sake, stop using that word. It makes me damned uncomfortable. And, no.'

'No what?'

'No, it may not be better. Owens is not a nice man, from what I've heard. A bit brutish.'

'Brutish? You mean—you mean he hurts her?'

Kit nodded. 'Knocks her about from what I hear.'

'Then we must do something immediately,' she said, striding towards the street. 'Do you have a vehicle?'

'Yes, but we are not going anywhere. I refuse. It would put her in even more danger anyway. Owens is hardly going to hand her over. Plus I absolutely refuse to put you in danger particularly when you have a husband to do that.'

'But, Kit, we must. Why come here at this ridiculous hour if you didn't mean to take action?'

'I—'

'No matter. I am going whether you come with me or not.'

'No.' He grabbed her arm. 'No! You don't even know his address. And I will not tell you. Look, I've done what I can, but I'm not going to risk your reputation. Or my own for that matter...'

'Yours?'

'Yes. About to make an offer actually.'

'You're what?' She gaped at him, surprise briefly stilling her. 'You mean an offer of marriage?'

Kit was like a rambunctious puppy and no more suited to the role of husband than one of his father's bird dogs.

'Lady Caroline de Witt. She has title, a dowry and remarkable eyes. Mater and Pater delighted, more with the dowry than the eyes. But I like the eyes. Very remarkable.'

'Good Lord, stop prattling. I am happy for you, but still I do not quite see why you cannot help me.'

'Rattling around with a married woman to places of ill repute not quite the thing. Need to be responsible. Almost a married man,' he said churlishly.

Sarah sighed. She knew Kit well enough to recognise when he would not be moved. He'd always had a stubborn streak. Besides, if Owens was as nasty as Kit thought, bringing him would be like expecting a Labrador puppy to do a man's work.

If she hoped to help her sister, she had only one choice.

Sebastian looked through the window of his bedchamber. He slept poorly most nights and usually pushed away retiring.

He held a glass of cognac and sipped it as he studied the dimly lit shapes of the garden's shrubs and trees. He wondered if he should seek the company of his wife and obliterate his thoughts in physical love.

But his desire for his wife was close to becoming an overwhelming need and that spoke of vulnerability. Outside, a cloud passed over the moon, casting weird shadows across the flagstones' white diamonds.

Later it seemed to him that he sensed the figure before seeing it. His flesh prickled. His hands tightened reflexively as he held his breath, stepping behind the curtain to better observe the garden.

The figure, small in stature and wrapped within a dark cloak, ran over the flagstones, cutting obliquely across the grass towards the residence. A French spy? Edwin miraculously returned?

The thoughts collided; tenuously balanced between dread and hope.

Then, as the individual neared the premises, the hood fell back, exposing a woman's pale face.

Recognition jolted through him.

Sarah.

His first thought was that she must have rescued a toad or some other creature. It was only as he looked past the garden that he noted a cabriolet in the street and recognised the crest.

His fingers tightened against the velvet curtain. More pain than he would have thought possible wrenched through him. His heart felt as if it had stopped and now beat more wildly.

He cursed as everything fell into place with horrid clarity. It made sense, of course. Why hadn't he realised it before? Kit had been unable to marry her, a penniless, illegitimate woman, but their affection had been obvious...

He was a fool. A cuckolded fool.

A cuckolded fool *again*.

With a conscious effort, Sebastian unclasped his fingers, stepping away from the window. Doubtless Kit was the reason she'd even agreed to the marriage. A married woman had much greater freedom than a spinster, particularly one within Mrs Crawford's home.

He finished his drink in one fiery gulp and walked across the chamber, throwing himself into the armchair and thrusting out his feet. Then, within a second, stood again, unable to remain still even for a moment.

'Sebastian!'

Her shout came from the corridor, loud enough to wake the dead. He opened the door and saw his wife running towards him. The cloak flapped about her and her hair appeared wildly dishevelled.

For a second, surprise softened his anger. Then it flared back, stronger than ever. The woman had given herself to that boy and now came running back to him.

'My lady?'

'Thank goodness you're still awake and dressed.'

'It would not appear that you missed me overly much.'

Sarah seemed not to notice his tone, but stopped in front of him, her hands gripping the lapels of his jacket. 'You must help.'

'Kit Eavensham cannot oblige?'

'What? No, no, he refused on account of Lady Caroline and her eyes. And I need to go there. Tonight. Who knows what he is doing to her?' Her eyes sparkled with tears and he could feel that her hands trembled.

'Your lover has taken another woman and you expect me to intervene? You're even worse than Alicia!'

'My what? Who?'

'Eavensham—I noticed his curricle. No doubt you will become sneakier with practice,' he said.

Her mouth dropped at his words. She let go of his lapels.

'At least you don't waste my time by denying that you had been out with Eavensham,' he said.

'Of course I was. He told me about Charlotte and Mr Owens. But we do not have time for this.' She ran a hand through her hair, which was already wild.

'I apologise if I am boring you.'

'Boring? Oh, for goodness' sake, stop drawling nonsense at me. I am not having, nor would I ever have, an affair with Kit Eavensham. I came here for help. I will not lose Charlotte for a second time. I *won't*.' Her voice quivered and he saw her jaw clench as though to compensate for the weakness.

Inhaling, she stepped away and turned her back to him, her arms crossed and shoulders tightly hunched in an attitude which was both angry and defensive.

I came here for help. The words circled his brain.

'Sarah,' he said finally, forcing himself to speak calmly. 'Why do you need help? Who is Charlotte?'

She turned. 'My sister.'

'Your sister?'

'Yes.' She spoke quickly, an urgent rush of words. 'My mother was not married to my father. She was his mistress. And prior to my father she was the mistress of another man. Charlotte is that man's child and my older sister or half-sister. When my mother died, Mr Crawford gave me shelter, but not Charlotte and now she is the mistress of a horrible man called Owens.'

Questions pounded through his head, but Sebastian pushed them away, holding on to the one clear fact.

He pulled the bell.

'What—what are you doing?' Sarah gasped.

'Preparing to rescue your sister, it would seem.'

Chapter Nineteen

'You will help?'

'Yes.'

'Now?'

'Yes,' he said.

'Thank you,' she said. The tears that she had been holding back fell now. She felt them track down her cheeks.

He shrugged. 'Likely it makes more sense to wait until morning, but—'

'What?'

'I happen to know he's on a losing streak and in a bad temper.'

'You know him?'

'I know of him.'

'Then absolutely we must go.' She grabbed his arm, already stepping towards the door.

'You stay here. I will look into the matter.'

She shook her head. 'No, I'll go with you. I must. She doesn't even know you.'

'Does she know you? When did you last see her?'

'Fourteen years ago, but she will remember me,' she said. 'She must. Besides, she likely fears men.'

Briefly, she thought he would challenge her, but then,

with a quick nod, he acquiesced. 'It is safer for her this way. We will take my curricle. It is faster.'

They travelled swiftly through dank streets lined with buildings, the outlines an indistinct grey within the night-time gloom. The street lamps were infrequent and the few people on the street appeared drunken or destitute. Occasionally she'd seen women on street corners with their desperate, brightly painted faces.

'You are right. This is quite dreadful,' she said, shivering.

Sebastian halted the vehicle. The stench was strong both from the river and the rubbish which lay rotting on the street. A rat scuttled by in the gutter. Sarah saw the quick movement of its silhouette in the dim light.

They approached the house, a small, brick structure with tattered lace curtains visible through dirty windowpanes. A cluster of wilted plants straggled from a window box.

There was something both brave and pathetic about those boxes with their wilted blooms.

Sebastian knocked; the noise loud, echoing within the night's stillness. They waited for what seemed like whole minutes. Sarah heard the clang of something falling in the neighbours' garden and felt the quick startled intake of her own breath.

Sebastian knocked again.

At last, the door handle turned. Without realising it, Sarah clutched Sebastian's arm. The door eased open and a pale woman stood on the threshold, framed within the narrow aperture. Her hair hung in long, lank ringlets and a dark bruise marked her cheek, swelling so that her left eye was almost closed.

Sarah caught her breath as a turbulent mix of emotions engulfed her: relief, sadness, anger. She swallowed. Tears smarted as she took in the familiar blue eyes set within that pale countenance which now looked so much older than her years.

But it was Charlotte. Her Charlotte.

Impulsively, Sarah stepped forward, then stilled as, eyes widened with fear, Charlotte backed away from them. Her expression showed no sign of recognition.

'He sent you here? Did he lose? Am I the prize?' she asked in a flat voice, devoid of curiosity.

'I... No,' Sebastian said.

'Charlotte,' Sarah whispered.

Now the woman angled her head to Sarah, staring at her in a strange, unfocused way. 'Who are you? How do you know my name? Does he want it with you as well?'

Hot colour rushed to Sarah's face as she understood the meaning of the words. 'Charlotte, don't say such things. Don't...don't you recognise me?'

'Should I?'

'I'm Sarah.'

'Sarah?' The woman gasped as if winded, one hand clutched at the faded dress while the other reached for the wall.

'Your—your sister. Please, you must remember me?' The conversation felt strange and surreal.

Sarah had envisaged this moment for ever, but this was so cruelly, so horribly different from the scene she had pictured. Yet, despite everything—the swollen face, the lewd connotations of speech and the dullness in the blue eyes— Sarah knew that this woman was Charlotte.

But she was also a stranger. There was a greyness to her complexion, as though all life and vibrancy had been drained from her.

'Sarah. Why are you here? You should not be,' Charlotte said, again speaking in a flat voice. Sarah could hear no trace of joy in her tone and even her fear seemed muted. It was as though exhaustion deadened her every emotion.

'I had to find you. I've dreamed of it since that last day.'

A carriage rolled by on the street. Charlotte straight-ened as if momentarily jarred into fearful animation by the brisk clip-clop of hooves. She bit her lip. 'You should go.'

'I can't. I've waited for ever to find you and I am not going now. We can help—'

Charlotte shook her head, her mouth working as if about to cry, the flatness of expression gone briefly in painful agitation. 'No, no. You can't. It is not safe for you or me. He mustn't see— Please, you must go. I am glad you are well, Sarah, but you cannot help me. I am beyond help. Look after yourself.'

With a sudden unexpected movement she slammed the door shut so quickly that neither Sebastian nor Sarah could intervene.

'Charlotte!'

Sarah stood on the doorstep and stared at the dull brown door with the dangling strips of paint and the unpolished bronze knocker.

'Charlotte, we could take you away from here. Please, please come out or let us in,' she said. Stinging tears spilled over from her eyes, washing down her cheeks.

She had never imagined this. She had considered the possibility that she might never find Charlotte or that she might learn that her sister was dead. But not this.

It felt as it had when she'd gone on an excursion into the country with her mother and had stood at the edge of a fast flowing river and felt the current suck at the sand and pebbles from between her toes.

Like the earth was falling away.

'What do I do now?' she asked.

'We go home,' Sebastian said.

'No.'

'With your sister.'

* * *

Sebastian knocked briskly. 'Miss...' he paused '...Miss Martin, we will stay here and hammer at the door until morning or the arrival of Mr Owens, whichever occurs first. Therefore, it might be best to allow us entry.'

After a moment, the door opened.

'Are you called Miss Martin?' he asked.

'Among other names,' she said, the merest trace of humour visible in her blue eyes, briefly reminding him of Sarah.

'I am Sebastian Hastings,' he said, omitting his title. 'Your sister's husband.'

'Then you must know or have heard of Mr Owens. Please leave me be and tell Sarah to...to leave me be.'

'I find my wife doesn't do what she is told. May we come in so that we are not talking on the steps? It would be safer.'

She nodded. They stepped into a narrow dimly lit hallway and from there into a sparsely furnished but clean parlour.

'Sit down,' Charlotte said.

They sat, the two sisters looking at each other with disbelieving eyes. For a moment, they just stared, taking in the other's appearance until Charlotte again broke the silence.

'Sarah, I am glad to see you, truly I am, and that you are well. I am sorry that I was ungracious. It is just I—I do not want Mr Owens to find you here. Really, it is better if you go now.' She ended in a quick nervous rush of speech, her voice dropping lower as though the drab walls had ears.

'We are not going,' Sarah said.

Charlotte turned to Sebastian in mute appeal. 'You must.'

'No, we mustn't,' he said with certainty.

It was not even about Sarah any more. There was a

vulnerability, a hopelessness about this woman which demanded action. 'If we do, Mr Owens will kill you.'

She touched her cheek self-consciously. 'He isn't that bad. He is always sorry afterwards.'

'I doubt his sorrow lasts. Nor will it mend broken bones. If you stay, he will kill you,' Sebastian repeated the harsh words gently but with firmness. They needed to be said. 'And I cannot allow that. It would distress my wife. You will leave with us.'

Charlotte trembled. Her glance roamed the small room in search of an exit, escape or solution. She swallowed. He saw the movement in her thin throat.

'I can't just leave.'

'Yes, you can. We will go to the carriage now. I will make it right with Owens tomorrow.'

He caught her frightened gaze.

Her fingers rubbed at the cheap fabric of her dress. It was clean, but he saw several rips neatly sewn. Her right arm, he noted now, was also swollen and bruised.

'Please,' Sarah said.

'What about my things?'

'Collect anything you absolutely need. Sarah can furnish you with anything else you require,' Sebastian said.

'What will your servants think?'

Sebastian shrugged. 'They will think what they are told to think. You and Sarah can decide how best to introduce you to the household.'

'As my sister,' Sarah said.

Charlotte shook her head, quickly and decisively. 'No. I will not bring disgrace to you.'

'Well, decide it between you, but later,' Sebastian said. 'Collect your belongings and let us leave. I would rather deal with Owens tomorrow when he is more likely to be sober than to run into him tonight.'

And Charlotte complied.

* * *

The whine of wheels and the clatter of horses moving too fast alerted them. Sebastian turned to see a high-sprung curricle careen about the corner.

He cursed, wishing the man to Hades. Thank goodness Sarah and Charlotte were already in the curricle. Perhaps they could still make a quick getaway. But Owens was already out of the carriage, lurching towards them on unsteady legs. He held a whip. It glinted under the street lamp.

'What do you want?' He slurred the words into a single blast of sound.

'Mr Owens?'

'What's that to you?'

'I wanted to talk to you. It will be to your advantage,' Sebastian said.

Owens stared at him for several seconds as though his whisky-infused brain needed the extra time to make sense of the words.

'Very well,' he said and nodded towards the house.

'I'll come, too,' Sarah said, leaning out of the vehicle.

'Fine with me,' Owens sneered in a way Sebastian did not like.

'You will stay here,' Sebastian told his wife.

'I could help—'

'You could do nothing but get in the way.'

'I am quite strong. You forget my life has not been one of leisure.'

'What do you think I am going to do?'

'Fight him. Attack him.'

He laughed shortly. 'No such drama. I will pay him. Now stay in the curricle and wait.

They travelled home swiftly. Sarah clutched her sister's hand. Charlotte did not pull away, but neither did she hold on. Indeed, she seemed in a state of shock, staring blankly at the passing streets.

Sebastian said little about his conversation with Owens, only remarking that it had been satisfactory and that they were safe. All of them.

Sarah exhaled as the distance between them and the desperate little house lengthened. The air held the cool stillness of dawn. Gradually, a grey-pink glow lit up the London skyline and as it grew Sarah knew the swell of euphoric wonder.

She had done the impossible. She had found Charlotte. She had found Charlotte and rescued her.

When they arrived home, Sarah took Charlotte to a bed-chamber immediately. She had intended to organise a bath and provide food, but Charlotte refused both, curling on the bed like a small, wounded child.

For a moment, Sarah stood, studying her sister's face in the dawn's grey light. She looked younger now, the lines of care and strain softening as she eased into sleep.

After gently covering her with a wool blanket, Sarah tiptoed into the hallway and closed the door with a muted clunk. Questions circled in her mind. There was so much she wanted to know and to say to Charlotte. But there was time enough for that. A lifetime of time.

She found Sebastian staring from the window in his bedchamber.

'Thank you,' she said as she slipped into the room.

He nodded, turning to her with cold appraising eyes.

'There has never been anything between me and Kit. You must believe me. He is like…like a little brother to me.'

'I believe you,' he said.

She stepped towards him, reaching out her hand, but his countenance remained hard. Her hand dropped with a soft thwack to her side. 'Then it is because I am a bastard—that is why you are looking at me like that.'

'No,' he said. 'I guessed as much when I first met you.'

'Then why? Why are you looking at me like that?' A frightening pain seemed to twist through her.

'You deceived me.'

The words struck her with almost physical force. Something hard and leaden solidified within the pit of her stomach.

'I didn't. I mean—'

'You have been sneaking around London and you did not tell me. That is deceit,' he said.

'To find my sister.'

'You lied to me like Alicia.'

'Alicia ran off with another man!'

He turned from her, picking up a brandy snifter from the dressing table and swallowing it in a single fiery gulp before staring again into the dimness of the early morning.

'The motivation does not matter. The fact remains you made choices which could have brought danger to this house…to my daughter.'

'I didn't. I would never hurt Elizabeth.'

'And Alicia would not knowingly have put Edwin or Elizabeth in harm's way. She was no monster—just a fool. She trusted the wrong man and got caught up in a revolution.'

'And you think I am like that? You liken a few excursions in London to that?'

'I think you did things under my roof without telling me. How can I protect you, Elizabeth or even your sister if you do not tell me the truth? If I do not know what you're doing or what danger you might bring to us?'

'You think Owens will seek revenge?'

'I think Owens is a small-time criminal who has been paid off and will slink back into the cesspool from which he came. But you didn't know that. And you were not honest.' He put down the snifter and turned as though to leave the room. 'I knew we did not have love, but I thought we had trust.'

That hurt. It surprised her how much it hurt. She stepped back, biting her lip as she tried to hold back the tears.

It should not hurt this much.

'However, I cannot undo what is done, but only take precautions to keep my family safe. You will not venture unaccompanied from the house,' he said.

'I am not a child.'

'No, you are a lady and my wife. It is neither safe nor appropriate for you to traipse around London unescorted. And no longer necessary, I presume, unless you have additional missing relatives?'

'I don't. And what about Charlotte?'

'What about her?'

'Can she stay?'

'Yes,' he said.

'Thank you and—um—Sebastian—I'm—I'm sorry I did not tell you or trust you.'

'So am I,' he said.

Sebastian sat within the chill quiet of his study. It was almost mid-morning, but he still had not ordered the fire to be lit or even eaten.

For weeks, she'd deceived him. She'd gone out and explored London's labyrinth of roads, hiding her doings, just like his mother and his wife.

He remembered the pain that had surged through him when he'd thought she'd been with Kit. It lingered still in the knowledge that she'd sought the lad's help. It muddied his reason and distracted his mind.

It was a weakness.

Standing, he went to the window and stared at the empty street.

His children; their needs, both emotional and physical, must come first. He could not risk distraction. He could not forgive deceit.

There were no white lies. No partial truths. No harmless falsehoods.

There were only lies.

They spoke little during the next few days. Sebastian was polite but unreachable as the northern star.

Sarah felt a deep thankfulness that she had found Charlotte, but at what cost? She had not even realised how much she valued Sebastian's company and welcomed the emotional intensity of their physical love, until she found herself bereft of both.

She realised also how few people he afforded any measure of trust.

And she had had it—at least in some small measure.

And lost it.

There was anger as well. It was deep-seated, tapping into the roots of her childhood. Always she had been judged. To her mother's servants she was the unfortunate result of illicit love but lacking her mother's beauty. To her mother, she was the plain daughter, ill-equipped to secure husband or lover. To Mr Crawford she was an inconvenient duty. To Mrs Crawford, she was a Christian duty and physical reminder of her husband's infidelity.

To Sebastian, she was a liar.

And, really, she was all of these and none of them. She was a person.

The days slipped by. Charlotte slept. Sarah told the servants she was an indigent relative come to stay and organised clothes for her. Sometimes, she and Charlotte talked of desultory things, flowers and needlepoint. Occasionally Sarah mentioned their childhood or tentatively asked about her sister's life after their mother's death, but Charlotte would turn away, tears shimmering in her eyes.

The one bright spot on this somewhat dim landscape was Elizabeth. The girl still had not spoken, but she rocked less and usually dismounted and sat at the table when Sarah visited.

Sometimes, the child played with Orion. The rabbit now had a pewter water dish and would lift it by the rim and toss it to the floor with a clatter. Then Elizabeth would pick it up and return it in an oddly opposite game of fetch.

Sometimes the girl would draw, filling the page with dark images of small rooms and bars. Sarah averted her gaze from the harsh reality of Elizabeth's truth, but felt it was better for the child to let these memories out than to keep them festering within.

Surprisingly they had few visitors. Harsh weather gripped the town and several people succumbed to colds. Even Lady Harrington was laid low, staying away until the following Wednesday when she sent a brisk note demanding Sarah's attendance at Mrs Frobisher's tea.

'It is vital that you are not seen to languish,' she wrote in her bold hand.

Once with Sarah in the carriage, her ladyship warmed to her theme. 'People are saying that Sebastian is spending long hours in his club which will not do,' she announced, her strident tones louder even than the carriage wheels' clatter.

'I rather think you might be talking to the wrong person, if you hope to change that.'

'I never "hope". I do. And it is imperative that people see him as committed to you and no longer seeking his son.'

'But he is,' Sarah said. 'Why pretend otherwise? I am finished with pretence.'

'That's as maybe. Meanwhile, he is also at the Frobishers'. Talking to Mr Frobisher, I believe.'

'And you hope that by bringing me to tea it will appear as though we are out together?'

'Indeed, I will not stay too long largely because I am easily bored. Therefore Sebastian will be duty-bound to take you home which will be good for everyone to observe.'

'And that is all that matters. Not what is reality, but what people think is reality.'

Lady Harrington looked at her sharply. 'Fiddlesticks. I only aim to control what people think. It is up to you to control the reality of your marriage.'

'I am afraid Sebastian has rather taken on that role.'

'Then you must wrestle it from him. It is all very well for men to think they are in control, but it is disastrous if they actually are.'

'And he accuses me of deceit.'

'Sebastian said you speak French?'

Sarah nodded, blinking at this abrupt change of subject.

'Many people do. Dreadful language. But at least you can talk to those *émigrés*. There are bound to be several. Mrs Frobisher is drawn to titles like bees to a honeypot, although that is not a very original expression and I do like to be original. However, it would seem that any information you could ascertain might endear you to Sebastian.'

Again Sarah felt her lips twitch. 'I might almost think that you like me.'

'You are not as bad as some,' Lady Harrington acknowledged. 'But don't let that go to your head. And stop plucking at your reticule or you will damage it. I know I am as rich as Croesus, but I abhor waste. Besides, I need to rest for the remainder of the journey and the rustling distracts.'

With these words, Lady Harrington leaned her powdered head on the cushions, allowing her eyes to close.

* * *

Mrs Frobisher's salon was the last word in elegance. Mirrors lined white walls and this, combined with high ceilings and tall windows, gave the room a feeling of space and light. Gold leaf decorated the door frames and pastel clouds festooned the high ceiling. Even the furniture appeared delicate; the tables had thin, spindly legs while the sofas were small and low to the ground.

Lady Harrington settled herself comfortably within a velvet chair next to several fashionable ladies and immediately launched into loud conversation about roses, although Sarah was uncertain what had prompted her choice of topic.

'It is absolutely no use being gentle to them. Have you never noted that the most humble cottages have the best roses? The key to roses is neglect. Cut them back in autumn and neglect them,' Lady Harrington announced.

'And have you an opinion on this, Lady Langford? I hear you are originally from the country,' a pale woman said. She had translucent skin and an air of tragedy so pronounced that Sarah wondered if she might be one of the promised *émigrés*.

Lady Harrington gave Sarah no opportunity to answer, instead suggesting that the entire party venture outside to observe the Frobishers' roses which had been recently pruned.

Dutifully, the other ladies rose and, as they departed the drawing room, Lady Harrington introduced her niece to their hostess, the pale sad woman, and to their fellow guests.

The garden proved wonderfully large by London standards and Sarah happily inhaled the scent of grass and earthy damp. She was too fresh from the country not to welcome these moments and to revel in the moist springiness of the grass under her feet and the touch of damp breeze.

As for the rose plants, they were not remarkable. Indeed, the bushes had been so severely trimmed that they resembled little more than bare stalks.

'They look like nothing now, but in summer they will be beautiful,' a slim woman said, stepping beside Sarah.

Comtesse Hubert—Sarah pulled the name out of the confusing mix of names which had been rattled off to her in the drawing room.

'I look forward to that, Madame La Comtesse,' Sarah replied, switching to French.

The woman smiled. 'It is nice to hear my language and you speak it well. We used to have a beautiful garden, too, you know.'

'You must miss your home.'

'I miss—I miss the way it used to be, but not the way it is now. There is fear everywhere. My husband is dead and I do not know about my sons.'

'I am sorry.'

The Comtesse gave a shrug as they continued to walk past the bare flower beds. 'The French are survivors. I am thankful to be here. To be alive.'

Sarah could think of little to say. Her heroine, Petunia, of course, never had this problem. Petunia rose to any occasion with aplomb.

'My mother was French. She was a survivor. I mean until she died,' Sarah said awkwardly.

'That is why you speak the language so well.'

'Yes, she taught me. She said I had best have accomplishments as I am no great beauty.'

'Brains last longer than beauty. Lord Langford is still looking for his son?'

Sarah hesitated.

Comtesse Hubert placed her hand on her arm, a feathered gesture of a touch. 'We are all friends here, *oui*?'

'Yes,' Sarah said.

'I also look.'

'For your sons?'

'And any of my family. I will let you know if I hear anything about the child,' the older woman said gently.

'Thank you.'

With a tiny nod, the Comtesse stepped away to rejoin the group, but Sarah lingered, conscious of a confused mix of emotion: pity, hope and an infinite sadness. How could it be right for children to be so cruelly embroiled within their parents' mess?

The other ladies now walked back towards the house, but Sarah felt reluctant to return. The company was pleasant enough, but she felt apart from them, like an oddity within their uniformity of hats and lace and desultory conversation.

She missed the country. She missed the smells and open spaces and the freedom to go as she pleased. She missed the steady common sense of the country folk and the useful tasks of feeding chickens and milking cows.

A sound, almost a whimper, caught her attention. She stiffened, angling her head. The sound came again, more distinct this time.

She stepped towards a small privet hedge and, looking over, noted a boy digging in the earth.

She paused, uncertain. The other ladies had re-entered the house and she would seem odd if she delayed, chatting to this boy.

But she couldn't ignore human suffering. She stepped closer, moving around the hedge. 'Hello? Can I help?'

The sobbing stopped. The boy jerked his head up. Tears trickled down to his chin, where they hung pendulous.

'What is your name?' Sarah asked.

He said nothing, staring at her as though half-fearing she was an apparition.

'I'm Sarah,' she said.

'Fred, miss.'

'Well, Fred, can you tell me what the trouble is.'

'Tell you? But yer a lady.' His dazed glance took in her gown.

'You could still tell me what's wrong.'

'But I ain't supposed to be 'ere talking to the likes of you.'

She smiled, leaning forward with a wink. 'I doubt I'm supposed to be talking to the likes of you, but I won't tell if you don't. Now, what's the trouble?'

The boy looked reluctant. The tears had left vertical lines, white demarcations cutting through the grime. ''Tis me dog, miss.'

'Yes?' she prompted.

'I'm sure it ain't yer problem, miss,' he repeated, frowning as he rubbed a tattered sleeve across his nose.

'Probably not, but I'd like to hear it. It would give me respite from worrying about my own problems and I am uncommonly fond of animals.'

''E got in the larder again and Mrs Cobbs, what's the cook, she says she's gonna git rid. Shoot 'im or poison 'im. She's a mean one.'

The boy blinked.

Sarah swallowed. She knew what it was like to depend on an animal for love.

'There's no one else who could look after him until Mrs…um…Cobbs gets over the larder incident?' she asked.

'Don't have no one, me. Never had no dad and me ma died and, well, Liver is me only friend and cook says she's gonna do it tonight.'

The tears spilled over again. Sarah produced her handkerchief, giving it to the boy. His eyes grew round and, even after taking the cloth, he made no use of it, holding it delicately between two grimy fingers.

'You can use it to blow your nose and wipe your eyes,' Sarah said.

The boy did so, dabbing uncertainly.

'What about a friend? Is there a friend who could hide the dog?' she asked after a moment.

He shook his head. 'I don't know nobody. Besides, everyone is afraid of Mrs Cobbs and the butler.'

'And Mrs Cobbs is usually a woman of her word? She doesn't make idle threats?'

'She always does what she says.'

'Right. Then I suppose we'd best do something,' Sarah said, standing abruptly.

'What?'

'Show me the animal for a start.'

'Huh?' the boy replied, his jaw dropped and he stared at her, eyes wide with disbelief. 'But you can't see 'im.'

'Why not?'

'Well, you're a lady.'

'Evidence that I can see him, if I choose, which I do.'

This logic made the boy's forehead wrinkle and he rubbed his face with his hand as though to clear his thoughts.

'But we'd have to go to the garden what's outside the servants' quarters,' he said, cocking his head presumably in that direction.

'Then we'll go. Only we'll have to be quick. Lead on, Macduff.'

'I'm Fred, not Macduff.' He spoke with firmness as though holding on to this indisputable fact in a world that had gone crazy.

'Of course, and what did you say your dog's name was?'

'Liver, on account that he's liver coloured and likes liver.' Fred got to his feet. He presented a thin figure with several inches of wrist protruding from the frayed cuffs of his shirt.

He led her around the side of the house to the kitchen garden.

'Do you—um—mind mud, my lady?' her young companion asked, as they paused.

'I—' Sarah hesitated, thinking of her slippers. 'Not at all,' she said gamely.

The boy whistled softly and Sarah heard the instant pad and rustle of paws as an animal bounded over the fallow soil. Its body was long and lank and it waved its feather duster of a tail in apparent ecstasy.

Fred patted the animal and the feather duster moved with greater wildness.

'Isn't he lovely?' the boy asked.

Sarah squinted, unsure if she would have used that adjective as the animal appeared undernourished and extremely dirty. 'He seems affectionate.'

'He is. And how were he supposed to know that the mutton chops was for the servants' tea?'

'It might have been better to ensure that Liver was not in the vicinity of mutton chops.'

'I do normally, 'cept 'e snuck in somehow whilst I was cleaning the boots. Besides, 'e's starving 'alf the time. There's nothing like starvation to make an animal desperate. She won't give 'im nothin'. I saves what I can from my own supper.'

His desolation and the obvious love between boy and dog touched her.

'What if I take him?' she asked impulsively.

Chapter Twenty

'You, miss?' He stared at her as though she'd suggested flying to the moon.

'Well, I don't have any animals in London. Except for Orion.'

'Orion?'

'My rabbit.'

'Are you going to eat the rabbit?'

'No,' she said.

'Liver might chase it.'

'I'll keep them separate.'

'You'd really save him and...and look after 'im?' he asked.

'I would.'

What was she doing? Goodness knew what Sebastian would say. Or the servants for that matter. First, Orion, Charlotte and now this stray dog.

But when it came to her animals she'd never let what others might say stop her and she refused to start now!

'What about yer 'usband? Or don't you have none.'

'I do,' Sarah said.

'But what'll 'e think, miss? Ma'am, I mean.'

An excellent question. Nothing good, she was sure.

'I'm not entirely certain, but he always knew I was eccentric.'

'I dunno about eccent—whatsit—but I thinks yer a saint, miss—um—ma'am, truly I do.' The boy's voice shook and he knelt beside the dog, slipping his arms about the animal's neck and hiding his face in the matted fur. 'Will you take 'im today?'

Sarah hesitated. She had come in Lady Harrington's carriage, but Sebastian was supposed to take her home. However, neither vehicle would be suitable transport.

'I don't know about today—'

'You gotta, miss, I mean, ma'am. Otherwise cook might git 'im. She'd niver believe me that a fine lady's going to rescue him. I don't believe it meself,' Fred said.

'I could make the arrangements tomorrow.'

'It'll be too late. Please.' His eyes were so full of hope and despair that Sarah could not disappoint.

'I'll take him today,' she said.

Sebastian saw his wife the instant he exited the study where he had been conversing with Mr Frobisher. She stood with several other ladies within the entrance.

His wife, however, looked distinctly different than the other ladies. Her cheeks were flushed. Her hair was messy. Grime and dirt ringed the hem of her skirt and several splotches of mud were apparent on her bodice.

Quite frankly, she looked appalling.

Anger flared within him. Must his wives both deceive him and make him the laughing stock of the *ton*?

'Lord Langford, so nice to see you. We were having a stroll before tea and her ladyship had a mishap in the rose garden,' Mrs Frobisher said.

The words were polite, but the tone was spiteful. Several of the other ladies tittered.

'It was actually in the kitchen garden that my mishap occurred,' his wife said, rather too loudly.

For some odd reason, her response mitigated his anger. It was so spirited and reminded him of the fox rescue. He felt his lips twitch.

'Sadly, she feels that she must now go home. Lady Harrington has left already and I was going to suggest my own carriage,' Mrs Frobisher said.

'So kind, but entirely unnecessary. I will, of course, transport her ladyship without delay,' he said, making his bow.

His carriage was summoned and, moments later, he stepped outside with his wife. He sniffed the air as they descended the steps.

She must have noted his expression. 'I may have a slight aroma on account of Liver.'

'Liver? They served liver at teatime?'

'My dog,' Sarah said.

'Your dog?'

'Um—yes.'

'To the best of my knowledge, we did not own a dog this morning. That has changed?'

'Yes.'

They stepped towards the carriage.

'Might I ask, given that I do not see a dog about your person, where this newly acquired animal now resides?'

She dropped her gaze and nodded towards the waiting vehicle. 'I suggested your carriage.'

Sebastian stared. He saw now that the carriage was rocking as if of its own volition and that a series of muffled yelps could be heard from within.

Dobbs stood at the door. 'Should I—um—open it, my lord?' he asked, his face falling into worried lines.

'I suppose so,' Sebastian said drily. 'If we hope to enter.'

The second the door opened, a dark streak of fur shot

out, scrabbling on the cobbles with a wild cacophony of yips and barks.

'Liver, no, sit,' Sarah said ineffectually. Whatever her prowess with animals, it clearly did not involve training.

Meanwhile the ladies had opened the front door to better enjoy the entertainment, he presumed.

Nor could he blame them. Sarah was now chasing the cur, her skirts clasped within her hands. The horses snorted, stamping the ground, while Dobbs's gaze swivelled between the horses to her ladyship, as if unsure of who was in the greater need of assistance.

At this moment, two footmen joined the milieu and the dog, thinking they were playing, jumped and barked, wagging its tail like a mad thing.

'Liver, sit!'

The voice was young, high and almost lost in the general hubbub.

The dog sat.

For a split second of amazement, silence fell and then everyone turned, of one accord, looking towards a young lad.

'Thank you, Fred,' Sarah said. 'You are most helpful.'

''E always listens to me.'

'I take it we have acquired the animal from you?' Sebastian ventured.

'Yes, sir, your lordship, sir. I mean I—I hope so, sir.'

The boy fixed him with round worried eyes and Sebastian was conscious that his wife also looked at him, her gaze almost beseeching.

In fact, he was quite the centre of attention as the bevy of ladies watched from the steps and Dobbs and the two footmen awaited further instructions.

'Then perhaps you might assist in removing the animal into the carriage,' he said.

With Dobbs's help, the boy got the animal into the carriage, telling it to 'sit' and 'stay'. Then he stepped back;

Sebastian saw he was a gangly creature, his wrists and ankles visible beneath his sleeves and trousers. 'Thank you, sir, my lord and…um…miss. I mean, ma'am.'

Tears glistened in boy's eyes and, as though conscious of scrutiny, he rubbed his sleeve across his eyes almost savagely.

Sarah, of course, noticed his distress.

'Look,' she said as Sebastian had known she would. 'I'm sure a boy like you could be very useful in any household. Maybe, if I contact your employer—'

'Wot? And come work for you?'

'Yes, well—'

'You're not just a saint. You're an angel, miss, I mean, ma'am—I mean, my lady.'

'We will postpone any such discussions for another day and leave now before that animal decides to cause further mayhem,' Sebastian said firmly, handing Sarah into the carriage.

Too late, of course. The animal had already made its mark on the interior. The air reeked. Nose smudges speckled the glass panes and a cushion had been ripped, disgorging its feathers.

The dog, apparently named Liver, stood with his nose thrust on to Sarah's knee while wagging its bedraggled plume of a tail inches from Sebastian's nose.

'Sit!' he ordered.

The animal lumbered up on to the cushioned seat and sat, spewing a fresh shower of feathers.

'Not there.' He pushed the animal to the floor.

'He believes himself human,' Sarah said, as though this were an entirely rational explanation.

'Hopefully, you'll disabuse him of the notion.'

'I am usually good at training animals. And I am sorry about all this, but I didn't know what else to do. Fred was desperate because the cook was going to kill him on account of the mutton chops.'

'Fred is the boy, I presume, to whom we have also offered employment.'

She nodded.

The coach pulled away from the Frobishers' entrance and gained momentum, swaying as it turned on to the London streets. The animal, obviously unused to travel, stopped barking and started to whimper.

Sebastian eyed him with some displeasure. He should be furious. Sarah had made herself, and him, a laughing stock. She had adopted this animal without consultation and it had already caused all manner of damage.

'I'm sorry,' she said at length. 'I know Liver made our exit conspicuous and adopting dogs was not in our agreement.'

'An oversight, no doubt,' he said.

Glancing across at her, he saw that she observed him with an unreadable expression. He raised his brows enquiringly.

'Are you always so calm, my lord? I do not know whether to be thankful or unnerved?' she asked.

'You would prefer that I rant?'

'It would be an indication that you are human, at least. It would be natural to be angry.'

But strangely now he did not feel angry—irritated maybe—but not angry. Moreover, he was aware of another, contradictory emotion. He glanced towards his wife as she bent over the animal. Her tousled hair fell on to her shoulders and her breasts hung in the loose free-flowing gown, now splashed with mud.

The mutt waved its dirty plume of a tail. The stench of its breath filled the carriage and strings of drool dangled from its jowls.

What manner of woman goes out to tea and brings back a cur?

A woman willing to break social convention, shock the *ton* and risk her husband's anger to save the heart of a small boy.

He was unsure of his emotion.

But it was not anger.

Naturally, Liver did not wait for Sebastian or Sarah to exit, but bounded from the carriage the moment the door opened. Gripping the tattered string attached to him, Sarah scrambled after him and was pulled towards the entrance as she shouted 'heel' to no effect.

The butler opened the door and Liver lunged inward.

'I will take him before he pulls you off your feet,' Sebastian said, grabbing the cord. 'And where are you planning for this sorry specimen to sleep?'

Sarah frowned. 'I'd suggest my room, but if he smells the rabbit—'

The word electrified Liver. Indeed, if Sebastian had not braced himself, he would have been dragged across the hall.

'Isn't he brilliant?' Sarah said. 'Did you see? He actually understood the word "rabbit".'

Liver made a second lunge.

'For goodness' sake, stop saying the word. Harding, get a footman to take him somewhere.' Sebastian handed over the rope.

'Yes, my lord. Where, my lord?'

'In the servants' quarters where there is no furniture to spoil. The animal is filthy.'

Harding gave the rope to one of the footmen who nodded, leaving in the direction of the servants' quarters. The dog followed, still waving his tail.

Sarah suppressed a giggle. The duo presented a comical image, the stiff-backed footman and scruffy canine.

It would be a wonderful scene, although of course Miss Petunia Hardcastle was too poised to land herself in such a situation.

She would tell Elizabeth and Charlotte. She tended to think of them as a duo now. Indeed, her sister often reminded her of Elizabeth with her quiet, closed-in expression and sad, haunted eyes which had seen too much.

Then, with a prickle of excitement, an idea struck her. It was crazy, of course, and yet despite its madness, the concept lured her with a faint, infinitesimal promise of success.

Animals had always helped her. Her gaze went to the now-empty passage. Maybe Liver could help. And if he did, if she helped Elizabeth, surely Sebastian would lose that shuttered expression he'd worn since the night they'd rescued Charlotte. Surely he would see her need to find her sister not an act of deceit, but of desperate love.

Chapter Twenty-One

Sarah wasted no time in putting her idea into motion. She woke next morning with a sense of urgency and purpose she had not known since her sister's rescue.

She ate a hurried breakfast, sent a message to Charlotte asking that she meet her in the servants' quarters and then clattered up the stairs to the nursery.

'I need help,' she announced, pushing open the door and entering the chamber.

Elizabeth sat on the rocking horse.

'Of course, my lady. What can I do?' the maid asked, dropping into a curtsy.

'Nothing. I need Elizabeth's help. I have acquired a dog.'

If the girl heard, she gave no sign. The maid's eyes widened, but she also said nothing.

'I met him yesterday. It belonged to a child, a boy, a boy named Fred. The dog smells. He needs a bath. But he is scared.' Sarah paused, slowing her voice and approaching Elizabeth.

After a moment, she continued, choosing her words with care. 'I do not like to see an animal scared or in pain and... and I know animals like you because Orion likes you. I think Liver, that is the dog's name, would like you. I think he would feel less frightened if there was a child about, someone who would remind him of his former owner.'

Sarah held her breath, forcing herself not to rush into the silence, to beg or pressure. The clock on the mantel ticked. The fire crackled. The maid shifted with a rustle of her cotton dress. Orion moved in his hutch, his hind paws making a soft thud as he hopped. Someone shouted in the street and a carriage rattled by.

Elizabeth continued the rhythmic rocking. The wooden rails creaked against the flooring. A fly buzzed against the windowpane.

Then, with measured movements, the girl slowed, dismounted and stepped towards the door.

Sarah's breath released with a whoosh as she followed the child. 'I think we'll bathe him in the servants' quarters. I'm not quite certain where or what to use. A tub, I guess.'

She finished the sentence a little flatly, realising that, like many of her projects, she'd not thought the process through entirely.

'Mr Harding has a tub to soak his bunions,' the maid suggested.

'Right. Thank you, we will go downstairs and wrestle the tub from Mr Harding and his bunions,' Sarah said.

The servants' quarters were located at the bottom of a narrow staircase. The kitchen was at least double the size of Mrs Crawford's with a red-flagstone floor, a ceiling studded with dark beams and a grey stone hearth taking up much of the far wall. The scent of cooking permeated the atmosphere and two maids chopped vegetables in unison.

Sarah sniffed the warm, oniony air. She'd always liked kitchens. Both in London and later at the Crawfords' home she'd spent many hours within those warm confines, finding them more comfortable than the upper floors.

Elizabeth's face did not change. Sarah saw no curiosity, distaste, interest or any other emotion pass across her features.

'My lady and…and Miss Elizabeth,' the cook said, curt-sying and rubbing her palms across the starched white cloth of her apron. 'Can we help you?'

'I'm looking for a bathtub in which to wash my dog. Actually, I'm looking for both the tub and the dog.'

'It's outside at present, but I'm sure one of the footmen could bathe the animal,' Mrs Lorring stated, entering the kitchen from the housekeeper's room.

To Sarah's surprise, she felt Elizabeth's movement beside her, shaking her head as though in protest.

'Miss Elizabeth is right,' she said as if the girl had spoken. 'We don't want to scare the animal. He used to belong to a boy, you know, and I think a child's presence would be reassuring. Miss Elizabeth and I will help bathe Liver, but I would like the bathtub please. Perhaps the one Mr Harding uses?'

'I am not entirely sure if I would advise the mistress of the house to wash a—a dog…' Mrs Lorring began, her long face falling into lines of disapproval.

'Then it is as well that I am not asking for your advice,' Sarah said.

The white enamel tub was placed in the kitchen. Charlotte and the servants boiled kettles over the huge fireplace, filling the tub with water and soap so that the kitchen became foggy with steam.

Occasionally, Sarah glanced at Elizabeth. The girl did not participate in filling the tub, but her gaze was not as unfocused as usual. Instead, she watched the proceedings, the hint of a smile curving her mouth.

The footman came back with Liver and the animal, re-sisting the man's futile attempts of control, ran into the kitchen.

Recognising his companion from the night previous,

he jumped at Sarah, almost bowling her into the tub, his ragged tail waving in a wild rotating movement which seemed to involve his entire hindquarters.

'Down!' she said.

He wagged his tail with even greater gusto, threatening to send the onions and several bowls flying.

'Liver, down and sit.'

She grabbed the frayed rope at his neck and pushed heavily on his buttocks.

'Sit,' she repeated, keeping the pressure on his haunches.

For a second, he seemed to understand. Taking advantage of the momentary quiet, Sarah made the introductions. 'Liver, this is Elizabeth. Elizabeth—Liver.'

Sarah had not expected Elizabeth to react, but slowly, cautiously, the girl's hand reached out. With a tentative touch, she ran her fingers through the tangles of Liver's fur. Briefly, time stilled and Sarah could hear the collective inhalation of breath from both herself and the staff.

Then Liver broke the spell, standing again and scrabbling madly across the floor where he collided with Charlotte who, showing sudden animation, grabbed him.

'He likely doesn't enjoy baths,' she said.

Sarah grinned. 'As I recall, most of your strays didn't.'

She was rewarded by her sister's answering smile. 'Remember that dreadful sausage dog?'

'Indeed. You rescued him from the park, but he insisted on hiding in tiny spaces and consequently getting stuck,' Sarah said.

'Then he tried to bite us when we rescued him.'

'Luckily Liver is much better behaved. Come on, boy. Bath time!'

On entering his house, Sebastian found the entrance hall deserted. He frowned, his body tightening in a jerk of apprehension.

'Harding?'

He heard no sound, other than his own voice echoing in the still hallway.

Striding briskly, he ascended the stairs to the second floor. It, too, was empty. He went to the nursery, but the fire had burned low and he could see neither Elizabeth nor the maid.

Elizabeth seldom left the nursery.

He heard sounds from downstairs and, heart thumping, descended quickly, hurrying through the baize door and into the kitchen. He stopped.

What—

Warm, soap-scented air met him. A white, sudsy object stood in a tub of water. Meanwhile Sarah—his own wife—bathed the animal. Her sister helped while the remainder of the servants hovered as though expecting a miracle of biblical proportions.

'My lady?'

Everyone jerked at his voice. His wife rubbed a reddened, sudsy hand across her forehead, leaving splatters of white lather dangling from her hair.

The dog, recognising his chance for freedom, burst into frenzied barks and leapt from the tub. Soap and water splattered everywhere in a blizzard of suds.

'Liver!' Sarah shouted.

Liver ran straight towards Sebastian, jumping at him, leaving wet, soapy paw prints against Sebastian's jacket.

'Down!' Sebastian thundered.

Surprisingly the dog obeyed, sprawling on the floor with its face on its paws.

'I refuse to keep this animal if it is going to create chaos and stop the regular running of this household. He needs to go—'

A small figure, squatting unnoticed by the tub, stood. Sebastian's jaw dropped. His voice trailed into silence. Eliz-

abeth was sodden to the skin with her hair a tangled mess
and her chin and nose white with lather.

A tiny smile twisted at her lips.

Something too close to pain to be joy struck at his chest.
He swallowed. Her face was not pale. Instead her skin
glowed pink. Her eyes were not unfocused. She was looking—actually looking—at the wet, sudsy animal now lying
at his feet on the floor.

'I—er—suppose you can keep on bathing him for now,'
Sebastian said. His voice, even to his own ears, had a dazed
quality.

His arms reached forward to touch his daughter, to hold
her, but then he caught Sarah's gaze and her wordless warn-
ing.

'Right—' he said, swallowing and allowing his hands to
fall back, conscious of an unfamiliar uncertainty. 'Look—
um—it appears I am the only person this crazy beast will
listen to, so I'd best remain here and ensure some measure
of order.'

'You're joining us?' Sarah asked.

'Yes, I think so,' he said.

He thought Elizabeth's smile grew, but maybe it was
wishful thinking.

He stripped off his jacket and handed it to Mrs Lorring,
who stood, grim-faced. He never had liked the woman.

Then he picked up the animal and returned him to the
tub with a splash. Liver smelled of wet dog mixed with
soap.

'Lizzy—' the name came out naturally '—if we hold
him down, could you rinse the soap off him?'

He felt her sudden stillness and wished he had not spoken so directly, but, to his surprise, she complied. Kneeling
at the side of the tub, she reached for the pewter tumbler.

She dipped it into the water and then splashed it over
the dog's fur so that trickles of water ran down his ears and

back. She did so again, using her hands to rub it through his sodden fur. The smile hovering about her lips grew.

Suddenly, with an energy born of desperation, Liver once again leapt out of the tub. He knocked Sarah off balance so that she half-fell against her husband. Sebastian caught her while his other arm grabbed his daughter, scooping them both up in a wet, soapy embrace.

Elizabeth did not bolt. She did not stiffen.

Sebastian's heart swelled. It was a physical sensation as though the organ truly had increased in size within his chest cavity. His throat hurt. He swallowed, conscious of an unnatural stinging in his eyes.

He pulled his wife closer.

'Not feeling so calm, my lady,' he muttered into Sarah's hair.

She stood with Elizabeth in his arms.

'You can always rant, if you want,' she said.

And, in the dim kitchen, he felt a sense of family and hope.

'I'm sorry,' Sebastian said later that night as she lay entwined with him in bed.

'Hmm?' Sarah nuzzled him, enjoying the warmth of his body and her growing desire as she pressed closer to him.

'I overreacted when I learned about Charlotte. I should not have expected you to share all aspects of your life with me when we were so little acquainted. I should have also realised how ashamed Mrs Crawford would have made you feel about your parentage.'

'And I am sorry. I wanted—I have always wanted to find Charlotte. It coloured my judgement. I felt I couldn't risk telling you. I thought you wouldn't marry me or that you might send me from London. Charlotte is the only person that has ever loved me, just for me.'

Sarah closed her eyes. Memories flickered through her

mind. Once, as a small child, she had wandered out on to the street. She remembered the terror of being small and lost within a world of carts, carriages, hooves, dogs, dirt, refuse, beggars.

But Charlotte had found her.

'And then when you did confide, I judged you,' he said.

'But you saved Charlotte.'

'I would have saved her anyway.'

'I know,' Sarah whispered into his chest.

They were silent. Sarah was conscious of an ease between them, a contentment almost. It seemed right, comfortable and reassuring to be curled against this warm, male body under the fresh sheets with the crackle of the fire, his heart and breath forming a rhythmic cadence.

'And thank you for today,' he said.

She smiled. 'You're thanking me for getting you soaked and ruining your shirt and jacket.'

'I am thanking you for hope. Elizabeth smiled.'

'She enjoyed herself. Did you see how she scrubbed that animal?'

'Within an inch of his life.' Sebastian chuckled. She felt the movement of his chest under her cheek.

'Sarah?'

'Hmm?'

'Today it felt—we felt—we felt like a family.'

She stilled, swallowing, conscious of an aching soreness in her throat. 'I've never really had a family.'

'You do now.'

'Sebastian…' She hesitated, shifting uncertainly. She did not want to offer false hope and yet she wanted to be honest. 'I need to tell you that I will do anything and everything for Elizabeth…and Edwin. And I want you to know that I spoke to Comtesse Hubert yesterday,' she concluded with a quick rush of words.

He stiffened. 'And?'

'She is also looking. For her sons. She will tell me if she finds anything.'

'You believe her?'

'That she will tell me if she can?'

'Yes.'

'I believe her,' she said.

'Thank you.'

'I will do whatever I can. I wish—'

'What?'

She shrugged. 'I just wish I could do more. I wish I were brave and beautiful like a romantic heroine able to do all sorts of daring exploits.'

He lifted himself on to his elbow and looked down on her. Slowly he bent his head so that his lips grazed her own.

'I prefer you like this. Being a romantic heroine might be rather exhausting and time consuming. Then you might not have time for this or this,' he murmured, kissing her nose and then trailing kisses along her cheekbone.

'Oh, no, Petunia has—' She stopped, biting her lip.

'Petunia? Haven't I heard that name before?'

She felt heat rush to her cheeks. 'It is—um—nothing, only foolishness.'

His smile widened, the genuine humour making him look younger. 'That I will not allow. One thing I know is that Sarah Martin is never foolish. Eccentric, maybe. Foolish, never.'

'Well, this is embarrassing and silly. You see I—um— write a little.'

'Write?'

'Yes, you know...stories. At first it was for practical reasons. I hoped to earn money.'

'I knew there would be an element of practicality.'

'But I never sold anything and really I just liked writing them,' she confessed.

'And Petunia is your main character.'

'One of them. She is quite brave and blonde with blue eyes, although she is unfortunately incarcerated at present. I need to determine how the hero will rescue her.'

'I think I might like to learn more about Petunia.'

She glanced up to see if she could discern mockery in his expression.

'Is Petunia based on yourself?' he added.

She shook her head. 'No, absolutely no. She is very beautiful and brave. Quite perfect.'

'A positive paragon, but I rather think I prefer the author.'

'You do?'

He nodded as he lowered his body on top of hers so that she felt encompassed in the long, heavy length of him.

'Hmm…because the author is warm.' He pressed a kiss to her lips. 'And her lips are soft. Her hair is like silk.' The kiss deepened.

'And,' he murmured, when he could speak again, 'she is real.'

This time the kiss's gentle intimacy ignited into passion. Heat and need and want suffused her. She lifted herself to him, moulding her body to his own.

'I want you,' she whispered. 'And I missed you.'

And he had missed her. He had missed not only her body but something more, something deeper. Her way of surprising him, amusing him and the way he felt around her—hopeful…younger…

His kisses trailed from her lips, down the satin skin of her throat and the swell of her breasts as he tried with his lips, hands and body to demonstrate that she was perfect, more perfect than any paragon. And they made love in a way which felt not only a merging of bodies, but a merging of souls.

Chapter Twenty-Two

St Margaret's Bay—Tuesday, one p.m.

Sebastian studied the paper he held between his thumb and forefinger.

He did not need to—the words were already ingrained in his mind.

The note had been delivered yesterday, its arrival following fast on whispered rumours that Beaumont had escaped. He was in England.

Sebastian stood from the breakfast table, imbued with restless energy. He paced to the window as though some answer might be visible in the still-empty streets.

He was a man on the brink of heaven…or hell. He rubbed at the scrap of paper still pinched between his fingers. It crackled. It was from the Lion. The seal was authentic.

It could mean that Edwin was safe.

It *must* mean Edwin was safe.

He stared at green shrubbery, hardly daring to think or hope. A man so close to resurrection while still conscious of hell's gate.

A month ago, any semblance of happiness had seemed an impossibility but now… If Edwin came home and Elizabeth recovered and Sarah—

He smiled, he couldn't help it. The past few days had been…nice. Like a holiday from real life. Lovemaking at night and excursions during the day. They had been to the British Museum yesterday. Elizabeth had come, too. Both Sarah and Elizabeth had been fascinated by that stuffed giraffe. His daughter had said nothing, but had stood quite still, studying it, forehead puckered, her concentration obvious. Then she had pulled out paper and pencil and, squatting, started to sketch. And Sarah had made up a story about a fashionable giraffe in need of a scarf who could find none suitably long until, with a spark of brilliance, he sewed several together.

And Sebastian had questioned how a giraffe could sew with hooves, so Sarah had retorted that it was a very rich giraffe and had had a tailor do the necessary sewing.

At that, Elizabeth had not only smiled, but giggled.

The day before that, they had been riding. Well, not really proper riding as Sarah had gone little faster than a trot and a slow trot at that. Sebastian smiled at the memory.

Even Fred, their new employee, had been a positive addition. He kept Liver under tight control, but also showed a respectful kindness and understanding to Elizabeth and the two had walked beside each other with the dog.

And this, all of this, felt so new, so precious, so impermanent.

Sebastian strode from the window to the fireplace and back.

The holiday was over.

Beaumont was back, if the rumour was to be believed. But what did Beaumont's arrival in England mean? How had the man escaped or had he brokered his escape with the Committee of Public Safety? Did he know something about the Lion? Could he be using Edwin to bait a trap?

The questions rattled around in Sebastian's brain like so many billiard balls.

But one thing was clear: Beaumont had taken everything from him once. Everything.

Tension snaked through Sebastian's shoulders. His head hurt as though squeezed in a vice. He could not lose Elizabeth again. He could not lose Edwin before he had even regained him. He could not lose Sarah, this woman who made him smile and hope and love.

His breath caught. Love?

Everything—the hedge, the pavement, the trees, the shrugs, even the glass pane—seemed to jerk, moving and vibrating as though shifted by some cosmic force.

Footsteps sounded in the hall. He straightened, scrunching up the note and, turning quickly, tossed it into the fire. It shrivelled, the writing briefly visible in the yellow flames before turning to ash.

A footman and Sarah entered.

'Good morning,' she said.

He nodded stiffly. He loved this woman. He loved this woman with her rabbits and dogs.

He *loved* this woman.

The footman poured coffee, leaving at Sebastian's abrupt signal. Sarah took her seat at the table, her forehead furrowed noting his unease. 'My lord?'

'I have decided that we should remove the household to visit Mrs Crawford.'

'What?' Her eyebrows rose, her jaw dropping, an expression which would have been comical except that he was in no mood to see humour. 'Everyone? Elizabeth and Charlotte? To Mrs Crawford's house.'

'Yes.'

'And Fred and Liver?'

Sebastian frowned. 'They need not come.'

'But Elizabeth and Fred have become friends. He is quite wonderful with her...' She paused, lifting her hands and then letting them drop. 'Which isn't important. Why would we be going to Mrs Crawford's? And when?'

'Today.'

'Today?' Her voice rose.

'Yes.'

'That's insane. I mean, we can't uproot Elizabeth like that and…why? What earthly reason would you have?'

'Your safety, my lady, and that of my child.'

'Safety? Is it Owens?'

'I…' He paused, rubbing his finger around the gilt edge of the coffee cup. It whined. 'Yes.'

'But Charlotte has been here for more than a week. And we haven't heard from him. You said he was desperate for money and quite happy with the financial arrangement you offered.'

'Owens is a greedy, unpleasant man. I have to leave town so I prefer to know that you were removed from here,' Sebastian said, then waited. She was too intelligent to accept the fallacy and yet, for her own protection, how could he tell her the truth?

'Surely we could go to your country estate. That would be more familiar to Elizabeth.'

'No.'

'No? Just like that?' Her voice rose in anger. 'No consultation? Why, even Mr Crawford would consult Mrs Crawford before making travel plans for her. And if you are so worried, why are you leaving anyway?'

'A business commitment.'

He saw the questions flicker across her face. Her gaze narrowed and then her expression cleared with dawning comprehension.

She ran to him, the movement so sudden that the chair scraped noisily over the floor as she jumped up. 'It's Edwin? You've heard something? Tell me.'

Her eagerness both touched and angered him. He wanted

to tell her. He wanted to share this mix of hope and dread.
She placed her hand on his jacket sleeve. He could feel the
warm pressure of her fingers through the cloth.

'Sarah, I am leaving London, for business, as I said. And
I want you and Elizabeth to be in a location which is not
connected with me. That is all you need to know.'

'But—if you tell me I could help. And I want to know.
I care about you and Elizabeth—'

Her persistence moved him. His own lies frustrated
him. His need to lie angered him. But he could not risk
her knowing too much. If this assignation was a trap, she
needed to be far away. If Beaumont planned to gain lever-
age over him, hoping he might betray the Lion, Sebastian
needed Sarah and Elizabeth somewhere the man would
never think to look.

And if, by awful circumstance, she were captured, true
ignorance would be her best defence.

'There is nothing more to tell.'

He saw her expression harden. Worse, he saw her hurt.
He wanted to hold her, to confide in her, but he could not.

She stiffened, physically stepping back from him.

'I thought—I thought we were a family.'

'We are.'

'No, a family helps each other. A family confides in each
other and trusts each other. Didn't you teach me that? Or
for you is it a one-sided thing? True for the wife and not
for the husband?'

'I will confide in you when there is something to confide and accept help when I need it. Right now, I do not. I
only require you to get Elizabeth ready and the boy, if you
wish. And your sister naturally.'

'And there is nothing else I can do?'

He shrugged. 'There is one thing.'

'Yes?'

'Ask no more questions.'

* * *

They made good time to the country. The swaying coach brought with it a confused muddle of emotion and a rush of memory. Sarah had felt so uncertain on their previous journey, neither spinster nor married lady. But this uncertainty had been balanced by a singularity of purpose. She needed to find her sister. There was simplicity in that desire. All else had waned, had been dwarfed into insignificance.

Now everything felt complicated. She had found Charlotte, but she had found also a stranger. She had embarked on a marriage as if it were a business contract, only to be mired in emotion.

Sarah looked out of the coach window where her husband rode, a tall stern figure.

She wanted so much more than a business contract. She hadn't expected to care, not like this, but she wanted—she wanted his confidence. She wanted his trust. She wanted—

His love.

Damn.

Her stomach lurched in a way which had nothing to do with the carriage's movement. She wanted his love because she loved him.

Of their own volition, her hands clutched at the fabric of her skirt. Her mind skittered away from the thought and yet, despite her impulsive rejection of it, she knew it was true.

And that was why it—why *everything*—hurt.

But when had this happened? When they'd made love? When he'd helped Charlotte? When they'd washed that bedraggled dog? When he'd relieved her of the basket in that frigid stream?

Or in recent days when she'd been floating on a deluded dream of happy families as though she'd stepped into her own manuscript?

But she was no Petunia. She never had ever been. Never would be. Never could be.

With effort, she forced her gaze away from the erect figure and back to her companions, her sister and Elizabeth.

Thankfully, Charlotte was looking much improved. Her face had some colour. The bruises had faded and the shadows under her eyes had lightened.

Elizabeth sat beside her. The two had formed a bond. Elizabeth seemed more relaxed in Charlotte's company; her jaw less tight and her lips more often twisting upwards.

Catching Sarah's glance, Charlotte leaned forwards, frowning, her hands twisting together. 'Will Mrs Crawford know who I am?' she asked, the words pushed through pale lips.

Sarah shook her head. 'Not if you don't want her to.'

'No.' A dull flush heated Charlotte's cheeks. 'Let me be a maid. I want to fade into the background. To become a piece of furniture.'

'Then you will start your career as a chair today,' Sarah said with whimsical humour. 'But not for ever. You are too beautiful and too strong to let evil win and if you always hide, evil will have won.'

'Hasn't it already won?'

'No,' Sarah said.

Tears shimmered in Charlotte's eyes, and a glittering drop trickled downwards, briefly sparkling in the sunlight slanting through the carriage window.

'You haven't cried before,' Sarah said.

Charlotte lifted her hand, wiping away the tear and glancing down at the dampness with a kind of wonder. 'I—um—felt dead inside. Dead people don't cry.'

'And now?'

'Not alive. But not dead. It hurts. You know, like when you are out in winter and your hands get so cold they hurt to warm up.'

'Eventually the hurting stops.'

'Unless they are so damaged by frostbite the fingers blacken.'

Sarah reached across, taking her sister's hand, a small and fragile thing. 'Not black. No frostbite,' she said.

Charlotte tightened her grip and for a wonderful moment, they clasped hands and Sarah felt again that connection, like they'd had when they were children.

Sebastian ordered a break for luncheon to change the horses, eat and give the travellers respite from the rattling wheels and lurching vehicle.

Naturally, Liver jumped out, relieved himself and then darted around the courtyard like an animal possessed. Fred proved little better. He had been riding outside, but still seemed unable to get enough of the open fields and pasture. He stared wide-eyed towards the open spaces, his nose pointed in the air like a dog himself.

'I've never been in the country. I never knew there could be so much green.'

'Then you'll love it with Mrs Crawford. It is even more beautiful. There is a brook, woods, a barn and the most delightful cows. I'll introduce you,' Sarah said.

'I don't know as I'd like that. Not that I'm afeared of cows or owt,' Fred hastened to add.

'Of course not,' Sarah replied. 'But you're bound to love Portia and Cleopatra. They are so gentle. I'll teach you to milk them.'

'You know as how to milk cows?' Fred asked.

'I do,' Sarah said and felt a foolish little thrill of pride at the boy's open and honest admiration.

'I think you are like a—a goddess or—a—an 'eroine, ma'am, I mean, my lady.'

'I don't think heroines milk cows,' Sarah said. Petunia

would certainly never sully her milk-white hands in such an occupation.

'Mine do,' Fred said.

When they resumed their journey, Sebastian joined them in the carriage, but he did not seem relaxed, sitting as upright and stiff against the cushioning as he had on his horse.

Elizabeth also seemed more remote, curled into the corner of the carriage with her face averted. Sarah wondered if perhaps this lengthy journey brought back memories of other travels.

'Elizabeth,' she said softly. 'I'll tell you a story, if you'd like. Sometimes a story helps to pass the time.'

Elizabeth shifted slightly to look at her and then, with careful, measured movements, pointed to Orion whose hutch had been placed within the far corner of the coach's interior.

'You want one about the rabbit family?'

Elizabeth made no concrete sign of encouragement, but angled her body forward, her face appearing less shuttered.

So Sarah told a rambling tale about Mr Rabbit who, having rescued his two babies, decided they needed to relocate to somewhere safer without hawks. They then travelled in a hollowed-out chunk of wood lined with dandelion fluff pulled by several muscular mice.

It was just as Mr Rabbit and his children were stopping for lunch that Sarah noted that Elizabeth's eyes had closed, the worry and anxiety on her face softening in repose.

Sebastian also watched his daughter. Catching his expression—the love, the pain, the hope there—Sarah glanced away. She felt as though she had intruded on a private grief.

A few days ago she might have had a right to be privy to his emotion. Or felt that she could help. Or even that he would accept her help.

But not now.

Chapter Twenty-Three

The party arrived at the Crawford residence in the early evening and Sarah found it wonderfully improved. Indeed, both her former guardian and Miss Sharples sat in the drawing room in front of a lit fire, albeit a small one.

'Lovely to see you. We got your message and were expecting you,' Miss Sharples said, her round face wreathed in smiles.

'Molly, it is so long since I have seen you,' Mrs Crawford said, confusing Sarah with her sister.

'It is nice to be here,' Sarah said gently, taking Mrs Crawford's fragile hand within her own.

'It has been too long, although I know it is hard for you to get away with the children. You are lucky to have children. Perhaps one day… I have always wanted a child.'

'I know,' Sarah said, her eyes glancing towards Miss Sharples, comforted to see the lady's sympathy.

'Your husband, is he here?'

'He is just making arrangements for the horses.'

'And how do you like the married state? It was all very sudden.'

'It is fine, ma'am,' Sarah said, unsure if she was now Molly or Sarah in her guardian's mind.

Mrs Crawford nodded.

At that moment, Sebastian pushed open the door and Sarah was again struck by the size of him. She had become accustomed to him in the larger rooms of their London residence, but here at the Crawfords' house he seemed bigger, taller, more intimidating.

It felt peculiar, disorientating, as the separate lives of girl and wife coalesced.

He made his bow.

'Langford, lovely to see you,' Mrs Crawford said. 'And you need not look surprised that I recall your name. Indeed, I am not quite in my dotage yet. I hope you are remembering to pray and to send frequent donations to the heathens.'

Apparently, she was Sarah again.

'Indeed, I remember them at every possible opportunity, ma'am,' Sebastian said.

'Your party has expanded. We will be hard pressed to find accommodations for so many and I hope you do not expect luxury.'

'Not at all. We appreciate that you made room for us at such short notice.'

'There is a child with you?'

'My daughter, Elizabeth. The maid took her up to bed, but she is looking forward to meeting you in the morning,' Sebastian explained.

'Maids are a luxury. I will not have this house become a Sodom and Gomorrah. I am tired. I am going to bed and I want to hear no more of maids and such.'

Taking her cane, Mrs Crawford moved briskly and determinedly from the room.

'That went well,' Sarah muttered, as the door closed.

'Don't you worry about that none, my lady,' Miss Sharples said. 'She is much more tractable when she lives in the past, which she does more and more these days. She was irritable just now because she realised she'd mistook you for her sister.'

'She looks better.'

'I find that she eats more and is more willing to have a fire when she thinks her husband is still alive. It is as though she steps back into that lifestyle and talks considerably less about the heathens.'

'Thank you,' Sarah said with sincerity. 'I appreciate everything you're doing. It is relief to know that you are here.'

'Don't mention it. Now, it is late. Would you like something to eat or should I show you to your room?'

With a start of surprise, Sarah realised that she would not be sleeping in her usual bedchamber, but in the guest chamber. Indeed, Charlotte would likely inhabit her former room under the eaves. Reluctantly, but also with guilty relief, Sarah had acquiesced to Charlotte's request to be introduced as a maid. She was not yet strong enough to cope with Mrs Crawford's vitriol.

And she was certain Charlotte was not.

'Bed,' Sarah said. 'And don't bother showing me up. I know the way.'

Odd to be a guest in her own home, Sarah thought, as she went through the familiar corridor and into the unfamiliar bedchamber.

It was more spacious than her own former room. A large window overlooked the stable and farm, the view framed with curtaining patterned with pink roses.

She sat on the bed. She had nothing to do at present. Her trunk had not yet been brought up. Charlotte was looking after Elizabeth. Sebastian was still outside and Fred had apparently adopted both Orion and Liver and was therefore looking after their needs.

She could visit Portia and Cleopatra, she supposed. Except they were likely settled for the night and, although not yet ready to sleep, she felt a heavy, physical exhaustion precluding movement.

Taking off her boots, she stretched on the bed, staring at

the white ceiling above her and trying to discern a pattern in the faint cracks marring the smooth paint.

Sebastian entered and she shifted, propping herself up slightly so that she could better see him. He moved abruptly, flinging himself into the seat and staring unseeingly at the low fire. He ran his fingers through his dark hair, the tension evident in his movements, the thrust of his legs towards the hearth and the tightness in his shoulders and jaw.

Outside the breeze pushed the tree boughs with a *shush... shush...shush*. The mournfulness matched her mood.

'Sarah,' he said at last, shifting his gaze to her.

'Mmm?'

'Thank you for the story in the carriage. Elizabeth liked it.'

'I like stories. They helped me.'

He drew his feet back from the fire and, hunching forward, placed his elbows on his knees. 'Sarah?'

'Yes.'

'If anything should ever happen to me, you will take care of Elizabeth?'

'Nothing will happen.'

'But...in case. We are neither of us children. Life comes with no absolutes.'

'Yes,' she said. 'I love her. She is my family and I hope I am hers. But why are you talking like that? What aren't you telling me?'

He shrugged. 'Things can happen—I just want to be sure.'

'I will always do my best for her.'

'Thank you.'

'You can't tell me anything more? Where you are going? How long will we stay here?' she asked, after a pause.

'Until I am back,' he said enigmatically.

'Hard to gauge as we do not know where you are going or even when you are leaving.'

'Tomorrow,' he said. 'I leave tomorrow.'

'And you want us just to wait?' Inaction was not natural to her.

'Yes.'

One single monosyllable and nothing more.

She frowned. Petunia's lover always told her everything. They shared their trials.

'Be careful,' she said.

'Always.'

She wanted to say more. But she was not Petunia. She could not make demands or expect partnership. She could not expect him to need her or want her and certainly not love her.

'I could do more,' she said.

'You have made Elizabeth smile. It is enough.'

Except it wasn't.

She was not a wife. She was not a partner. They were not a family—at least not in the full sense of the word.

Sebastian left next morning.

He ordered Sarah to remain inside and so, angry and hurt, she stood by the window within the bedchamber, peering at the familiar courtyard and ramshackle barn. Sebastian was travelling on horseback. The horse stood, already saddled, its chestnut coat glossy in the morning sun. She saw no sign of curricle or carriage.

Sarah shivered. The air was cool despite the fire.

Why was he travelling on horseback and with no vehicle or groom? She could only presume he needed the speed or secrecy.

Moments later, Sebastian stepped from the house towards the stable. He wore dark, nondescript clothes and strode towards the animal, with that long-legged fluidity of his.

Briefly, the handsomeness of his lean length, broad

shoulders and angular profile almost hurt. She wondered if he would look back at her or gesture farewell.

The horse leaned forward, nuzzling him as he patted its neck, pulling some form of treat from his pocket. Then with typical grace he swung up into the saddle.

Her hand tightened against the curtaining, the other reaching to the pane as though she could touch him through the glass. The surface was cool and slightly damp against her fingertips.

Then, without a glance in her direction, Sebastian nudged the animal forward.

And they were gone.

A hollow pit formed in Sarah's belly which had nothing to do with hunger. She leaned into the window. She swallowed, her throat aching and tight.

He was heading into danger. Had not his question about Elizabeth proved just that? Yet he had not looked up. He had given her no thought, no backward glance.

Tears stung as she stared at the rutted lane, empty now save for the black crows and the puddles from last night's rain.

Sarah did not hear Elizabeth's approach. Indeed, only the clatter of Liver's claws on the hard wood alerted her to the girl's presence. The two were inseparable.

Sarah turned as Elizabeth stepped with dainty movements across the floor. Elizabeth stopped beside her and, by common consent, they looked back through the window into courtyard.

Then, with a tiny movement and rustle of cloth, something wonderful happened.

Elizabeth placed her small, warm hand into Sarah's. It was compact, the skin smooth and her fingers relaxed.

'You dear,' Sarah whispered, holding her breath, fearful that even breathing might shatter the moment.

A tear brimmed over, trickling down her cheek, but whether it was a tear of joy or pain, she didn't know.

For a brief, beautiful moment, they stood within the still quiet, connected.

It was a flicker of movement, a flash of brown against the green which caught Sarah's attention. Something stirred on the lane set behind the bushes to the left of the stable. She froze, rubbing away the tears as she stared with sudden urgency.

Nothing moved, except a cockerel strutting across the courtyard and a stable cat slinking after its prey. She exhaled. Her breath misted the window.

Then, she saw it again, the blurred image of man and horse. She wiped clear the window, staring at the man and horse as they exited the bushes, briefly silhouetted against the stable's grey wood. The animal was dark brown, thin with big hip bones and ungainly movements. The man wore dark clothes and a dark hat. He did not approach the house or even glance in its direction, but took the path Sebastian had taken.

'It's him,' Elizabeth said. Her hand tightened, her fingers gripping hard into Sarah's flesh.

'Who?' Sarah asked, the urgency of the moment overshadowing the joy or even the recognition that Elizabeth had spoken.

'Him,' she said. Her voice was low, rusty with disuse and threaded with anguish.

Looking down, Sarah saw such distress within Elizabeth's expression that it felt like a physical blow.

'The man that took you?' Sarah asked.

'Yes.'

Chapter Twenty-Four

'You're certain?'

Elizabeth nodded. The colour had drained from her face and her eyes were dark with fear. Sarah's stomach dropped. Everything—the whitewashed walls, the fire and flowered curtains—swayed in a jerky, panicked dance.

She turned back, gazing at the now-empty road. The man was trailing Sebastian. He must be. But why? To what end? She felt her breathing quicken. Tension twisted through her shoulders and neck. Her heart drummed, fast and furious, like the gallop of hooves.

Sebastian must be warned. But how? How could she warn Sebastian when she didn't know his route or final destination?

Inhaling, she forced herself to calm, to breathe, to think. The only solution was to follow either Sebastian or that man. She must hold on to her practicality and move with swift efficiency and logic.

Just then, Elizabeth twisted around, grabbing Sarah's other hand as well. Her fingers were ice cold, but strong and tight. She stared at Sarah with peculiar intensity, her eyes wild against the ashen skin.

'Stop him,' she said.

* * *

Miss Sharples sat at the table and looked up when Sarah and Elizabeth entered the morning room.

'I'm glad to see you,' she said, sipping her tea. 'Would you like a cup—'

'Something has come up which necessitates my immediate departure.'

'Indeed, so I hear. It sounds as though a "council of war" is required.'

'A what?' Sarah was startled.

Miss Sharples's lips had compressed into a firm line. 'To warn his lordship and prevent that evil man from doing further mischief.'

'You—you what? How did you know?'

'Fred told me.'

'How would he know?' Sarah asked.

'I listens at doors,' the boy said, bobbing up from the floor beneath the table where he had been sitting with Liver.

'You were listening at my bedchamber.'

'Actually, I was sitting in the stairwell waiting for someone to git up this morning. I'd heard the master come downstairs. Then 'e leaves and I sees Miss Elizabeth go into yer room so I thought I oughta listen, figure out what's going on.'

This speech was said without pause for breath and came in a single blast of sound. For a second, both Sarah and Miss Sharples fell silent as though trying to interpret the rush of words.

'That's as maybe,' Miss Sharples said at last, taking her napkin and wiping any residue of tea from her lips. 'And we will deal with Fred's morals at a later date. At present, we need to determine the best course of action. Firstly, I imagine you intend to follow his lordship and I think I should accompany you, Lady Langford.'

'You should accompany me?' Sarah repeated.

'It would be inappropriate for you to travel unaccompanied.'

'I don't care for propriety—'

'Indeed, however, we must assume that Mr—what is his name?'

'Beaumont,' Elizabeth whispered.

'Right, that Mr Beaumont might recognise you if he has been keeping your London household under surveillance. However, it is doubtful that he would have seen me, which would allow me to secure lodging and food without attracting notice. I assure you I can be decidedly nondescript.' Her plump red cheeks bunched like shiny apples with pleasure at this statement.

'I am not lacking skills in that department either,' Sarah said. 'And even if I were, I cannot leave Elizabeth here with only Charlotte and Mrs Crawford.'

'I'd help,' Fred interjected. 'That is, if you don't need me and Liver with you.'

'No.' Both Sarah and Miss Sharples spoke together, then laughed, the tension breaking in momentary humour.

'Besides, if both his lordship and Beaumont are on horseback then I must also travel that way, or I will never keep up,' she said, conscious of an uneasy lurch within her stomach. Mr Crawford had taught her when she had moved to the country and she had ridden again a few days ago. She had an adequate seat, but she would never ride with the ease of the aristocracy.

'We could go directly to his lordship and intercept him at his destination,' Miss Sharples suggested. 'As opposed to following Mr Beaumont.'

'I can't. I do not know his destination,' Sarah said flatly. *Because he does not trust me.*

The words hung unspoken, but as obvious to Sarah as though they had been emblazoned across the walls and ceiling.

Miss Sharples frowned, drumming her fingers against the wood table. 'I do not ride,' she admitted reluctantly.

Sarah reached across the table towards the other woman. 'And I need you to stay here. Charlotte is not yet well and Elizabeth—'

She left the sentence unfinished.

'But it is not appropriate for you to travel alone. And on horseback.'

Sarah stilled the other woman's fingers with her hand. 'And there are some things more important than propriety. You must stay. You must make sure Elizabeth and Charlotte are safe.'

'That is your decision as mistress?'

'Yes,' Sarah said, conscious of a flicker of surprise. She had never before seen herself as a leader or an individual capable of leadership. 'Yes, that is my decision.'

After a moment, Miss Sharples nodded. 'Very well.'

'Good. Now, I'd best go quickly before I lose track of him.'

'What horse will you take?' Miss Sharples asked, standing also.

Sarah paused. Sebastian had the only horse suitable for riding. The new horse he had purchased for her was still in London. 'I will write a note to Eavensham. They have one who is both docile and fast.'

She paused, glancing at Elizabeth who now sat on the floor next to Fred with her arm draped over Liver.

'Elizabeth—' She knelt beside her. 'You know I don't want to leave you, but I can't think of any other option. I think I must follow Beaumont.'

'Stop him,' Elizabeth repeated.

'I will try.'

Elizabeth nodded, her face still ashen.

'You will be all right?' Sarah asked.

'Yes.'

* * *

The next hour passed in a flurry of activity. Clothes were grabbed and pushed into a valise. Fred was dispatched to Eavensham to fetch the horse and Elizabeth fell back into silence and sat watching Sarah, stroking Liver.

'I'll do everything I can to warn him and bring him home,' Sarah said softly.

'Thank you,' Elizabeth whispered, her voice softly husky.

Sarah squeezed the girl's hand and pressed a kiss against her hair.

To Mrs Crawford, Sarah said only that she had business out of town. 'Miss Sharples and Charlotte will look after you. And there is still Mrs Tuttle to cook for you.'

'I hope you will knit,' Mrs Crawford said, rather vaguely.

'Pardon?'

'In the coach. It is a good way to pass the time and will help the heathens.'

'I will knit,' Sarah said gently. 'And you will eat well and stay warm. We need you to keep strong so you can continue with your good work.'

'That is what that new lady says.'

'Miss Sharples?'

'I suppose. Sometimes names are hard to remember.'

Finally Fred returned, leading the mare, a gentle, hard-working animal called Minerva. With Fred's help, they strapped Sarah's few belongings behind her on the saddle. Then she mounted the animal. As always, she felt that momentary twist of fear at her sudden height and the horse's swaying movement.

'I wish his lordship had not sent his groom back to London,' Miss Sharples said, her kindly face cast into worried lines.

'Well, he did and he must have had his reasons,' Sarah

said. 'Besides, one rider will move more swiftly and inconspicuously than two.'

With a final wave, Sarah directed Minerva towards the laneway. Fortunately for the first few miles there was really only one road. After that, she must hope to pick up their trail. She could assume, she supposed, that Sebastian was heading towards the coast. Although that might not prove entirely helpful, Sarah realised, as she considered the numerous routes and sea towns dotting the British shore.

After two hours, she approached a small town located at a crossroads.

'Our first decision,' she muttered to Minerva.

She'd stop and give Minerva some water. It was likely, she supposed, that Beaumont and Sebastian's mounts would have required refreshment. Besides, Minerva needed a drink.

As she entered the inn's courtyard, she noted that a stagecoach had recently arrived and its occupants milled across the flagstones, as did several chickens, giving the place a bustling atmosphere.

Minerva sidestepped a little skittishly and Sarah again felt that nervous pulse of fear. She would never ride again, that is, if she made it out of this alive.

Dismounting, she handed the reins to a groom. Her rear felt bruised and every muscle hurt so that she almost winced visibly as she walked into the inn. It was small, dark, crowded and no one had any recollection of either gentleman.

Now what? She supposed, given that there were only two roads, she had a fifty per cent chance of choosing correctly.

She left the inn's darkness quickly, glad to get into the comparative freshness of the yard, which smelled of grass and manure as opposed to stale ale.

On impulse, she asked the servants if they might have

seen either Sebastian or Beaumont and, to her great relief, met with success. A stable hand with tufts of blond hair and a poor complexion nodded and removed a long shaft of straw from his mouth.

'I remembers the one. A short fellow. And nasty. Kicked his horse and didn't give me so much as a halfpenny.'

'Did he mention where he might be going?'

The lad replaced the straw, chewing for several moments. 'Dover, I'm thinking.'

At dusk Sarah stopped for dinner and secured a room. She hated the delay, but her animal was exhausted. Besides, her own body hurt with every movement and she knew she was not a sufficiently good rider to travel in the dark.

Surprisingly, despite both her worry and pain, Sarah slept soundly and only awakened at the maid's knock. For a second, she was unsure of her location and stared blankly at the ceiling and the spartan furnishings visible in the grey predawn light. As memory flooded back, she sat up, almost crying aloud at the pain in her back and muscles.

The maid entered, bringing with her the hot water and the small breakfast Sarah had requested, eyes round saucers of curiosity. Sarah supposed the inn did not frequently receive unattached ladies riding on horseback. Nor, she thought, would she advocate this manner of locomotion.

After thanking the maid, she splashed water on her face and dressed quickly. With her worry no longer muted by heavy exhaustion, the urgency grew. Who knew how far the two gentlemen were ahead? As experienced horsemen, they could well have ridden through the night. Spurred by this thought, she urged Minerva into a canter, forcing down the fear that made her back ache and her hands clammy.

The sun was up now, lighting the green fields, squat houses and barns which dotted the countryside; a chequerboard of pastures, some green and others dark rectangles of rich dirt.

And beyond—as yet not visible—was the sea.

Sarah had never been to the seaside, at least not in the manner of an excursion, although she had glimpsed the London docks as a child.

Petunia had, of course. Petunia had smelled sea air and dabbled her toes within the chill waters.

The ocean presented itself first as a band of shimmering silver, too ephemeral to be real. Squinting, she leaned forward as though this movement could afford a better view.

'The ocean—I never thought I would see it,' she whispered to Minerva, struck by the need to share the moment with another living soul.

Gradually that wonderful luminescent band widened. The air changed so that the tangy salt mixed with the pastoral scent of grass. Then the fields gave way to buildings and the road became busier. A cart loaded with rattling milk cans headed towards the town and a carriage, likely the property of local gentry, lumbered by.

The town itself was a confusing mass of narrow, twisting of roads each lined with houses or crammed with shops leading towards the wide sweep of the harbour.

She continued down one twisting avenue until she was halted by the sea. She could see the back ends of fishing boats heading towards deeper waters and clusters of women and children dug for clams along the shore.

What next?

She fiddled uncertainly with the reins. If Sebastian hoped to meet Edwin, it was only logical that he would need to be close to the shore.

But she could hardly make Minerva pace the promontory and expect to remain inconspicuous. Besides, the animal needed water and she did not wish to remain in the saddle for any longer than absolutely necessary.

She'd find Minerva lodging and food and then she supposed she could do little more than keep the shore and docks under observation, hopefully without getting any undue attention. Inaction again. And yet what else could she do? Run about calling for Sebastian or Beaumont as she would a stray dog?

She approached a suitable establishment and the landlord emerged, walking towards her with a rolling gait as though his current occupation was but a break in a lifetime of seafaring. The top of his head was bald, but encircled by surprisingly thick brown hair, giving him a monklike appearance.

At first he did not appear hospitable, but Sebastian's sovereigns soon found Minerva a comfortable stall and fresh hay, also securing Sarah a bedchamber where she could leave her valise and freshen up.

The window looked out on to the harbour and she stood for several minutes, staring at the ocean's movement, the constant rise and fall of the waves, its pewter finish broken occasionally with a white skim of foam.

Her body ached. The long hours of travel made her feel as though she was still moving and, after her impetuous journey, she felt a heavy glumness, a certainty that she had raced here for no purpose.

Had Sebastian or Beaumont even come to Dover? She had only the vague thoughts of a pimply stable boy—hardly conclusive evidence. And she thought also of the vast emptiness of the British coast, imagining the pebble beach tripled and quadrupled a hundred times.

Edwin might arrive at any spot or cove. Or he might not be arriving at all. Maybe Sebastian was seeking counsel with the English Lion.

If only she knew... If only he had confided in her... If only...

Chapter Twenty-Five

Sebastian felt as though he'd been waiting for ever, crouched within this hidden cove. His legs, already stiff from riding, now ached from enforced immobility. He was chilled from the damp wind coming off the Channel and his eyes smarted from straining against the grey seas.

At times he started, certain he'd heard footsteps, but it proved to be nothing more than a seabird, the rustling wind or perhaps a rat or small animal foraging under the bushes.

His emotions swung from hope to despair with the regularity of a clock's pendulum. He'd been told to come here, but it could mean all manner of things: that his child was alive or that his child was dead, that the Lion had secured a boat and they were going to France or that he had secured a boat and Edwin was being brought here—

Brought home.

The journey had gone smoothly enough. He'd changed his horse only once and arrived in the early morning hours at St Margaret's Bay.

Here he'd been met by an old fisherman, a taciturn individual who made little sound except for a steady squelch as he chewed his tobacco and a guttural clearing of his throat at intermittent intervals.

He'd brought Sebastian to his home and pointed to a straw pallet. Sebastian had rested there until the fisherman woke him. After giving him water and bread, the man had led him out and they had traversed down the steep winding path to this cove.

'You's to stay here,' the fisherman said when they reached the shore.

Then, with no further words, he left. His footsteps disappeared up the cliff with the scrabble of boots on loose rock.

Sebastian rolled his shoulders and rubbed a hand over his tired eyes. Sometimes they played tricks on him and he'd see a white sail. But each time this had proven to be naught but an illusion, a seagull or white-capped wave.

The sun moved across the sky into mid-morning, its orb a bright disc through a layer of high clouds which had formed, obscuring the clear skies of early morning.

Then he saw something. He straightened, shifting forward. It was the merest flicker of white against the ocean. He waited for it to turn into a gull. Or a wave. It didn't. He stood, pressing his hand against his forehead to shadow his eyes from the water's glare. He stepped to the shoreline, as though those few feet would bring the object into clearer focus. The wind blew cool and damp against his cheeks. The waves slapped against the rocks and a gull cried mournfully.

It was—he'd swear to God it was.

A sail.

His pulse hammered. His chest felt tight and his mouth dry. Hope effervesced inside him. Mixed with fear. The emotions coalescing into a cold sludge within his gut.

The sail drew closer now. His eyes smarted. His tongue cleaved to the roof of his mouth. Every muscle in his body tautened and his breath came in quick pants as he waited.

On the brink of heaven or hell.

* * *

Sarah exited the inn. She walked towards the harbour, standing at the base of the promontory. From this aspect, she could see children running over the rocks, seagulls circling and fishermen sitting on upturned crates as they sewed torn nets.

The splashing of waves was punctuated by the gulls' haunting cries and the unhurried clank, clank, clank as an elderly man hammered nails into his boat's upturned hull.

The sea had retreated with the tide, baring the pebble beach dotted with tide pools and rocks. The seaweed-coated pebbles formed a green band at the waterline and the air was heavy with fish and seaweed.

Sarah stood staring at the scene, conscious of a heavy, exhausted sense of anticlimax. Sebastian and Beaumont could be anywhere. They could be miles from here or in brutal combat around the next curve.

For more than half an hour, she stood staring at the foreshore. She did so, not with any sense of purpose, but rather because she could think of no alternate course of action.

Then a movement caught her attention. A man walked on the beach, stepping under the jetty and navigating between the thick wooden pylons.

With sudden energy she traversed the promenade to where the jetty jutted across the pebbled shore and into the sea. After a moment, she saw the man emerge from under the wooden structure. She didn't recognise him, but his back was to her. Besides, she had not seen Beaumont's face clearly yesterday.

However, he seemed the right size and shape and wore a similar oversized coat.

He was certainly not a fisherman.

She watched as the man continued along the pebbled shore. Was it her imagination or did his actions and the way he glanced to the sea speak of stealth?

Sarah hesitated. He might be anyone; a harmless bird-watcher or local innkeeper.

Or Beaumont.

There was no logical way of knowing.

Sarah believed in logic and yet it was not infallible. She remembered that instinctive gut level, knowing when her foxes were close or how to tend to an injured rabbit.

It had made little logical sense and yet she had known.

Straightening her shoulders, she made her decision.

The wooden planks, damp and worn, felt uneven under her feet as Sarah hurried down the quay. It broadened at its end into a square and, in one corner, she saw a cleaning station, stained with fish blood. The smell of fish was strong. Nearby, two men and a woman had spread their nets, darning the rips with thick black string. A barrel of fish guts occupied a third corner and an empty wine bottle had rolled close to the edge of the planking.

'Excuse me,' Sarah said.

The man looked up, his eyes a weak, watery blue.

'I wanted to buy your net.'

'You wot?' he asked.

Sarah opened her reticule, producing a coin.

'I'll sell you mine an' all,' the woman said, smiling to reveal a single yellowed tooth.

'No, but I'd like your shawl, please. Of course I will pay.'

The woman gave a cackle. 'You wot?'

Sarah handed out another coin. 'And I'll give you more for that bottle.'

'Wot bottle?'

Sarah nodded towards the wine bottle.

'It's empty,' the woman said.

'That's fine.'

All three stared at her.

'It takes all sorts,' the woman said at last.

'But if we could hurry. Here.' Sarah handed the woman a coin and bent to pick up the bottle. The glass was cold and sticky from the spilled wine.

'You want my shawl and all?' the woman reiterated.

'Yes.'

The woman took it off, pushing it towards Sarah. It was loosely knitted, the wool felt greasy to the touch and smelled of fish, sweat and alcohol.

'Thank you.' Sarah draped it about her shoulders, squashing a shudder. Then, picking up the net, she held it bunched in front of her so that it hid the fabric of her dress.

The three individuals continued to stare at her, their faces masks of blank confusion.

'Thank you,' Sarah said again and, with a hurried nod of farewell, she walked back down the quay and clambered over the rocks and on to the pebbled beach.

For a moment, she couldn't see the man. Indeed, the expanse of rock and cliff and sea seemed the epitome of emptiness. A panicked disappointment twisted though her. Had she delayed too long in the manufacture of this ludicrous disguise?

Then a movement caught her eye and she saw a dark, male silhouette turn against the grey sea.

Keeping her head bent and her movements slow, she shuffled forward, her hand clenched about the empty bottle and her gaze downcast as though scavenging for firewood. Her shoes sank into the damp sand, the pebbles pressing hard against the soles.

Ahead, she saw the man near a series of dilapidated huts huddled within the shadow of the tall white cliffs. She glanced towards these structures with little interest, then froze, her hands tightening against the fish net with a lurch of panic.

There were three figures hunched behind the huts. They

wore dark uniforms and she saw the glint of knives or bayonets.

French soldiers. They must be. But what should she do? Were they here to catch this man or did they aim to entrap someone coming from sea? And, if the latter, how best to warn him?

Keeping the stooped posture of an old woman and gripping the bottle, Sarah hobbled in the direction of the huts, swaying as though drunken.

She continued this way until she stood quite close to the squat structures. Then she sat on a log, shawl wrapped about her hair as she raised the bottle to her lips, pretending to drink. From this angle she could look both out to sea and also monitor any action from the huts behind her.

And so she sat for what felt like hours in this ludicrous, dangerous farce, pretending not to notice them while they pretended not to exist. The minutes dragged with painful slowness. The log felt even harder, the uneven lumps and bumps pressing into her rear. She shifted, her eyes watering from her constant scanning of the blank ocean.

The minutes dragged, yet it was likely not more than half an hour before she saw it. Her stomach twisted even tighter so that it seemed to have morphed in a hard, leaden rock. Something stuck in her throat and her breath quickened, her heartbeat drumming.

A boat, a dinghy really, approached. It was white and powered only by oars which stuck out from its sides like miniature sticks.

It did not travel directly across the Channel, but rather rounded the corner as though coming from elsewhere further up the British coastline.

Sarah again pretended to drink. Her hand shook. The sticky rim of the bottle rattled against her chin.

It might be nothing more than a fisherman, she told

herself, or even a smuggler, sneaking in French brandy or some such thing.

The boat came closer and she could see that there were two occupants, one tall and the other small and huddled within the stern. She could see also the shimmer of wet oars as a weak shaft of sunlight pierced the sullen clouds. She could hear the splash as the oarsman sliced through the water with quick, urgent strokes.

She clutched the bottle so tightly that her fingers ached. Who was it? Could it be Sebastian and Edwin?

What could or should she do? What would Petunia do?

She squinted seaward, a heavy certainty lining her stomach. Intellectually, she recognised there were any number of explanations for the tiny vessel and its occupants, but intellect didn't matter. She knew, deep in her gut, it was them—Edwin and Sebastian. And, with every moment, they were rowing closer, moving ever nearer to a trap, to the crouched men in their tri-colour uniform.

To Beaumont.

With sudden desperation, she stood. Lurching unsteadily, she stumbled over the pebbles towards the water's edge.

'Ahoy, there!' she shouted, her words slurred.

The oarsman had his back to her. The boat was quite close now, so close she could see his dark, wind-tousled hair.

A seagull circled.

'Ahoy!' she shouted again. Her voice cracked.

She heard a curse from behind her and a rock flew past her ear, hitting the pebbled shore with a sharp crack. Another hit her shoulder. She stumbled.

But somehow that sharp pain galvanised her, making everything only more real and imminent. With sudden energy, she ran into the water, sliding and staggering on the slimy pebbles under her feet.

'It's a trap. Go!' she screamed.

The boat did not stop.

Floundering, she lurched towards it. Her sodden skirts weighed her down as she pushed forward, waving the bottle now gripped so tightly within her hand that she could not have released it even if she had wanted.

The man lifted the oars, a glistening stream of water slid down the wood, dripping into the sea. In its stern she saw a small form, huddled under a blanket.

'Leave! He's here.' She plunged forward, clutching on to the gunnels of the boat as its bottom grated over the pebbly shore.

The oarsman thrust aside his oars and stood—a strong, tall figure.

Sebastian.

Sebastian climbed over the bow and stepped into the shallow waters.

Chapter Twenty-Six

The storm broke.

Figures rushed from behind huts, bayonets drawn and
glinting. An old woman was shouting. Someone leapt at
him. Sebastian saw a flash of metal and felt the bite of steel
at his shoulder. He staggered and, in a moment of clarity,
saw Beaumont's face.

Another man had made it into the water, somehow circling behind him. He grabbed Sebastian, his fingers tight
at his throat. Sebastian gagged, thrusting his elbow back
against the softness of the man's gut.

The crazy fish woman who had shouted was struggling
to stand. She threw something, a rock maybe, and must
have struck his attacker because the man's hands loosened
and he stumbled backwards.

In that moment of respite, Sebastian took in the scene.
Two French soldiers were fighting each other. One would
be one of the Lion's men, but in disguise.

The moment ended as Beaumont rose up again. Ignoring the pain in his shoulder, Sebastian struck him. He felt
his fist contact the man's face. He heard the crack of bone
and felt the give of soft tissue and the warmth of the man's
blood.

A savageness coursed through him.

With his next blow, Sebastian felt the man's jaw crack as Beaumont fell, sprawling within the shallows.

The fishwife—

She must have been hit. The woman lay face down in the water, surrounded by the black cloud of her shawl. She'd drown. Sebastian stumbled forward, grabbing her arm and pulling her ashore. But before he could tend to her, he heard his name and a wild thrashing within water.

Damn. Beaumont had pulled himself from the shallows and now lunged towards the dinghy, which had been pushed back out to sea in the fighting and was floating some feet away. Grabbing the gunnel, Beaumont turned towards the shore, raising a knife. The steel glittered.

'I'll kill him!' His words were slurred. He had lost his front teeth and blood filled his mouth, dribbling blackly down his chin. 'I'll kill Edwin. Tell me his name or I'll kill him.'

Aiming at the blanket, Beaumont slashed wildly. 'Tell me the Lion's name!' he shouting, bringing the blade down. Again. And again.

'No!' Like a crazed animal, the woman ran through the waves. She held a bottle within her hand. She struck Beaumont's head with such force that the glass split in two, shattering against the gunnels in a myriad of shards.

Beaumont slumped, falling backwards and on to Sebastian so that he held him in a macabre dance.

'Edwin? Is he okay?' the woman shouted, turning towards him.

Dear God in heaven…

'Sarah!' He threw the unconscious man to the shore. 'What are you doing here?'

'Him—he followed you,' she gasped.

He stepped to her. 'Are you hurt?'

She shook her head, although he saw red welts on her cheek and forehead, and blood dripped from her hand.

'Your hand. Here.' He thrust a handkerchief at her and she took it, wrapping it about her palm.

'Don't worry about me. What about Edwin? Did Beaumont cut him?'

'No.' Sebastian said. 'No.'

Turning, he waved to the Lion's man. 'Tie Beaumont up. And you have the others secured?'

The man nodded, cocking his head to where two soldiers lay, trussed like Christmas geese.

'Right,' Sebastian said once Beaumont had also been tied. His breath caught. Hope, fear, joy was overwhelming.

'Ready?' he asked huskily.

The man nodded and Sebastian uttered a piercing whistle.

Sebastian stepped to Sarah, placing his arm about her. Suddenly glad she was here, glad they could share this moment together.

'Look.' He pointed out to sea. A second small white boat came into view. It moved slowly, the intermittent splash of its oars audible over the water's stillness.

Now that the moment was upon him, there was a surreal quality—as though time had slowed. His tongue felt dry and large within his mouth. His throat tightened. His breath came in quick pants. His heart thundered.

He took Sarah's hand, the one which was uninjured, holding it tightly.

Behind him, he was vaguely aware of the Lion's man questioning his captives, the men's curses and the crunch of footsteps across pebbles. But it was background noise, inconsequential as chatter at a dance.

The boat was so close now that Sebastian could see the oarsman's broad back. He could see his muscled forearms, the boat's plank construction and the movement of the oarlocks. He could see...

A small figure suddenly stood. He waved wildly as the boat rocked. 'Father!'

That wonderful, beautiful word.

His heart exploded. 'Edwin!'

His legs burst into movement. He plunged into the water, thrashing and stumbling over the pebbles.

Edwin still stood, the boat rocking with his movement.

Then Sebastian was there. He reached up and Edwin threw himself at him, clinging like a limpet as they hugged and laughed and cried.

Tears ran down Sarah's face as she saw the child, his face hidden in Sebastian's broad shoulders, his legs and arms wound tight around his father's torso.

Catching sight of Sebastian's face, her heart squeezed with a joy that was also pain. She swallowed, turning to give them privacy. But, with a generosity she found touching, Sebastian waded up the beach, still holding the child.

'Sarah,' he said, his voice hoarse and trembling with emotion. 'Sarah. This is Edwin.'

He put the boy down and Edwin stood, looking at her with wide, uncertain eyes—grey, like his sister's. Sarah smiled. 'I am glad to meet you and I am so glad you are safe.'

The boy looked at her, his expression unreadable. His hands hung awkwardly at his sides, too long for the short jacket he wore.

'Where's Elizabeth?' he asked.

'Safe with a relative of mine. She will be so, so happy to see you.' An inadequate word. 'And I am so, so happy to see you and meet you.' Also inadequate.

The boy nodded, allowing himself a small, tentative smile.

'But, Sarah, how did you even get here and why?' Sebastian asked after a moment.

He still held Edwin's hand, as though unwilling to release it even for a second.

'We saw Beaumont following you moments after you left.'

'From the Crawfords'?'

'Yes.'

'But how did you know it was him?'

She smiled with a pulse of pure happiness. 'Elizabeth told us.'

'She spoke?'

'Yes.'

'Thank you.' He stepped closer to her, enfolding her in his arms and pressing a kiss against her temple. Then he reached for his son, pulling him into an embrace.

They stood clinging to each other. Sebastian wore a rough knitted sweater and Sarah could feel the wool and hear the thump of his heart as she lay her head against his chest.

She could feel Edwin's small form, perhaps edging slightly away and she couldn't blame him. He hardly knew her.

But the family was whole. Edwin had returned. Elizabeth would recover. Sebastian might never love her, but he would feel joy at his son's return and the happiness of his daughter's renewed health.

And it would be enough. It was enough.

A piercing whistle startled them back to reality. Looking over his son's head, Sebastian saw two parish constables approaching, truncheons bared.

'Good, the law is here. They can deal with this lot.' He glanced back at Beaumont and the two French soldiers who now sat trussed and impotent.

Sarah and Edwin also turned.

The constables were almost upon them when Sebastian

heard a stifled sob and saw his son sink to the ground, his whimpers feral.

'What is it? Are you in pain? Were you hurt?' Sebastian asked, bending over the boy.

He made no response, but huddled more tightly over his knees. Again Sebastian was struck with that confused powerlessness. Edwin looked so small, so vulnerable, so afraid.

Sebastian watched as Sarah knelt beside the boy. She spoke in the sing-song voice Sebastian had heard her use with animals.

'They are not soldiers, Edwin. They are officers of the law. They won't hurt you or your father. They are here to take away the bad people. To take away Beaumont.'

Her one hand hovered above his tousled head, as though wanting to touch, but knowing that he was not yet ready.

'And, indeed,' she continued still in gentle, rhythmic tones, 'it is well that they are here. That way they can do their jobs while we return to the inn and get warm and dry.'

The boy's position eased. His shoulders dropped as the tension lessened. He lifted his head a bit so that they could see his forehead and huge eyes.

As though disturbed by the boy's motion, something moved and a small creature could be seen, peaking from the frayed edges of his sleeve.

'What the— What is that?' Sebastian asked sharply.

The boy moved quickly, cupping his hand over the creature, his white face turning dull red.

'What is it?' Sebastian asked again.

'Please, I know it is vermin, but can I keep it?'

'Vermin?'

Sarah laughed. 'It's a mouse.'

Edwin's eyes widened and he bit his lip as though fighting back tears. 'Please, ma'am, don't make me get rid of him.'

'Get rid? Of course not,' Sarah said. 'He is more than

welcome. A mouse, a rabbit and a dog. Together we will drive your poor father mad.'

At that, Sebastian laughed, a spontaneous belly roar and the boy stared round-eyed as if now fearing they were all insane.

'You see,' Sarah explained, her voice soft and gentle, 'I have a habit of bringing home stray animals. I have a dog called Liver and a rabbit called Orion and I am absolutely thrilled to be adding to the menagerie.'

With a choked cry, the boy, forgetting all shyness, flung his arms about her neck. Sebastian watched, his heart so full that his chest hurt and wetness dampened his eyes.

'Thank you,' he whispered to fate or God or whatever had brought about this miracle.

After the arrival of the constables, everything blurred into instructions and concern. They were escorted back to the inn where Sebastian secured additional rooms, ordering baths and food. A doctor came and stitched Sebastian's shoulder and bandaged Sarah's hand.

Once the doctor had left, Sarah wrote to Miss Sharples and Elizabeth and ordered clothes for Edwin so that he might travel in greater comfort.

After this, the justice of the peace came with more questions and Sarah had to retell her story until her mouth felt dry, her head ached and it was far too late to depart on their journey that day.

Sarah wished they could have left. The inn had provided for their every comfort, but she wanted to get back to Elizabeth and Charlotte. She wanted to see the family whole and to remind herself that, just as Sebastian had found his son, she had found her sister.

And yet she found her relief mixed with a heavy, lacklustre and nagging despondency.

Sitting alone beside the crackling fire, Sarah pulled her blanket more closely about her and tried to make sense of her own emotions. They made little sense. After all, her happiness that both Edwin and Sebastian were safe was huge and genuine.

And yet...

Sarah sighed, staring absently through the window opposite. The curtains were drawn and through the pane she could see the reflection of the fire mixed with the twilight gloom and circling gulls. The sound of the ocean was a constant, sad, moaning sound.

She decided that she did not like the sea.

She liked green fields, dotted with friendly cows, not this oppressive grey of clouds and rocks and water.

But it was not only the sea. It was the inescapable fact that Sebastian had married her to help in Edwin's release and to aid in Elizabeth's recovery.

The first had now been accomplished. The second was well in hand.

This meant, therefore, that Sebastian had landed himself with a wife who would serve little purpose in his current life. A wife who lacked money, looks, wit or social standing.

He did not even trust her.

And now, with his children safe, Sebastian would wish to return to a life of politics and balls. He needed a suitable woman at his side—not a drab little nobody with a penchant for rescuing stray animals.

Even daydreams of Petunia could not distract her. Petunia only made her feel more inadequate, as though her own imagination was mocking her with her heroine's violet eyes and blonde curls.

Sarah leaned back, trying to sleep, but the wind made the casement windows rattle, magnifying the sea's roar.

Two thoughts circled in her mind, giving her no peace. Firstly, the reasons Sebastian had married her were null and void.

And, secondly—she loved Sebastian.

Chapter Twenty-Seven

A knock sounded at her door. Edwin entered. He held a candle which illuminated his face with a flickering glow and wore what must have been Sebastian's nightshirt. It was several sizes too large and trailed on the floor so that all that she could see of his legs were quick glimpses of toes.

He looked unsure, shifting his weight and eyeing her from those serious dark eyes which formed a startling contrast to his blond curls.

'I couldn't sleep,' he said.

'I know that feeling. Did you want to sit here for a while?' she asked.

'I guess.' He put down the candle and sat beside her.

'Sometimes, I didn't want to sleep after my mother died,' she said.

'Why?'

'I'd have bad dreams or when I woke up I would have forgotten she was dead and the remembering made it worse.'

'I don't want to sleep,' he said.

'Because you have bad dreams?'

He shook his head, his fingers twisting in the fabric of his shirt. 'Because I think this is a dream and if I sleep it will end and...and I'll be back.'

'I've felt that, too,' she said. 'But you know what I do?'

He shook his head.

She took his hand, stilling its movement and holding it gently within her own. 'I hold on to something that I know is real, even if everything else feels like a dream. So I want you to feel the warmth of my hand. That is real. I am real. Your father is real.'

'Can I stay here for a while?'

'Yes. And you do not have to sleep. Sometimes it's nice to just sit in the quiet.'

'Over there, I couldn't decide which I hated most—night or day. The tumbrils didn't roll by at night and I couldn't hear the awful cheering of the crowds, but then at night...'

'At night it is too quiet, too dark and too lonely with nothing to distract your thoughts,' Sarah said.

Edwin moved closer and she felt the nodding of his head against her chin. 'Except when people moaned or cried. Sniffy, my mouse, made things better. I'm glad you understand about him.'

'When I was little I had to live in a new place. There weren't any other children so I made friends with the stable cats.'

'And now you live with Father?'

'Yes, and Elizabeth. We will start back tomorrow and you will see her.'

'And are you going to leave like Mother did?'

Sarah started at the abrupt question. 'No. I will stay with you and Elizabeth and...and your father.'

'Because you love him?'

The boy twisted his body to meet her gaze, staring up with such intensity she could not lie. 'Because I love him.'

'And he loves you?'

'I...' She paused.

She wanted to lie. The boy needed, deserved security and yet under the dark scrutiny of that gaze she could not tell even that harmless fib. 'I...we...we have a good relationship founded on mutual respect,' she said.

Gracious, she sounded like she'd swallowed one of those dreadful ladies' journals...whole.

'He loves you.'

The deep, husky timbre of Sebastian's voice filled the candlelit room.

Sarah jerked her head about, looking towards the door. He stood within the doorway, his tall frame and broad shoulders silhouetted against the light from the wall sconce in the hall outside.

'I'm glad,' Edwin said. 'I think I'll like you as a step-mother.'

'Which shows uncommonly good sense.' Sebastian strode into the room. 'Now, why don't you go back to bed?'

Edwin pulled a face. 'I can't sleep.'

'I'll tuck you in and you can give it another try,' Sebastian said, scooping the boy from the sofa.

Nestling against his father's shoulder, he looked very young and very sleepy and Sarah did not think he would be long awake.

'Sleep tight,' she said.

'You do not believe me?'

'Pardon?'

Sebastian had re-entered the room, striding across the bare floorboards and sitting beside her on the spot left vacant by his son.

'You do not believe that I love you?' he repeated.

Heat flushed into her cheeks. She looked down at her hands as they played nervously with the cloth of her dress. 'I think you wanted to reassure Edwin and I—um—think you might care in a comfortable, old-slipper way.'

'You are comparing me to footwear?'

'I think I am comparing myself to footwear,' she said

with an attempt at levity. 'I am saying you might care for me in a comfortable way. And it is for the best. Fairy-tale romance is really better in books—'

Angling his body, he faced her more squarely and took her hands within his own. 'I love you, Sarah. The feeling has nothing to do with slippers, old or otherwise.'

She shook her head, squashing a ludicrous, bubbling, fizzing hope. 'No, I am not the sort of woman that a man loves.'

'And what sort of woman does a man love?' He leaned forward. A lock of dark hair fell into his eyes and she longed to brush it back and to run her fingers along his angled jaw and kiss the bruise left by Beaumont's fist.

'One that is beautiful, mysterious, witty,' she said, forcing herself to focus.

'Ah, you mean Petunia. You do not believe that you are my very own Petunia?'

'Definitely not. I am not the stuff from which romantic heroines are made.'

He reached forward, gently stroking her chin and lifting it so that she had to meet his gaze, dark and intent.

'The only difference between you and Petunia is that you are a real woman and I happen to like my women real.'

She frowned, shifting nervously. He didn't mean…he couldn't mean… Her glance sheared away from the intensity of his gaze because she couldn't…wouldn't believe… or hope.

She smiled, forcing her voice to trill lightly. 'Lud, you do not need to espouse any devotion to me. It is not necessary. I will do my best to be a good mother to Elizabeth and Edwin. Indeed, I am certain we will be very content together.'

'A family of contented slippers. Is that what you feel for me, Sarah? A gentle affection? Compassion and caring?'

No! She wanted to yell it from the rooftops. No! Of

course it wasn't. There was nothing gentle about her feelings. They roared through her, surged through her. They encompassed and swamped every other emotion in a rush of desire and pain and joy and love.

But she would say none of this. It felt that if she gave her feelings voice, they would triple and quadruple and she would lose herself in them and lose any hope of comfortable contentment.

'I care for you,' she said.

'Like an old slipper?'

'Yes,' she said. 'Exactly—like an old slipper.'

Old slipper, my foot. Sebastian didn't want to be her old slipper. He didn't want their marriage to be one of comfort and damned convenience.

He glared at the fire in his bedchamber as though bearing it particular malice. Picking up the poker, he stabbed at the coals and a shower of sparks chased into the chimney.

He thrust the poker aside so that it clanged against the grate.

He loved her, damn it.

Maybe he'd loved her from that first moment when he'd found her clutching the cursed rabbit.

But did she really love him? Could she love him?

Or was the more pertinent question, would she allow herself to love him? Or was she so limited by the pigeonhole she had created for herself?

A thought struck him. A grin tugged at his mouth, the heavy, leaden weariness lifting.

'Hell,' he said, his smile broadening. 'I think I'll do it.'

Sarah awoke the next morning with the sense of being watched.

Jerking awake, she peered blearily about the unfamiliar chamber, disorientated and momentarily afraid. Then she saw her husband seated on a chair close to the bed. A fire crackled within the hearth and bright, early morning sun filtered through the window.

'Sebastian, how long have you been there?' she asked.

'I was waiting for you to wake. I need to read you something.'

There was something unusual about him, a repressed excitement, a tension. It was in the set of his jaw, the curve of his lips and the expression in his gaze.

'About Beaumont?' She raised herself on her elbow and saw now that he held a sheaf of pages.

'No,' he said. 'More pleasant. It is a story.'

'A story? You need to read me a story?'

'Most urgently,' he said. 'Because this is a story about a woman. It is a story about a woman with long brown hair, deep, dark, endless grey eyes, pale porcelain skin and lips meant for kissing. It is a story about a woman who rescues stray animals and believes in hopeless causes. It is also a story about a man who falls deeply, hopelessly and passionately in love with her.'

Sarah swallowed. A lump had formed in her throat and her eyes stung. 'But—'

'Shh,' he said, bending forward and pressing his fingers to her lips. Huskily, he started to read. 'Once upon a time there was a man who no longer believed in love. He didn't believe in romance or in happy endings. Life had kicked the romance out of him and he wanted to hear no more of it.

'But then he met someone. He met a true flesh-and-blood woman, a woman who was beautiful inside and out, a woman who would risk everything for those she loved. Indeed, he met a woman who was a heroine in every sense of the word.

'This woman taught him to hope. She taught him to laugh. She taught him that cows had feelings and that foxes deserve second chances. Most of all she taught him to believe in happy endings. She taught him to love.'

The tears fell now, coursing unchecked down her cheeks. Very slowly, he leaned into her, pressing his lips against her cheeks and kissing away the tears.

'I love you, Sarah. I love that you drag stray animals home. I love that no one is too dirty or too poor for you to love. I love that you made my son's mouse as welcome as my son. I love you, everything about you.'

He cupped her chin, pressing his lips to her mouth, a soft, gentle, intimate touch. 'Do you believe me?' he whispered.

'I—yes.'

'And I'm sorry I didn't trust you before—that I didn't tell you where I was going and that I didn't accept your help. It is not that I didn't love you, but I wanted—I needed—to keep you safe. I didn't...I couldn't lose you.'

'I'm here,' she said. 'I'll never leave.'

'I know. You would do nothing to hurt this family. But—' he still cupped her face, looking at her with his dark, serious gaze '—there is something I need to know.'

'What?'

'Could you...could you grow to love me a bit?'

With shock, she saw his raw vulnerability and realised what it had taken to lay himself bare.

She flung her arms about him, losing all restraint. She ran her fingers through the thickness of his hair, kissing his cheeks, his chin and his lips.

'I already love you,' she said.

They kissed with passion and with the wonderful feeling of coming home and of belonging. Unheeded, the pages fell, scattering across the floor.

Sarah and Sebastian didn't care. They had each other and were living their own, very real, happily ever after.

Epilogue

The journey home seemed slow, lengthened by Edwin's every impatient rustle. At times he fell asleep but, when awake, he pressed his nose to the windowpane as though by staring at each passing field he could make their hired coach move faster.

But at last they swayed over the familiar rutted lane and, as they swung around that last curve, Sarah saw the small square stone house, its front garden dotted with rust-coloured chickens. Behind them both Miss Sharples and Charlotte flapped their aprons in their direction in an apparent desire to encourage them into the henhouse.

Fortunately, the coach avoided both the chickens and the two ladies and pulled safely to a halt within the courtyard.

Even before they had ceased moving, Edwin had flung open the door, leaping from the coach and running towards the front door.

'Lizzy! Lizzy!' he shouted.

The front door flung open. The girl flew across the ground with a speed of movement Sarah had not thought possible. She flung her arms about her brother so that they spun around the courtyard in a joyful caper of arms and legs, punctuated by wild yelps of excitement.

Tears smarted in her eyes. Sarah swallowed, her throat

aching. Sebastian reached for her hand, his touch saying all he could not put into words: joy, love, thankfulness.

At that moment, Liver loped out from the house, followed by Fred. The dog let out a volley of barks, his excitement so great that even Fred's firm command had no impact.

Sarah knew she would remember this moment for ever. There were the children cavorting in their wild dance, Miss Sharples and Charlotte still chasing the chickens while Liver ran around them all in wild, crazed circles, sending up showers of dust with his massive paws. Meanwhile Fred followed him, making occasional lunges for his lead while Mrs Crawford stood in the doorway, clutching her knitting as though to ward off the chaos.

Central to it all, more important than all the rest, she felt the warm loving pressure of her husband's hand and its promise of for ever.

She held tight to him, and standing on tiptoes, whispered into his ear, 'I have rescued Petunia from her tower.'

'Pardon?'

'All she had to do was rescue herself, which she accomplished most handily.'

* * * * *

If you enjoyed this story, make sure you read Eleanor Webster's fantastic debut
NO CONVENTIONAL MISS